EVERYMAN,

I WILL GO WITH THEE,

AND BE THY GUIDE,

IN THY MOST NEED

TO GO BY THY SIDE

EVERYMAN'S POCKET CLASSICS

STORIES OF MOTHERHOOD

EDITED BY DIANA SECKER TESDELL

EVERYMAN'S POCKET CLASSICS

Alfred A. Knopf New York London Toronto

THIS IS A BORZOI BOOK
PUBLISHED BY ALFRED A. KNOPF

This selection by Diana Secker Tesdell first published in
Everyman's Library, 2012
Copyright © 2012 by Everyman's Library
A list of acknowledgments to copyright owners appears at the back
of this volume.

All rights reserved. Published in the United States by Alfred A. Knopf,
a division of Random House, Inc., New York, and in Canada by
Random House of Canada Limited, Toronto. Distributed by
Random House, Inc., New York. Published in the United Kingdom
by Everyman's Library, Northburgh House, 10 Northburgh Street,
London EC1V 0AT, and distributed by Random House (UK) Ltd.

US website: www.randomhouse.com/everymans

ISBN: 978-0-307-95779-5 (US)
978-1-84159-611-2 (UK)

A CIP catalogue reference for this book is available from the
British Library

Typography by Peter B. Willberg

Typeset in the UK by AccComputing, North Barrow, Somerset

Printed and bound in Germany by GGP Media GmbH, Pössneck

STORIES OF
MOTHERHOOD

Contents

RON CARLSON

BLOOD AND ITS RELATIONSHIP TO WATER

THE NOISE EDDIE makes when he first wakes for his two a.m. feeding is closest to a fanbelt slipping, a faint periodic squealing, which like a loose fanbelt doesn't signal an emergency; it just means that if not looked to soon, there is going to be real trouble. In Eddie's case, if we linger in our bed too long, the sound becomes a wail similar to that of straining power steering in some late-model Fords. Some Fairlane will try a U-turn on a side street and you hear that low scream near the front axle.

At six weeks, Eddie's also developing a strange growl that he uses primarily when we try to burp him; it is as if he's trying to fake one so as to get back to the bottle. And at night sometimes, as the fanbelt slips into the power steering wail, he'll throw in a little growl as counterpoint, just to show us he's beginning to do things on purpose.

He also has a four-note nasal coo, which is the sweetest noise ever created. He coos whenever the bottle is plugged in his mouth, and sometimes he coos for a moment or two after he's eaten, as his eyes roll sleepily back in his lids.

We know his every peep, every soft snort (he has two), and we listen to him and study these noises because like any parents, we take them as signs of life. We go to the crib at all hours and listen for the feather breath, the muted sigh, some small sound. But we are also keen because Nancy is looking for a sign of love. She hangs on his every glance, tic, start; he's smiled a couple of times now and when he has,

Nancy has called me into the room where she stands with his little head in her hands, while she sobs and sobs. 'He smiled,' she says. 'He smiled at me.' She has fallen in love with Eddie so profoundly that our house seems a new place, and she needs some small sign of love in return.

I know she's going to get one, but she is not so sure. Eddie came to our house in the arms of my lawyer's wife, Bonnie, when he was two days old. Bonnie, who has four children of her own, was weeping, and repeating again and again: 'He's so beautiful, so perfect.' It was the moment of transfer that changed Nancy, utterly. She had been cool. She had been hopeful, surely, but also steady and reasonable, and then when Bonnie put Eddie in Nancy's arms, it was as if the infant carried 50,000 volts of some special electricity. Nancy sat down with her eyes on his little face, and her mouth became a scared line. I stood there wishing she would just cry instead of looking like she was about to start crying.

And it's been that way for six weeks. A solemnity has crept into our lives as my wife, the dearest soul I know, waits to see if this adopted child will love her. Hey, I've talked to her, and obviously, logic has no place in the deal. So my wife listens to the baby and watches his face the way astronomers stare into the deepest heavens for the first sign of a new star.

Tonight, when Sam came over, in fact, was the first time Nancy has relaxed enough to drink a beer, and I think by the time he left after midnight, she'd had four. Sam loves kids and just the way he held Eddie and how obviously happy he is for us to have a baby put Nancy at ease.

I brought a chair in from the dining-room and we sat in the kitchen and Sam tried to remember when Robbie and Juney were babies. He told a funny story about how Rob wouldn't stop crying at night and the doctor had told them just to let him cry. But a neighbor, suspecting child abuse, had called the police. It had happened twice. Now Robbie is fifteen and works for me weekends, mowing the lawn and washing the cars. He lives with his mother.

After his ten o'clock bottle, Eddie went to bed, bunching himself on his arms and knees like a bug. When I returned to the kitchen, Nancy had opened another beer and had her feet up under herself on the chair. Sam had opened the window and pulled out his cigarettes. Something was up.

Well, with our old friend Sam, it's always Vicky. They've been divorced over three years, but he feels that she still conducts her life around a massive and undiminished hatred for him. 'It's no Sun Valley this summer,' he said, blowing smoke like a strong secret out the window. He smokes differently since we've gotten the baby. 'It's her option, as always, and she says that she and Jeff are taking the kids to San Diego for five weeks after the Fourth. She's known since Thanksgiving about my time off and my plans to let Juney learn to ride, but all of a sudden, she's got this craving to take the kids on her honeymoon. Rob and Juney are acting funny, like it was my fault, like if I'm really their father why don't I just make it happen.'

Sam lifted an empty beer can and deposited his cigarette, tilting the can to extinguish the butt. I remember Vicky smirking when he did that; she always called him a 'bo-ho,' her joke for *bohemian*.

'Rob sure is getting to be a handsome young man,' Nancy said.

'Now that is undisguised flattery,' I said to Sam. 'He looks just like you.' And Rob does. What is most affecting, however, is that Rob *walks* just like Sam, and when we play one on one in the driveway, Rob has the same fake-left-go-right move that Sam uses. I haven't told him about it yet, because with my age, I need the little advantage.

'I wonder if Eddie will look like us,' Nancy said, hugging her knees in her chair.

'He already does,' Sam said. 'The poor little guy has that problem already.' He reached for his cigarettes, showed them to us. 'How we doing with the smoke?'

'You're all right, Sam. None's blowing in here,' Nancy said.

'I look more like my father than my brother Tim does,' Sam said, lighting up and shaking the match in front of the window opening. 'Tim's even six inches shorter than both of us.' He laughed. 'I think it pisses him off.'

'It sure forced him to become an outside shooter,' I said. I reached behind Nancy into the fridge. 'Beer?'

'One more, then I gotta go,' Sam said. 'Last hearing on the rate hike tomorrow; the public defender better be sharp.'

'Tim's not adopted,' Nancy said, taking the beer from me. 'Is he?'

'No. He and Irene came along after Mom and Dad had adopted me and Carrie.'

I took a chance. 'Nancy's a little worried, Sam,' I said. 'How...'

'How do you feel about *your* parents?' Nancy said.

Sam looked up, his face confused, and then he looked over at Nancy, huddled on her chair. His face rose into a large grin. 'You're kidding,' he said. 'Nan, you're worried? Come on. She's kidding, right?' Sam leaned on his elbows toward Nancy. 'Well, don't worry. He's your little boy and he'll always be your boy. Look at me. I love my parents and I love my kids; it's my wife I can't abide.' Sam laughed and stuck the cigarette back in his mouth. 'She's the one who grew up to hate me.'

Sam stood up. 'I gotta go. Thanks for the beer. I'll call

you late tomorrow and give you the play by play of the hearing.'

'What will you do if you can't take the kids to Sun Valley?'

'Plan two. Stay around here. Drink beer with you guys. Teach Eddie about women and how to ride a bike.'

'Go on,' Nancy said. 'You're not finished. What's the punchline?'

Sam shrugged and opened the door. 'Once you learn to ride a bike, you never forget.'

After Sam left I asked Nancy if she felt better.

'Sam's a good guy,' she said. 'And I should probably drink more beer; this is the first time my back has let go since the baby got here.'

'What about this. You go to bed and I'll listen for the baby,' I said, clearing the counter.

'My son,' she smiled, briefly hugging me, her head against my chest. 'Please listen for my son.'

It was twelve minutes after two when the fanbelt began to squeal, just a short touch and then another, then the real sound of a fanbelt slipping. I mean, it is so close I could tape it and convince people of car trouble. Nancy was out so cold with the worry and fatigue of six weeks that in the half light we have from the hall she could have been the definitive photograph of sleep deprivation.

You see a kid that small in his crib and it looks like someone sleeping on a jailhouse floor and you don't wonder about *any* sound he may make. I slipped my hand under Eddie's head just as the fanbelt was rising into power steering trouble and we ducked quickly into the kitchen. He quieted for the ride into the new room, and the quick flash from the fridge door turned his head in curiosity for the moment that allowed me to retrieve the bottle and stick it in the warmer.

Since we'd had the baby, I'd become used to standing naked in the kitchen at night with Eddie in my arms.

The standing-zombie fatigue was worst the third week and now in the sixth it had settled to just my eyes and knees, a low burning. My head rocked slightly and I kept my eyes closed, drifting through the routine.

While Eddie was still too amazed at being whisked around to cry, I changed him, and when I pulled the heavy wet diaper away from under him, he swam happily in the air for a moment, punching softly into the dark. By the time I had him powdered and diapered, he was squealing again, each breath a wonderful, powerful compression, focused and building.

In the kitchen, the bottle was ready. I found it without reaching twice, unplugging the warmer as an afterthought, the kind of motion that in ten years I would forget I had committed a thousand times. With a quick flip I had milk on my wrist, and then of all the easy connections and coincidences in the universe, the baby's mouth found the nipple easiest of all. And as I walked around my own house naked as they say Adam was, holding my son, I heard cooing, edged by a kind of purring slurp, and one or two real, honest deep breaths.

In the dark living-room, I sat in the corner of the old couch, holding Eddie, and listened until he snorted two or three times and then gasped, a sharp little gasp, and I knew that two ounces were down, and we could try for a little air. I stood him against my chest and patted his back while he squirmed and growled, his head bobbing in search of the bottle. Then he grew quiet, which always is a good sign. He stood, head away from my body, as if he was listening for something, and then it came: a belch, a good two-stage belch, which he delivered partially in my ear and which sounded exactly like a lawn mower coming around the corner of a house. After that, his head bobbed some more, poking me about the face, and he was ready for more dinner.

I had already fallen asleep twice during the feeding, but sometime during the second burping, Eddie really woke me up with his head. He was bumping against my face softly, working his mouth like a little fish, whining a little bit, when I felt him swing back into space. I had a good hold of him, so I wasn't too worried, when *wham!* his forehead hammered my nose. I saw a quick flash and my eyes filled with tears that burned and burned. I must have started or moved somehow, because I felt Eddie wet me right through the diaper leg, which – out of a kind of misguided concern – I always leave a little loose.

Eddie was fussing and I stood and walked him around the room for a minute, too tired to change him, too tired to go to bed. My head felt strange, kind of empty. And finally I gave up in the middle of our second lap and sat back on the couch. Leaning there I burned with fatigue, wet and warm, and headed toward three o'clock.

Once or twice I thought about getting up, drying us off, and going back to bed, but my head was light and I was tired to the bone. Eddie began to sleep there on my chest, evenly against me, each breath a bird wing in the night sky. I pulled the TV quilt over us and leaned back into warm sleep myself.

It's funny about love, about how you think you're in love or how you may think you know your capacity for love, and suddenly somebody like Eddie comes along and shows you whole new rooms in your heart. I never thought Nancy would be nervous about making this baby belong to us; and when I saw that she was, that she wanted fiercely for him to be ours in every way, I started getting nervous, because I didn't know how to help her.

When I woke there was crying. This was no gentle revving of the small engines of crying. This was roaring, and then I opened my eyes and it was Nancy. She had a hand on my forehead and all I could see in her face was her open mouth in a gasp so full of horror and fear as to seem counterfeit. Her eyes were wide, crystalline, unblinking. In the late dawn light, she looked as though she had bad news for me.

Then I looked down. Eddie lay on my chest in a thick mess which included the blanket, both my hands, my side, and a good portion of the couch cushion. It was blood. I reached up and felt the crust of blood on my neck and chin. My head ached slowly, a low-grade ice-cream headache, and I felt my swollen nose with my fingers. All the time, I realized, my other hand had been feeling Eddie sleep.

'It's okay, Nan,' I said in a thick voice. 'I had a bloody nose.' She sat on her heels next to me, her hands now clasped in her lap, her lower lip clipped fast in her teeth. 'Eddie's okay. He's still sleeping, see?' I tried to lift Eddie up just a little to show his breathing face to her, and when I tried that, I realized we were stuck. My nose had bled over everything, blood that would be on the couch for generations, and now a thin layer of blood had glued Eddie to my belly and chest.

When you lie naked in an empty bathtub with your son attached to your abdomen by the stickiness of your very blood, and your wife gingerly sponges you apart with luke-warm water, there is a good chance you too will wake the baby. Eddie opened his eyes in the warm wash of water and lifted his head, as he's learning to do. His eyes tracked the strange space, while Nancy squeezed water between us, and then he saw his mother and made the most extraordinary gesture of tilting his head in recognition, his mouth pursing comically as if to say, *Please, Mom, spare me this indignity.*

And she did. With a noise of her own, something between

a sigh and a cough, Nancy reached down for her child. His body awash with blood and water, Eddie hopped into his laughing mother's arms. There was no question about it this time: he put his arms around her laughing neck and, in a happy, bucking hug, he grabbed her hair.

LYDIA DAVIS

WHAT YOU LEARN
ABOUT THE BABY

Idle

You learn how to be idle, how to do nothing. That is the new thing in your life – to do nothing. To do nothing and not be impatient about doing nothing. It is easy to do nothing and become impatient. It is not easy to do nothing and not mind it, not mind the hours passing, the hours of the morning passing and then the hours of the afternoon, and one day passing and the next passing, while you do nothing.

What You Can Count On

You learn never to count on anything being the same from day to day, that he will fall asleep at a certain hour, or sleep for a certain length of time. Some days he sleeps for several hours at a stretch, other days he sleeps no more than half an hour.

Sometimes he will wake suddenly, crying hard, when you were prepared to go on working for another hour. Now you prepare to stop. But as it takes you a few minutes to end your work for the day, and you cannot go to him immediately, he stops crying and continues quiet. Now, though you have prepared to end work for the day, you prepare to resume working.

Don't Expect to Finish Anything

You learn never to expect to finish anything. For example, the baby is staring at a red ball. You are cleaning some large radishes. The baby will begin to fuss when you have cleaned four and there are eight left to clean.

You Will Not Know What Is Wrong

The baby is on his back in his cradle crying. His legs are slightly lifted from the surface of his mattress in the effort of his crying. His head is so heavy and his legs so light and his muscles so hard that his legs fly up easily from the mattress when he tenses, as now.

Often, you will wonder what is wrong, why he is crying, and it would help, it would save you much disturbance, to know what is wrong, whether he is hungry, or tired, or bored, or cold, or hot, or uncomfortable in his clothes, or in pain in his stomach or bowels. But you will not know, or not when it would help to know, at the time, but only later, when you have guessed correctly or many times incorrectly. And it will not help to know afterwards, or it will not help unless you have learned from the experience to identify a particular cry that means hunger, or pain, etc. But the memory of a cry is a difficult one to fix in your mind.

What Exhausts You

You must think and feel for him as well as for yourself – that he is tired, or bored, or uncomfortable.

Sitting Still

You learn to sit still. You learn to stare as he stares, to stare up at the rafters as long as he stares up at the rafters, sitting still in a large space.

Entertainment

For him, though not usually for you, merely to look at a thing is an entertainment.

Then, there are some things that not just you, and not just he, but both of you like to do, such as lie in the hammock, or take a walk, or take a bath.

Renunciation

You give up, or postpone, for his sake, many of the pleasures you once enjoyed, such as eating meals when you are hungry, eating as much as you want, watching a movie all the way through from beginning to end, reading as much of a book as you want to at one sitting, going to sleep when you are tired, sleeping until you have had enough sleep.

You look forward to a party as you never used to look forward to a party, now that you are at home alone with him so much. But at this party you will not be able to talk to anyone for more than a few minutes, because he cries so constantly, and in the end he will be your only company, in a back bedroom.

Questions

How do his eyes know to seek out your eyes? How does his mouth know it is a mouth, when it imitates yours?

His Perceptions

You learn from reading it in a book that he recognizes you not by the appearance of your face but by your smell and the way you hold him, that he focuses clearly on an object only when it is held a certain distance from him, and that he can see only in shades of gray. Even what is white or black to you is only a shade of gray to him.

The Difficulty of a Shadow

He reaches to grasp the shadow of his spoon, but the shadow reappears on the back of his hand.

His Sounds

You discover that he makes many sounds in his throat to accompany what is happening to him: sounds in the form of grunts, air expelled in small gusts. Then sometimes high squeaks, and then sometimes, when he has learned to smile at you, high coos.

Priority

It should be very simple: while he is awake, you care for him. As soon as he goes to sleep, you do the most important thing you have to do, and do it as long as you can, either until it is done or until he wakes up. If he wakes up before it is done, you care for him until he sleeps again, and then you continue to work on the most important thing. In this way, you should learn to recognize which thing is the most important and to work on it as soon as you have the opportunity.

Odd Things You Notice About Him

The dark gray lint that collects in the lines of his palm.

The white fuzz that collects in his armpit.

The black under the tips of his fingernails. You have let his nails get too long, because it is hard to make a precise cut on such a small thing constantly moving. Now it would take a very small nailbrush to clean them.

The colors of his face: his pink forehead, his bluish eyelids, his reddish-gold eyebrows. And the tiny beads of sweat standing out from the tiny pores of his skin.

When he yawns, how the wings of his nostrils turn yellow.

When he holds his breath and pushes down on his diaphragm, how quickly his face turns red.

His uneven breath: how his breath changes in response to his motion, and to his curiosity.

How his bent arms and legs, when he is asleep on his stomach, take the shape of an hourglass.

When he lies against your chest, how he lifts his head to look around like a turtle and drops it again because it is so heavy.

How his hands move slowly through the air like crabs or other sea creatures before closing on a toy.

How, bottom up, folded, he looks as though he were going away, or as though he were upside down.

Connected by a Single Nipple

You are lying on the bed nursing him, but you are not holding on to him with your arms or hands and he is not holding on to you. He is connected to you by a single nipple.

Disorder

You learn that there is less order in your life now. Or if there is to be order, you must work hard at maintaining it. For instance, it is evening and you are lying on the bed with the baby half asleep beside you. You are watching *Gaslight*. Suddenly a thunderstorm breaks and the rain comes down hard. You remember the baby's clothes out on the line, and you get up from the bed and run outdoors. The baby begins crying at being left so abruptly half asleep on the bed. *Gaslight* continues, the baby screams now, and you are out in the hard rainfall in your white bathrobe.

Protocol

There are so many occasions for greetings in the course of his day. Upon each waking, a greeting. Each time you enter the room, a greeting. And in each greeting there is real enthusiasm.

Distraction

You decide you must attend some public event, say a concert, despite the difficulty of arranging such a thing. You make elaborate preparations to leave the baby with a babysitter, taking a bag full of equipment, a folding bed, a folding stroller, and so on. Now, as the concert proceeds, you sit thinking not about the concert but only about the elaborate preparations and whether they have been adequate, and no matter how often you try to listen to the concert, you will hear only a few minutes of it before thinking again about those elaborate preparations and whether they have been adequate to the comfort of the baby and the convenience of the babysitter.

Henri Bergson

He demonstrates to you what you learned long ago from reading Henri Bergson – that laughter is always preceded by surprise.

You Do Not Know When He Will Fall Asleep

If his eyes are wide open staring at a light, it does not mean that he will not be asleep within minutes.

If he cries with a squeaky cry and squirms with wiry strength against your chest, digging his sharp little fingernails into your shoulder, or raking your neck, or pushing his face into your shirt, it does not mean he will not relax in five minutes and grow heavy. But five minutes is a very long time when you are caring for a baby.

What Resembles His Cry

Listening for his cry, you mistake, for his cry, the wind, seagulls, and police sirens.

Time

It is not that five minutes is always a very long time when you are caring for a baby but that time passes very slowly when you are waiting for a baby to go to sleep, when you are listening to him cry alone in his bed or whimper close to your ear.

Then time passes very quickly once the baby is asleep. The things you have to do have always taken this long to do, but before the baby was born it did not matter, because there were many such hours in the day to do these things. Now there is only one hour, and again later, on some days, one hour, and again, very late in the day, on some days, one last hour.

Order

You cannot think clearly or remain calm in such disorder. And so you learn to wash a dish as soon as you use it, otherwise it may not be washed for a very long time. You learn to make your bed immediately because there may be no time to do it later. And then you begin to worry regularly, if not constantly, about how to save time. You learn to prepare for the baby's waking as soon as the baby sleeps. You learn to prepare everything hours in advance. Then your conception of time begins to change. The future collapses into the present.

Other Days

There are other days, despite what you have learned about saving time, and preparing ahead, when something in you relaxes, or you are simply tired. You do not mind if the house is untidy. You do not mind if you do nothing but care for the baby. You do not mind if time goes by while you lie in the hammock and read a magazine.

Why He Smiles

He looks at a window with serious interest. He looks at a painting and smiles. It is hard to know what that smile means. Is he pleased by the painting? Is the painting funny to him? No, soon you understand that he smiles at the painting for the same reason he smiles at you: because the painting is looking at him.

A Problem of Balance

A problem of balance: if he yawns, he falls over backward.

Moving Forward

You worry about moving forward, or about the difference between moving forward and staying in one place. You begin to notice which things have to be done over and over again in one day, and which things have to be done once every day, and which things have to be done every few days, and so on, and all these things only cause you to mark time, stay in one place, rather than move forward, or, rather, keep you from slipping backward, whereas certain other things are done only once. A job to earn money is done only once, a letter is written saying a thing only once and never again, an event is planned that will happen only once, news is received or news passed along only once, and if, in this way, something happens that will happen only once, this day is different from other days, and on this day your life seems to move forward, and it is easier to sit still holding the baby and staring at the wall knowing that on this day, at least, your life has moved forward; there has been a change, however small.

A Small Thing with Another Thing, Even Smaller

Asleep in his carriage, he is woken by a fly.

Patience

You try to understand why on some days you have no patience and on others your patience is limitless and you will stand over him for a long time where he lies on his back waving his arms, kicking his legs, or looking up at the painting on the wall. Why on some days it is limitless and on others, or at other times, late in a day when you have been patient, you cannot bear his crying and want to threaten to put him away in his bed to cry alone if he does not stop crying in your arms, and sometimes you do put him away in his bed to cry alone.

Impatience

You learn about patience. You discover patience. Or you discover how patience extends up to a certain point and then it ends and impatience begins. Or rather, impatience was there all along, underneath a light, surface kind of patience, and at a certain point the light kind of patience wears away and all that's left is the impatience. Then the impatience grows.

Paradox

You begin to understand paradox: lying on the bed next to him, you are deeply interested, watching his face and holding his hands, and yet at the same time you are deeply bored, wishing you were somewhere else doing something else.

Regression

Although he is at such an early stage in his development, he regresses, when he is hungry or tired, to an earlier stage, still, of noncommunication, self-absorption, and spastic motion.

Between Human and Animal

How he is somewhere between human and animal. While he can't see well, while he looks blindly toward the brightest light, and can't see you, or can't see your features but more clearly the edge of your face, the edge of your head; and while his movements are more chaotic; and while he is more subject to the needs of his body, and can't be distracted, by intellectual curiosity, from his hunger or loneliness or exhaustion, then he seems to you more animal than human.

How Parts of Him Are Not Connected
He does not know what his hand is doing: it curls around the iron rod of your chair and holds it fast. Then, while he is looking elsewhere, it curls around the narrow black foot of a strange frog.

Admiration
He is filled with such courage, goodwill, curiosity, and self-reliance that you admire him for it. But then you realize he was born with these qualities: now what do you do with your admiration?

Responsibility
How responsible he is, to the limits of his capacity, for his own body, for his own safety. He holds his breath when a cloth covers his face. He widens his eyes in the dark. When he loses his balance, his hands curl around whatever comes under them, and he clutches the stuff of your shirt.

Within His Limits
How he is curious, to the limits of his understanding; how he attempts to approach what arouses his curiosity, to the limits of his motion; how confident he is, to the limits of his knowledge; how masterful he is, to the limits of his competence; how he derives satisfaction from another face before him, to the limits of his attention; how he asserts his needs, to the limits of his force.

HAROLD BRODKEY

LAURA

LAURA WAS BENDING over, trying without much hope to touch her toes, when the baby began to cry again. Laura's eyes, always warm and luminous, turned warmer and more luminous; at that moment, with her back bent, arms hanging straight down, and her head cocked to one side, she slid back into her childhood and its pleasantly queer perspectives. Somehow, her mother had always managed to be irritated when Laura assumed such postures (of course, her mother had been practically the only person who was impervious to her beauty); Laura could almost feel the vaguely desperate maternal hands pulling at the back of her dress. 'Stand up, Laura. Stand up this instant. You're making a spectacle of yourself.' But that was precisely what Laura had wanted to do; she would look at all the faces turned toward her, and she would *know* that she, Laura, was bending over imitating a monkey. She could almost feel her tail. 'It's me, Mother!' she'd say, delighted and surprised, and afterward her mother could go on scolding her for hours without ever penetrating the wonderful foliage of reveries and thoughts that had sprung up from her successful maneuver.

The baby's voice in a series of faint cries announced that hunger, like the tide, was coming in.

'If that damn child doesn't shut up, I'll strangle it!' Laura said. Hardly a second passed before she jerked upright in a spasm of guilt. Oh, you are a terrible person, she thought, and fled to the mirror, but no, her face was the same – kind, gentle, and infinitely calm. Laura leaned forward and touched the spot on the mirror behind which her lovely lips so provokingly lurked untouchable. Soon the cries would be demanding, but now they were gentle – little invitations to her mother to fondle her, to wade in the baby's need. Laura, refusing to give up the mirror, sighed because she would never know the pleasure that others had touching her lips. The trouble with beauty was that one could never enjoy it all by oneself in private, and one couldn't go on forever imitating a monkey in public, and so what was one to do?

'Be an actress,' Laura crooned, standing beside her daughter's crib. 'Be an actress, wee thing, and be lovely on the stage, where it earns you money,' she sang, in soft lullaby tones. The baby bent its tiny six-week-old body in an arch, and the eyes flashed open for an instant, but the figure at the edge of the crib wasn't bending down. 'Poor poverty-stricken child!' Laura said. The baby began to bawl. Her pink hands grew purplish and knotted with tension; her wrinkled eyelids pressed into her cheek; her almost nonexistent nose distended in hungry rage.

'Grow up tough,' Laura whispered. 'Grow up tough and mean. Learn to get your own way. Cry harder. Make me pick you up.' She bent over the crib, staring at her tiny daughter, hardly breathing, waiting for the coercive power of the other's life to force her to touch her, to calm her. But the baby was simply crying in some lonely universe where tire irons float in space. Poor Laura watched, being a Theban – no, Spartan – woman staring at her offspring exposed on a deserted hill while the moon watched and said nothing.

Laura was waiting for a sign from God or one of the gods (any omen would do) or a flash of inspiration – something mystical, like Saint Theresa – that would tell her what to do. The baby's very destiny was at stake. Surely a child of hers would have a destiny – a bird that came and watched over it, a guardian fairy with no other duties, who lurked in the shadows until midnight and then carried the child to Oberon's palace, where the walls were woven of vines and inlaid with grapes and ripe fruit. . . . No, Laura thought, her large, square hands joined in the peasant's gesture of hope-lessness, she didn't want a guardian spirit; she wanted to devote her entire existence to the child.

The baby cried on, still in its lonely void just before Genesis, before the earth is formed, where nothing has been named yet, and there is only the mother's face and the mother's breast, like the sun and the moon. But the crying was softer now, temporarily eased by the orbital warmth of another presence, and Laura looked down, aware that she was afraid. Her hands moved upward and pressed against her eyes, but the fear oozed through, in brighter and brighter streams. Laura impulsively reached for the baby. But I mustn't pick it up when I'm disturbed, she thought. I'll frighten it. Her hands lay twitching near the crying baby's head. Just holding it will comfort me. *Why can't I think?*

Tears streamed down Laura's face. She withdrew her hands from the baby's crib and pressed them one into the other, for warmth. She knew she was overtired. Every three hours, all through the day and night, Laura nursed the baby. In bright light, her face was gray with fatigue, and sometimes parts of her body would begin to twitch, as her hands were doing now; sometimes it was her leg, and sometimes her shoulder, and she couldn't control them.

'But I wanted to be a mother!' Laura cried. 'At least, I think I did.' She let herself sink wearily to the floor until her face peered at the baby's through the bars of the crib. 'Baby, don't cry. Mother's here. And you just ate. I can't feed you again. I haven't enough milk yet, anyway. Look, baby, Mummy's making faces at you.' The baby cooed faintly between sobs. 'Please tell me you're crying just for exercise. Please? Tell me I haven't ruined you.'

There were bottles for supplementary feeding in the ice-box downstairs. You take the bottle and loosen the cap so the bottle won't explode, and put it in a pan of water and heat it. Then you test it on your wrist. . . . No, Laura thought grimly, I won't. The baby and I'll work it out together. A voice in the back of her mind said, 'You're being romantic, Laura. You're being silly. Your baby's crying, and you think silly thoughts about motherhood and how you're going to be a natural mother.' The voice was her husband's.

'That's not true,' Laura said desperately. 'I don't think anything. I don't know how to think. That's my whole problem.'

Once, her husband had told her (they'd been lying side by side in bed, looking out their window at a particularly large and beautiful moon), 'Darling, you're so absurdly romantic. No one else says "I belong to you" and means it, the way you do. Do you know what I think?'

'What?' Laura had said, with an expression of hurt but secretly feeling pleasure at being the subject of the discussion.

'When you were little, you never developed defenses, the way normal people do. You were too spoiled. You never had to save yourself. You could always run to someone and smile at them, and they'd love you – as I do.'

'That's not so,' Laura said. But she remembered how her father's face had softened when she clambered on his knee and raised her pudgy hands for him to kiss. ('Mummy says I'm a bad girl.' 'Maybe you are,' her father had said, but he had laughed.)

'I was a very lonely child,' Laura said to her husband, lying there in the bright moonlight. *How pure it is*, she thought; *if only I could wear it.*

'Laura,' her husband cried, 'you only say that because you read it somewhere!' Tears gathered in her eyes, in the moonlight – because he was right, and it was depressing.

Since her husband hated her to cry, she stuffed her hand into her mouth so he couldn't hear her. And then, because she feared that he might not understand that she didn't blame him for anything, she bit her ring finger – pressed her teeth as hard as she could until the skin broke and the blood welled out warm and soothing. Laura lay for a moment savoring the pleasure of sacrifice, and then she turned and held out her hand to her husband. 'See how much I love you.'

'Laura!' he cried in exasperation, but the exasperation disappeared in laughter, and he rolled over so she could put her arms around him – she was almost as big as he was – and stroke him as one strokes a dog, until he stopped worrying and lay warm and placid on her shoulder. 'I deserve you because I put up with you,' he murmured.

But he *is* right, Laura thought now. I have a bad character; I have flaws. The baby was entranced with her faces. It reached out its tiny hand and gripped her nose. The fingernails were sharp and scratched at the tender membrane in her nostrils. Laura smiled and made noises at the baby. Surreptitiously, with one hand, she tested her breast, but there wasn't enough milk.

'Please don't cry any more,' Laura said. 'The milk is almost here. Just a few more minutes.'

She stood up and lifted the baby and held it on her shoulder and began to walk around the room with it, singing nonsense songs. Outside, the sky was turning purple and the locust trees down the block were swaying delicately. Soon her husband would come home and tell her what to do, persuade her to use the bottled supplement. Laura was

perspiring gently. But the baby was already ruined, of course;
she didn't love it. It was too much trouble. She didn't love
anything. The baby was riding on her shoulder, a strange
little lump that made noises. Laura began to stride around
the room, and the song she was singing suddenly marched
into a menacing minor key:

> 'Lumpen, lumpen, little lumpen
> On my shoulder you are bumpen . . .'

The telephone rang. The baby gave a startled little leap.
In sudden distaste, Laura half slung, half dropped the baby
in its crib and ran to the telephone; she was going to talk to
the outside world. How wonderful telephones were! She flew
down the steps. Behind her, the baby began to make small
noises. 'She's just exercising,' Laura said aloud, to the hall
mirror. She picked up the telephone. 'Oh, it's you, Mother.'
Cars moved up and down the street, the shadows were sliding eastward, and out of the dining-room window the sun
lay in the west, ripe and glowing. 'No, I'm not tired, Mother.
I don't want you to come over and help. . . . Mother, please.
. . . Yes, that's the baby crying. . . . Mother, I don't want that
awful nurse back. . . . I don't care if my waist hasn't gone back
to normal. I mean I *do* care, but not now. . . . Mother, I have
to go. . . .'

The baby was bawling again, and her mother was in the
middle of an expostulation, but nothing mattered, thank
God, because her breasts were full. Dreamily, not thinking,
or even knowing what she was doing, she slipped the receiver
on its hook. It was important to tiptoe, to move very quietly,
in order not to spill the happiness. You have to be happy
when you feed your baby; otherwise, the milk is poisoned or
something.

The crying had such a needy sound, but how could it be

desperate or frightened when she had her milk full in her breasts? Laura's hands unfolded into the crib, like flowers opening, and nestled the baby. Laura's sloppy dress slithered on her shoulders as she wiggled, and finally it fell free. One was supposed to wash the nipple with boiled water and antiseptic cotton, but 'After all,' Laura whispered, 'Mother's germs are nice germs.' The tiny head cradled itself in her hand; the tiny mouth clutched the nipple. Laura giggled amiably, aimlessly, and settled herself in the rocker she'd bought in a junk shop for two dollars, over her husband's objections. The chair began to move gently. The baby sucked. Laura smiled down at her nether heart and said, 'You'll give me back to me, won't you? When you don't need me.' And then she laughed, because her daughter looked so fierce clutching at the nipple and eating.

BARBARA KINGSOLVER

ISLANDS ON THE MOON

ANNEMARIE'S MOTHER, MAGDA, is one of a kind. She wears sandals and one-hundred-percent-cotton dresses and walks like she's crossing plowed ground. She makes necklaces from the lacquered vertebrae of non-endangered species. Her hair is wavy and long and threaded with gray. She's forty-four.

Annemarie has always believed that if life had turned out better her mother would have been an artist. As it is, Magda just has to ooze out a little bit of art in everything she does, so that no part of her life is exactly normal. She paints landscapes on her tea kettles, for example, and dates younger men. Annemarie's theory is that everyone has some big thing, the rock in their road, that has kept them from greatness or so they would like to think. Magda had Annemarie when she was sixteen and has been standing on tiptoe ever since to see over or around her difficult daughter to whatever is on the other side. Annemarie just assumed that she was the rock in her mother's road. Until now. Now she has no idea.

On the morning Magda's big news arrived in the mail, Annemarie handed it over to her son Leon without even reading it, thinking it was just one of her standard cards. 'Another magic message from Grandma Magda,' she'd said, and Leon had rolled his eyes. He's nine years old, but that's only part of it. Annemarie influences him, telling my-most-embarrassing-moment stories about growing up with a mother like Magda, and Leon buys them wholesale, right along with nine-times-nine and the capital of Wyoming.

For example, Magda has always sent out winter solstice cards of her own design, printed on paper she makes by boiling down tree bark and weeds. The neighbors always smell it, and once, when Annemarie was a teenager, they reported Magda as a nuisance.

But it's April now so this isn't a solstice card. It's not homemade, either. It came from one of those stores where you can buy a personalized astrology chart for a baby gift. The paper is yellowed and smells of incense. Leon holds it to his nose, then turns it in his hands, not trying to decipher Magda's slanty handwriting but studying the ink drawing that runs around the border. Leon has curly black hair, like Magda's – and like Annemarie's would be, if she didn't continually crop it and bleach it and wax it into spikes. But Leon doesn't care who he looks like. He's entirely unconscious of himself as he sits there, ears sticking out, heels banging the stool at the kitchen counter. One of Annemarie's cats rubs the length of its spine along his green hightop sneaker.

'It looks like those paper dolls that come out all together, holding hands,' he says. 'Only they're fattish, like old ladies. Dancing.'

'That's about what I'd decided,' says Annemarie.

Leon hands the card back and heads for fresh air. The bang of the screen door is the closest she gets these days to a good-bye kiss.

Where, in a world where kids play with Masters of the Universe, has Leon encountered holding-hands paper dolls? This is what disturbs Annemarie. Her son is normal in every obvious way but has a freakish awareness of old-fashioned things. He collects things: old Coke bottles, license-plate slogans, anything. They'll be driving down Broadway and he'll call out 'Illinois Land of Lincoln!' And he saves string. Annemarie found it in a ball, rolled into a sweatsock. It's as

46

if some whole piece of Magda has come through to Leon without even touching her.

She reads the card and stares at the design, numb, trying to see what these little fat dancing women have to be happy about. She and her mother haven't spoken for months, although either one can see the other's mobile home when she steps out on the porch to shake the dust mop. Magda says she's willing to wait until Annemarie stops emitting negative energy toward her. In the meantime she sends cards.

Annemarie is suddenly stricken, as she often is, with the feeling she's about to be abandoned. Leon will take Magda's side. He'll think this new project of hers is great, and mine's awful. Magda always wins without looking like she was trying.

Annemarie stands at the kitchen sink staring out the window at her neighbors' porch, which is twined with queen's wreath and dusty honeysuckle, a stalwart oasis in the desert of the trailer court. A plaster Virgin Mary, painted in blue and rose and the type of cheap, shiny gold that chips easily, presides over the barbecue pit, and three lawn chairs with faded webbing are drawn up close around it as if for some secret family ceremony. A wooden sign hanging from the porch awning proclaims that they are 'The Navarrete's' over there. Their grandson, who lives with them, made the sign in Boy Scouts. Ten years Annemarie has been trying to get out of this trailer court, and the people next door are so content with themselves they hang out a shingle.

Before she knows it she's crying, wiping her face with the backs of her dishpan hands. This is completely normal. All morning she sat by herself watching nothing in particular on TV, and cried when Luis and Maria got married on *Sesame Street*. It's the hormones. She hasn't told him yet, but she's going to have another child besides Leon. The big news in Magda's card is that she is going to have another child too, besides Annemarie.

When she tries to be reasonable – and she is trying at the moment, sitting in a Denny's with her best friend Kay Kay – Annemarie knows that mid-forties isn't too old to have boy-friends. But Magda doesn't seem mid-forties, she seems like Grandma Moses in moonstone earrings. She's the type who's proud about not having to go to the store for some little thing because she can rummage around in the kitchen drawers until she finds some other thing that will serve just as well. For her fifth birthday Annemarie screamed for a Bubble-Hairdo Barbie just because she knew there wouldn't be one in the kitchen drawer.

   Annemarie's side of the story is that she had to fight her way out of a family that smelled like an old folks' home. Her father was devoted and funny, chasing her around the house after dinner in white paper-napkin masks with eyeholes, and he could fix anything on wheels, and then without warning he turned into a wheezing old man with taut-skinned hands rattling a bottle of pills. Then he was dead, leaving behind a medicinal pall that hung over Annemarie and followed her to school. They'd saved up just enough to move to Tucson, for his lungs, and the injustice of it stung her. He'd breathed the scorched desert air for a single autumn, and Annemarie had to go on breathing it one summer after another. In New Hampshire she'd had friends, as many as the trees had leaves, but they couldn't get back there now. Magda was vague and useless, no protection from poverty. Only fathers, it seemed, offered that particular safety. Magda reminded her that the Little Women were poor too, and for all practical purposes fatherless, but Annemarie didn't care. The March girls didn't have to live in a trailer court.

Eventually Magda went on dates. By that time Annemarie was sneaking Marlboros and fixing her hair and hanging around by the phone, and would have given her eye teeth for as many offers – but Magda threw them away. Even back then, she didn't get attached to men. She devoted herself instead to saving every rubber band and piece of string that entered their door. Magda does the things people used to do in other centuries, before it occurred to them to pay someone else to do them. Annemarie's friends think this is wonderful. Magda is so old-fashioned she's come back into style. And she's committed. She intends to leave her life savings, if any, to Save the Planet, and tells Annemarie she should be more concerned about the stewardship of the earth. Kay Kay thinks she ought to be the president. 'You want to trade?' she routinely asks. 'You want my mother?'

'What's wrong with your mother?' Annemarie wants to know.

'What's wrong with my mother,' Kay Kay answers, shaking her head. Everybody thinks they've got a corner on the market, thinks Annemarie.

Kay Kay is five feet two and has green eyes and drives a locomotive for Southern Pacific. She's had the same lover, a rock 'n' roll singer named Connie Skylab, for as long as Annemarie has known her. Kay Kay and Connie take vacations that just amaze Annemarie: they'll go skiing, or hang-gliding, or wind-surfing down in Puerto Peñasco. Annemarie often wishes she could do just one brave thing in her lifetime. Like hang-gliding.

'Okay, here you go,' says Kay Kay. 'For my birthday my mother sent me one of those fold-up things you carry in your purse for covering up the toilet seat. "Honey, you're on the go so much," she says to me. "And besides there's AIDS to

49

think about now." The guys at work think I ought to have it bronzed.'

'At least she didn't try to *knit* you a toilet-seat cover, like Magda would,' says Annemarie. 'She bought it at a store, right?'

'Number one,' Kay Kay says, 'I don't carry a purse when I'm driving a train. And number two, I don't know how to tell Ma this, but the bathrooms in those engines don't even *have* a seat.'

Annemarie and Kay Kay are having lunch. Kay Kay spends her whole life in restaurants when she isn't driving a train. She says if you're going to pull down thirty-eight thousand a year, why cook?

'At least you had a normal childhood,' Annemarie says, taking a mirror-compact out of her purse, confirming that she looks awful, and snapping it shut. 'I was the only teenager in America that couldn't use hairspray because it's death to the ozone layer.'

'I just don't see what's so terrible about Magda caring what happens to the world,' Kay Kay says.

'It's morbid. All those war marches she goes on. How can you think all the time about nuclear winter wiping out life as we know it, and still go on making your car payments?'

Kay Kay smiles.

'She mainly just does it to remind me what a slug I am. I didn't turn out all gung-ho like she wanted me to.'

'That's not true,' Kay Kay says. 'You're very responsible, in your way. I think Magda just wants a safe world for you and Leon. My mother couldn't care less if the world went to hell in a handbasket, as long as her nail color was coordinated with her lipstick.'

Annemarie can never make people see. She cradles her chin mournfully in her palms. Annemarie has surprisingly fair skin for a black-haired person, which she is in principle. That particular complexion, from Magda's side of the family, has dropped unaltered through the generations like a rock. They are fine-boned, too, with graceful necks and fingers that curve outward slightly at the tips. Annemarie has wished for awful things in her lifetime, even stubby fingers, something to set her apart.

'I got my first period,' she tells Kay Kay, unable to drop the subject, 'at this *die-in* she organized against the Vietnam War. I had horrible cramps and nobody paid any attention; they all thought I was just dying-in.'

'And you're never going to forgive her,' Kay Kay says. 'You ought to have a T-shirt made up: "I hate my mother because I got my first period at a die-in."'

Annemarie attends to her salad, which she has no intention of eating. Two tables away, a woman in a western shirt and heavy turquoise jewelry is watching Annemarie in a maternal way over her husband's shoulder. 'She just has to one-up me,' says Annemarie. 'Her due date is a month before mine.'

'I can see where you'd be upset,' Kay Kay says, 'but she didn't know. You didn't even tell me till a month ago. It's not like she grabbed some guy off the street and said, "Quick, knock me up so I can steal my daughter's thunder."'

Annemarie doesn't like to think about Magda having sex with some guy off the street. 'She should have an abortion,' she says. 'Childbirth is unsafe at her age.'

'Your mother can't part with the rubber band off the Sunday paper.'

This is true. Annemarie picks off the alfalfa sprouts, which she didn't ask for in the first place. Magda used to make her wheat-germ sandwiches, knowing full well she despised sprouts and anything else that was recently a seed. Annemarie

51

is crying now and there's no disguising it. She was still a kid when she had Leon, but this baby she'd intended to do on her own. With a man maybe, but not with her mother prancing around on center stage.

'Lots of women have babies in their forties,' Kay Kay says. 'Look at Goldie Hawn.'

'Goldie Hawn isn't my mother. *And* she's married.'

'Is the father that guy I met? Bartholomew?'

'The father is not in the picture. That's a quote. You know Magda and men; she's not going to let the grass grow under *her* bed.'

Kay Kay is looking down at her plate, using her knife and fork in a serious way that shows all the tendons in her hands. Kay Kay generally argues with Annemarie only if she's putting herself down. When she starts in on Magda, Kay Kay mostly just listens.

'Ever since Daddy died she's never looked back,' Annemarie says, blinking. Her contact lenses are foundering, like skaters on a flooded rink.

'And you think she ought to look back?'

'I don't know. Yeah.' She dabs at her eyes, trying not to look at the woman with the turquoise bracelets. 'It bothers me. Bartholomew's in love with her. Another guy wants to marry her. All these guys are telling her how beautiful she is. And look at me, it seems like every year I'm crying over another boyfriend gone west, not even counting Leon's dad.' She takes a bite of lettuce and chews on empty calories. 'I'm still driving the Pontiac I bought ten years ago, but I've gone through six boyfriends and a husband. Twice. I was married to Buddy twice.'

'Well, look at it this way, at least you've got a good car,' says Kay Kay.

'Now that this kid's on the way he's talking about going

for marriage number three. Him and Leon are in cahoots, I think.'

'You and Buddy again?'

'Buddy's settled down a lot,' Annemarie insists. 'I think I could get him to stay home more this time.' Buddy wears braids like his idol, Willie Nelson, and drives a car with flames painted on the hood. When Annemarie says he has settled down, she means that whereas he used to try to avoid work in his father's lawnmower repair shop, now he owns it.

'Maybe it would be good for Leon. A boy needs his dad.'

'Oh, Leon's a rock, like me,' says Annemarie. 'It comes from growing up alone. When I try to do any little thing for Leon he acts like I'm the creature from the swamp. I know he'd rather live with Buddy. He'll be out the door for good one of these days.'

'Well, you never know, it might work out with you and Buddy,' Kay Kay says brightly. 'Maybe third time's a charm.'

'Oh, sure. Seems like guys want to roll through my life like the drive-in window. Probably me and Buddy'll end up going for divorce number three.' She pulls a paper napkin out of the holder and openly blows her nose.

'Why don't you take the afternoon off?' Kay Kay suggests. 'Go home and take a nap. I'll call your boss for you, and tell him you've got afternoon sickness or something.'

Annemarie visibly shrugs off Kay Kay's concern. 'Oh, I couldn't, he'd kill me. I'd better get on back.' Annemarie is assistant manager of a discount delivery service called 'Yesterday!' and really holds the place together, though she denies it.

'Well, don't get down in the dumps,' says Kay Kay gently. 'You've just got the baby blues.'

'If it's not one kind of blues it's another. I can't help it. Just the sound of the word "divorced" makes me feel like I'm dragging around a suitcase of dirty handkerchiefs.'

Kay Kay nods.

'The thing that gets me about Magda is, man or no man, it's all the same to her,' Annemarie explains, feeling the bitterness of this truth between her teeth like a sour apple. 'When it comes to men, she doesn't even carry any luggage.'

The woman in the turquoise bracelets stops watching Annemarie and gets up to go to the restroom. The husband, whose back is turned, waits for the bill.

The telephone wakes Annemarie. It's not late, only a little past seven, the sun is still up, and she's confused. She must have fallen asleep without meaning to. She is cut through with terror while she struggles to place where Leon is and remember whether he's been fed. Since his birth, falling asleep in the daytime has served up to Annemarie this momentary shock of guilt.

When she hears the voice on the phone and understands who it is, she stares at the receiver, thinking somehow that it's not her phone. She hasn't heard her mother's voice for such a long time.

'All I'm asking is for you to go with me to the clinic,' Magda is saying. 'You don't have to look at the needle. You don't have to hold my hand.' She waits, but Annemarie is speechless. 'You don't even have to talk to me. Just peck on the receiver: once if you'll go, twice if you won't.' Magda is trying to sound light-hearted, but Annemarie realizes with a strange satisfaction that she must be very afraid. She's going to have amniocentesis.

'Are you all right?' Magda asks. 'You sound woozy.'

'Why wouldn't I be all right,' Annemarie snaps. She runs a hand through her hair, which is spiked with perspiration, and regains herself. 'Why on earth are you even having it done, the amniowhatsis, if you think it's going to be so awful?'

'My doctor won't be my doctor anymore unless I have it. It's kind of a requirement for women my age.'

A yellow tabby cat walks over Annemarie's leg and jumps off the bed. Annemarie is constantly taking in strays, joking to Kay Kay that if Leon leaves her at least she won't be alone, she'll have the cats. She has eleven or twelve at the moment.

'Well, it's probably for the best,' Annemarie tells Magda, in the brisk voice she uses to let Magda know she is a citizen of the world, unlike some people. 'It will ease your mind, anyway, to know the baby's okay.'

'Oh, I'm not going to look at the results,' Magda explains. 'I told Dr Lavinna I'd have it, and have the results sent over to his office, but I don't want to know. That was our compromise.'

'Why don't you want to know the results?' asks Annemarie. 'You could even know if it was a boy or a girl. You could pick out a name.'

'As if it's such hard work to pick out an extra name,' says Magda, 'that I should go have needles poked into me to save myself the trouble?'

'I just don't see why you wouldn't want to know.'

'People spend their whole lives with labels stuck on them, Annemarie. I just think it would be nice for this one to have nine months of being a plain human being.'

'Mother knows best,' sighs Annemarie, and she has the feeling she's always had, that she's sinking in a bog of mud. 'You two should just talk,' Kay Kay sometimes insists, and Annemarie can't get across that it's like quicksand. It's like reasoning with the sand trap at a golf course. There is no beginning and no end to the conversation she needs to have with Magda, and she'd rather just steer clear.

* * *

55

The following day, after work, Kay Kay comes over to help Annemarie get her evaporative cooler going for the summer. It's up on the roof of her mobile home. They have to climb up there with the vacuum cleaner and a long extension cord and clean out a winter's worth of dust and twigs and wayward insect parts. Then they will paint the bottom of the tank with tar, and install new pads, and check the water lines. Afterward, Kay Kay has promised she'll take Annemarie to the Dairy Queen for a milkshake. Kay Kay is looking after her friend in a carefully offhand way that Annemarie hasn't quite noticed.

It actually hasn't dawned on Annemarie that she's halfway through a pregnancy. She just doesn't think about what's going on in there, other than having some vague awareness that someone has moved in and is rearranging the furniture of her body. She's been thinking mostly about what pants she can still fit into. It was this way the first time, too. At six months she marched with Buddy down the aisle in an empire gown and seed-pearl tiara and no one suspected a thing, including, in her heart-of-hearts, Annemarie. Seven weeks later Leon sprang out of her body with his mouth open, already yelling, and neither one of them has ever quite gotten over the shock.

It's not that she doesn't want this baby, she tells Kay Kay; she didn't at first, but now she's decided. Leon has reached the age where he dodges her kisses like wild pitches over home plate, and she could use someone around to cuddle. 'But there are so many things I have to get done, before I can have it,' she says.

'Like what kind of things?' Kay Kay has a bandana tied around her head and is slapping the tar around energetically. She's used to dirty work. She says after you've driven a few hundred miles with your head out the window of a locomotive you don't just take a washcloth to your face, you have to wash your *teeth*.

'Oh, I don't know.' Annemarie sits back on her heels. The metal roof is too hot to touch, but the view from up there is interesting, almost like it's not where she lives. The mobile homes are arranged like shoeboxes along the main drive, with cars and motorbikes parked beside them, just so many toys in a sandbox. The shadows of things trail away everywhere in the same direction like long oil leaks across the gravel. The trailer court is called 'Island Breezes,' and like the names of most trailer courts, it's a joke. No swaying palm trees. In fact, there's no official vegetation at all except for cactus plants in straight, symmetrical rows along the drive, like some bizarre desert organized by a child.

'Well, deciding what to do about Buddy, for instance,' Annemarie says at last, after Kay Kay has clearly forgotten the question. 'I need to figure that out first. And also what I'd do with a baby while I'm at work. I couldn't leave it with Magda, they'd all be down at the Air Force Base getting arrested to stop the cruise missiles.'

Kay Kay doesn't say anything. She wraps the tarred, spiky paintbrush in a plastic bag and begins to pry last year's cooler pads out of the frames. Annemarie is being an absent-minded helper, staring into space, sometimes handing Kay Kay a screwdriver when she's asked for the pliers.

With a horrible screeching of claws on metal, one of Annemarie's cats, Lone Ranger, has managed to get himself up to the roof in pursuit of a lizard. He's surprised to see the women up there; he freezes and then slinks away along the gutter. Lone Ranger is a problem cat. Annemarie buys him special food, anything to entice him, but he won't come inside and be pampered. He cowers and shrinks from love like a blast from the hose.

'How long you think you'll take off work?' Kay Kay asks.

'Take off?'

'When the baby comes.'

'Oh, I don't know,' Annemarie says, uneasily. She could endanger her job there if she doesn't give them some kind of advance notice. She's well aware, even when Kay Kay refrains from pointing it out, that she's responsible in a hit-or-miss way. Once, toward the end of their first marriage, Buddy totaled his car and she paid to have it repaired so he wouldn't leave her. The next weekend he drove to Reno with a woman who sold newspapers from a traffic island.

Annemarie begins to unwrap the new cooler pads, which look like huge, flat sponges and smell like fresh sawdust. According to the label they're made of aspen, which Annemarie thought was a place where you go skiing and try to get a glimpse of Jack Nicholson. 'You'd think they could make these things out of plastic,' she says. 'They'd last longer, and it wouldn't smell like a damn camping trip every time you turn on your cooler.'

'They have to absorb water, though,' explains Kay Kay. 'That's the whole point. When the fan blows through the wet pads it cools down the air.'

Annemarie is in the mood where she can't get particularly interested in the way things work. She holds two of the pads against herself like a hula skirt. 'I could see these as a costume, couldn't you? For Connie?'

'That's an idea,' Kay Kay says, examining them thoughtfully. 'Connie's allergic to grasses, but not wood fibers.'

Annemarie's bones ache to be known and loved this well. What she wouldn't give for someone to stand on a roof, half-way across the city, and say to some other person, 'Annemarie's allergic to grasses, but not wood fibers.'

'I'll mention it,' Kay Kay says. 'The band might go for it.'

Connie Skylab and the Falling Debris are into outlandish looks. Connie performs one number, 'My Mother's Teeth,' dressed in a black plastic garbage bag and a necklace of sheep's molars. A line Annemarie remembers is: 'My mother's teeth grow in my head, I'll eat my children's dreams when she is dead.'

Connie's mother is, in actual fact, dead. But neither she nor Kay Kay plans to produce any children. Annemarie thinks maybe that's how they can be so happy and bold. Their relationship is a sleek little boat of their own construction, untethered in either direction by the knotted ropes of motherhood, free to sail the open seas. Some people can manage it. Annemarie once met a happily married couple who made jewelry and traveled the nation in a dented microbus, selling their wares on street corners. They had no permanent address whatsoever, no traditions, no family. They told Annemarie they never celebrated holidays.

And then on the other hand there are the Navarretes next door with their little nest of lawn chairs. They're happy too. Annemarie feels permanently disqualified from either camp, the old-fashioned family or the new. It's as if she somehow got left behind, missed every boat across the river, and now must watch happiness being acted out on the beach of a distant shore.

Two days later, on Saturday, Annemarie pulls on sweat pants and a T-shirt, starts up her Pontiac – scattering cats in every direction – and drives a hundred feet to pick up Magda and take her to the clinic. There just wasn't any reasonable way out.

The sun is reflected so brightly off the road it's like driving on a mirage. The ground is as barren as some planet where it rains once per century. It has been an unusually dry spring, though it doesn't much matter here in Island Breezes, where the lawns are made of gravel. Some people, deeply missing the Midwest, have spray-painted their gravel green.

Magda's yard is naturally the exception. It's planted with many things, including clumps of aloe vera, which she claims heals burns, and most recently, a little hand-painted sign with a blue dove that explains to all and sundry passers-by that you can't hug your kids with nuclear arms. When Annemarie drives up, Magda's standing out on the wooden steps in one of her loose India-print cotton dresses, and looks cool. Annemarie is envious. Magda's ordinary wardrobe will carry her right through the ninth month.

Magda's hair brushes her shoulders like a lace curtain as she gets into the car, and she seems flushed and excited, though perhaps it's nerves. She fishes around in her enormous woven bag and pulls out a bottle of green shampoo. 'I thought you might like to try this. It has an extract of nettles. I know to you that probably sounds awful, but it's really good; it can repair damaged hair shafts.'

Annemarie beeps impatiently at some kids playing kickball in the drive near the front entrance. 'Magda, can we please not start right in *immediately* on my hair? Can we at least say, "How do you do" and "Fine thank you" before we start in on my hair?'

'Sorry.'

'Believe it or not, I actually *want* my hair to look like something dead beside the road. It's the style now.'

Magda looks around behind the seat for the seat belt and buckles it up. She refrains from saying anything about Annemarie's seat belt. They literally don't speak again until they get where they're going.

At the clinic they find themselves listening to a lecture on AIDS prevention. Apparently it's a mandatory part of the services here. Before Magda's amniocentesis they need to sit with the other patients and learn about nonoxynol-number-9 spermicide and the proper application of a condom.

'You want to leave a little room at the end, like this,' says the nurse, who's wearing jeans and red sneakers. She rolls the condom carefully onto a plastic banana. All the other people in the room look fourteen, and there are some giggles. Their mothers probably go around saying that they and their daughters are 'close,' and have no idea they're here today getting birth control and what not.

Finally Magda gets to see the doctor, but it's a more complicated procedure than Annemarie expected: first they have to take a sonogram, to make sure that when they stick in the needle they won't poke the baby.

'Even if that did happen,' the doctor explains, 'the fetus will usually just move out of the way.' Annemarie is floored to imagine a five-month-old fetus fending for itself. She tries to think of what's inside her as being an actual baby, or a baby-to-be, but can't. She hasn't even felt it move yet.

The doctor rubs Magda's belly with Vaseline and then places against it something that looks like a Ping-Pong paddle wired for sound. She frowns at the TV screen, concentrating, and then points. 'Look, there, you can see the head.'

Magda and Annemarie watch a black-and-white screen where meaningless shadows move around each other like iridescent ink blots. Suddenly they can make out one main shadow, fish-shaped with a big head, like Casper the Friendly Ghost.

'The bladder's full,' the doctor says. 'See that little clear spot? That's a good sign, it means the kidneys are working. Oops, there it went.'

'There what went?' asks Magda.

'The bladder. It voided.' She looks closely at the screen, smiling. 'You know, I can't promise you but I think what you've got here...'

'Don't tell me,' Magda says. 'If you're going to tell me if it's a boy or a girl, I don't want to know.'

'I do,' says Annemarie. 'Tell me.'

'Is that okay with you?' the doctor asks Magda, and Magda shrugs. 'Close your eyes, then,' she tells Magda. She holds up two glass tubes with rubber stoppers, one pink and the other blue-green. She nods at the pink one.

Annemarie smiles. 'Okay, all clear,' she tells Magda. 'My lips are sealed.'

'That's the face, right there,' the doctor says, pointing out the eyes. 'It has one fist in its mouth; that's very common at this stage. Can you see it?'

They can see it. The other fist, the left one, is raised up alongside its huge head like the Black Panther salute. Magda is transfixed. Annemarie can see the flickering light of the screen reflected in her eyes, and she understands for the first time that what they are looking at here is not a plan or a plot, it has nothing to do with herself. It's Magda's future.

Afterward they have to go straight to the park to pick up Leon from softball practice. It's hot, and Annemarie drives distractedly, worrying about Leon because they're late. She talked him into joining the league in the first place; he'd just as soon stay home and collect baseball cards. But now she worries that he'll get hit with a ball, or kidnapped by some pervert that hangs around in the park waiting for the one little boy whose mother's late. She hits the brakes at a crosswalk to let three women pass safely through the traffic, walking with their thin brown arms so close together they could be holding hands. They're apparently three generations of a family: the grandmother is draped elaborately in a sari, the mother is in pink slacks, and the daughter wears a bleached denim miniskirt. But from the back they could be triplets. Three long braids, woven as thin and tight as ropes, bounce placidly against their backs as they walk away from the stopped cars.

'Was it as bad as you thought it would be?' Annemarie asks Magda. It's awkward to be speaking after all this time, so suddenly, and really for no good reason.

'It was worse.'

'I liked the sonogram,' Annemarie says. 'I liked seeing it, didn't you?'

'Yes, but not the other part. I hate doctors and needles and that whole thing. Doctors treat women like a disease in progress.'

That's Magda, Annemarie thinks. You never know what's going to come out of her mouth next. Annemarie thinks the doctor was just about as nice as possible. But in fairness to Magda, the needle was unbelievably long. It made her skin draw up into goose pimples just to watch. Magda seems worn out from the experience.

Annemarie rolls down the window to signal a left turn at the intersection. Her blinkers don't work, but at least the air conditioning still does. In the summer when her mobile home heats up like a toaster oven, the car is Annemarie's refuge. Sometimes she'll drive across town on invented, insignificant errands, singing along with Annie Lennox on the radio and living for the moment in a small, safe, perfectly cooled place.

'I'd have this baby at home if I could,' says Magda.

'Why can't you?'

'Too old,' she says, complacently. 'I talked to the midwife program but they risked me out.'

The sun seems horribly bright. Annemarie thinks she's read something about pregnancy making your eyes sensitive to light. 'Was it an awful shock, when you found out?' she asks Magda.

'About the midwives?'

'No. About the pregnancy.'

Magda looks at her as if she's dropped from another planet.

'What's the matter?' asks Annemarie.

'I've been trying my whole life to have more babies. You knew that, that I'd been trying.'

'No, I didn't. Just lately?'

'No, Annemarie, not just lately, forever. The whole time with your father we kept trying, but the drugs he took for the cancer knocked out his sperms. The doctor told us they were still alive, but were too confused to make a baby.'

Annemarie tries not to smile. 'Too confused?'

'That's what he said.'

'And you've kept on ever since then?' she asks.

'I kept hoping, but I'd about given up. I feel like this baby is a gift.'

Annemarie thinks of one of the customers at Yesterday! who sent relatives a Christmas fruitcake that somehow got lost; it arrived two and a half years later on the twelfth of July. Magda's baby is like the fruitcake, she thinks, and she shakes her head and laughs.

'What's so funny?'

'Nothing. I just can't believe you wanted a bunch of kids. You never said so. I thought even having just me got in your way.'

'Got in my way?'

'Well, yeah. Because you were so young. I thought that's why you weren't mad when Buddy and I had to get married,

64

because you'd done the same thing. I always figured my middle name ought to have been Whoops.'

Magda looks strangely at Annemarie again. 'I had to douche with vinegar to get pregnant with you,' she says.

They've reached the park, and Leon is waiting with his bat slung over his shoulder like a dangerous character. 'The other kids' moms already came ten hours ago,' he says when he gets into the car. He doesn't seem at all surprised to see Magda and Annemarie in the same vehicle.

'We got held up,' Annemarie says. 'Sorry, Leon.'

Leon stares out the window for a good while. 'Leon's a stupid name,' he says, eventually. This is a complaint of his these days.

'There have been a lot of important Leons in history,' Annemarie says.

'Like who?'

She considers this. 'Leon Russell,' she says. 'He's a rock and roll singer.'

'Leon Trotsky,' says Magda.

Annemarie has heard all about Leon Trotsky in her time, and Rosa Luxemburg, and Mother Jones.

'Trotsky was an important socialist who disagreed with Stalin's methodology,' Magda explains. 'Stalin was the king-pin at the time, so Trotsky had to run for his life to Mexico.'

'This all happened decades ago, I might add,' Annemarie says, glancing at Leon in the rear-view mirror.

'He was killed by his trusted secretary,' Magda continues. 'With an axe in the head.'

'Magda, please. You think he'll like his name better if he knows many famous Leons have been axed?'

'I'm telling him my girlhood memories. I'm trying to be a good grandmother.'

'Your girlhood memories? What, were you there?'

'Of course not, it happened in Mexico, before I was born. But it affected me. I read about it when I was a teenager, and I cried. My father said, "Oh, I remember seeing that headline in the paper and thinking, What, Trotsky's dead? *Hal* Trotsky, first baseman for the Cleveland Indians?"'

'Live Free or Die, New Hampshire!' shouts Leon at an approaching car.

Magda says, 'Annemarie's father came from New Hampshire.'

Annemarie runs a stop sign.

It isn't clear to her what's happened. There is a crunch of metal and glass, and some white thing plowing like a torpedo into the left side of the Pontiac, and they spin around, seeing the same view pass by again and again. Then Annemarie is lying across Magda with her mouth open and her head out the window on the passenger's side. Magda's arms are tight around her chest. The window has vanished, and there is a feeling like sand trickling through Annemarie's hair. After a minute she realizes that a sound is coming out of her mouth. It's a scream. She closes her mouth and it stops.

With some effort she unbuckles Magda's seat belt and pulls the door handle and they more or less tumble out together onto the ground. It strikes Annemarie, for no good reason, that Magda isn't a very big person. She's Annemarie's own size, if not smaller. The sun is unbelievably bright. There's no other traffic. A woman gets out of the white car with the New Hampshire plates, brushing her beige skirt in a businesslike way and straightening her hair. Oddly, she has on stockings but no shoes. She looks at the front end of her car, which resembles a metal cauliflower, and then at the two women hugging each other on the ground.

'There was a stop sign,' she says. Her voice is clear as a

66

song in the strange silence. A series of rapid clicks emanates from the underside of one of the cars, then stops.

'I guess I missed it,' Annemarie says.

'Are you okay?' the woman asks. She looks hard at Annemarie's face. Annemarie puts her hand on her head, and it feels wet.

'I'm fine,' she and Magda say at the same time.

'You're bleeding,' the woman says to Annemarie. She looks down at herself, and then carefully unbuttons her white blouse and holds it out to Annemarie. 'You'd better let me tie this around your head,' she says. 'Then I'll go call the police.'

'All right,' says Annemarie. She pries apart Magda's fingers, which seem to be stuck, and they pull each other up. The woman pulls the blouse across Annemarie's bleeding forehead and knots the silk sleeves tightly at the nape of her neck. She does this while standing behind Annemarie in her stocking feet and brassière, with Magda looking on, and somehow it has the feeling of some ordinary female ritual.

'Oh, God,' says Annemarie. She looks at the Pontiac and sits back down on the ground. The back doors of the car are standing wide open, and Leon is gone. 'My son,' she says. The child inside her flips and arches its spine in a graceful, hungry movement, like a dolphin leaping for a fish held out by its tail.

'Is that him?' the woman asks, pointing to the far side of the intersection. Leon is there, sitting cross-legged on a mound of dirt. On one side of him there is a jagged pile of broken cement. On the other side is a stack of concrete pipes. Leon looks at his mother and grandmother, and laughs.

Annemarie can't stop sobbing in the back of the ambulance. She knows that what she's feeling would sound foolish put into words: that there's no point in living once you understand that at any moment you could die.

She and Magda are strapped elaborately onto boards, so they can't turn their heads even to look at each other. Magda says over and over again, 'Leon's okay. You're okay. We're all okay.' Out the window Annemarie can only see things that are high up: telephone wires, clouds, an airplane full of people who have no idea how near they could be to death. Daily there are reports of mid-air collisions barely averted. When the ambulance turns a corner she can see the permanent landmark of the Catalina Mountains standing over the city. In a saddle between two dark peaks a storm cloud spreads out like a fan, and Annemarie sees how easily it could grow into something else, tragically roiling up into itself, veined with blinding light: a mushroom cloud.

'Magda,' she says, 'me too. I'm having a baby too.'

At the hospital Magda repeats to everyone, like a broken record, that she and her daughter are both pregnant. She's terrified they'll be given some tranquilizer that will mutate the fetuses. Whenever the nurses approach, she confuses them by talking about Thalidomide babies. 'Annemarie is allergic to penicillin,' she warns the doctor when they're separated. It's true, Annemarie is, and she always forgets to mark it on her forms.

It turns out that she needs no penicillin, just stitches in her scalp. Magda has cuts and serious contusions from where her knees hit the dash. Leon has nothing. Not a bruise.

During the lecture the doctor gives them about seat belts, which Annemarie will remember for the rest of her life, he explains that in an average accident the human body becomes as heavy as a piano dropping from a ten-story building. She has bruises on her rib cage from where Magda held on to her, and the doctor can't understand how she kept Annemarie from going out the window. He looks at the two of them, pregnant and dazed, and tells them many times over that they are two very lucky ladies. 'Sometimes the strength of motherhood is greater than natural laws,' he declares.

The only telephone number Annemarie can think to give them is the crew dispatcher for Southern Pacific, which is basically Kay Kay's home number. Luckily she's just brought in the Amtrak and is next door to the depot, at Wendy's, when the call comes. She gets there in minutes, still dressed in her work boots and blackened jeans, with a green bandana around her neck.

'They didn't want me to come in here,' Kay Kay tells Annemarie in the recovery room. 'They said I was too dirty. Can you imagine?'

Annemarie tries to laugh, but tears run from her eyes instead, and she squeezes Kay Kay's hand. She still can't think of anything that seems important enough to say. She feels as if life has just been handed to her in a heavy and formal way, like a microphone on a stage, and the audience is waiting to see what great thing she intends do with it.

But Kay Kay is her everyday self. 'Don't worry about Leon, he's got it all worked out, he's staying with me,' she tells Annemarie, not looking at her stitches. 'He's going to teach me how to hit a softball.'

'He doesn't want to go to Buddy's?' Annemarie asks.

'He didn't say he did.'

'Isn't he scared to death?' Annemarie feels so weak and confused she doesn't believe she'll ever stand up again.

Kay Kay smiles. 'Leon's a rock,' she says, and Annemarie thinks of the pile of dirt he landed on. She believes now that she can remember the sound of him hitting it.

Annemarie and Magda have to stay overnight for observation. They end up in maternity, with their beds pushed

69

close together so they won't disturb the other woman in the room. She's just given birth to twins and is watching *Falcon Crest*.

'I just keep seeing him there on that pile of dirt,' whispers Annemarie. 'And I think, he could have been dead. There was just that one little safe place for him to land. Why did he land there? And then I think, *we* could have been dead, and he'd be alone. He'd be an orphan. Like that poor little girl that survived that plane wreck.'

'That poor kid,' Magda agrees. 'People are just burying her with teddy bears. How could you live with a thing like that?' Magda seems a little dazed too. They each accepted a pill to calm them down, once the doctor came and personally guaranteed Magda it wouldn't cause fetal deformity.

'I think that woman's blouse was silk. Can you believe it?' Annemarie asks.

'She was kind,' says Magda.

'I wonder what became of it? I suppose it's ruined.'

'Probably,' Magda says. She keeps looking over at Annemarie and smiling. 'When are you due?' she asks.

'October twelfth,' says Annemarie. 'After you.'

'Leon came early, remember. And I went way late with you, three weeks I think. Yours could come first.'

'Did you know Buddy wants us to get married again?' Annemarie asks after a while. 'Leon thinks it's a great idea.'

'What do you think? That's the question.'

'That's the question,' Annemarie agrees.

A nurse comes to take their blood pressures. 'How are the mamas tonight?' she asks. Annemarie thinks about how nurses wear that same calm face stewardesses have, never letting on like you're sitting on thirty thousand feet of thin air. Her head has begun to ache in no uncertain terms, and she thinks of poor old Leon Trotsky, axed in the head.

'I dread to think of what my hair's going to look like when these bandages come off. Did they have to shave a lot?'

'Not too much,' the nurse says, concentrating on the blood-pressure dial.

'Well, it's just as well my hair was a wreck to begin with.'

The nurse smiles and rips off the Velcro cuff, and then turns her back on Annemarie, attending to Magda. Another nurse rolls in their dinners and sets up their tray tables. Magda props herself up halfway, grimacing a little, and the nurse helps settle her with pillows under her back. She pokes a straw into a carton of milk, but Annemarie doesn't even take the plastic wrap off her tray.

'Ugh,' she complains, once the nurses have padded away on their white soles. 'This reminds me of the stuff you used to bring me when I was sick.'

'Milk toast,' says Magda.

'That's right. Toast soaked in milk. Who could dream up such a disgusting thing?'

'I like it,' says Magda. 'When I'm sick, it's the only thing I can stand. Seems like it always goes down nice.'

'It went down nice with Blackie,' Annemarie says. 'Did you know he's the one that always ate it? I told you a million times I hated milk toast.'

'I never knew what you expected from me, Annemarie. I never could be the mother you wanted.'

Annemarie turns up one corner of the cellophane and pleats it with her fingers. 'I guess I didn't expect anything, and you kept giving it to me anyway. When I was a teenager you were always making me drink barley fiber so I wouldn't have colon cancer when I was fifty. All I wanted was Cokes and Twinkies like the other kids.'

'I know that,' Magda says. 'Don't you think I know that? You didn't want anything. A Barbie doll, and new clothes,

71

but nothing in the way of mothering. Reading to you or anything like that. I could march around freeing South Africa or saving Glen Canyon but I couldn't do one thing for my own child.'

They are both quiet for a minute. On TV, a woman in an airport knits a longer and longer sweater, apparently unable to stop, while her plane is delayed again and again.

'I knew you didn't want to be taken care of, honey,' Magda says. 'But I guess I just couldn't accept it.'

Annemarie turns her head to the side, ponderously, as if it has become an enormous egg. She'd forgotten and now remembers how pain seems to increase the size of things. 'You know what's crazy?' she asks. 'Now I want to be taken care of and nobody will. Men, I mean.'

'They would if you'd let them. You act like you don't deserve any better.'

'That's not true.' Annemarie is surprised and a little resentful at Magda's analysis.

'It *is* true. You'll take a silk blouse from a complete stranger, but not the least little thing from anybody that loves you. Not even a bottle of shampoo. If it comes from somebody that cares about you, you act like it's not worth having.'

'Well, you're a good one to talk.'

'What do you mean?' Magda pushes the tray table back and turns toward her daughter, carefully, resting her chin on her hand.

'What I mean is you beat men off with a stick. Bartholomew thinks you're Miss America and you don't want him around you. You don't even miss Daddy.'

Magda stares at Annemarie. 'You don't know the first thing about it. Where were you when he was dying? Outside playing hopscotch.'

That is true. That's exactly where Annemarie was.

72

'Do you remember that upholstered armchair we had, Annemarie, with the grandfather clocks on it? He sat in that chair, morning till night, with his lungs filling up. Worrying about us. He'd say, "You won't forget to lock the doors, will you? Let's write a little note and tape it there by the door." And I'd do it. And then he'd say, "You know that the brakes on the car have to be checked every so often. They loosen up. And the oil will need to be changed in February." He sat there looking out the front window and every hour he'd think of another thing, till his face turned gray with the pain, knowing he'd never think of it all.'

Annemarie can picture them there in the trailer: two people facing a blank, bright window, waiting for the change that would permanently disconnect them.

Magda looks away from Annemarie. 'What hurt him wasn't dying. It was not being able to follow you and me through life looking after us. How could I ever give anybody that kind of grief again?'

The woman who just had the twins has turned off her program, and Annemarie realizes their voices have gradually risen. She demands in a whisper, 'I didn't know it was like that for you when he died. How could I not ever have known that, that it wrecked your life too?'

Magda looks across Annemarie, out the window, and Annemarie tries to follow her line of vision. There is a parking lot outside, and nothing else to see. A sparse forest of metal poles. The unlit streetlamps stare down at the pavement like blind eyes.

'I don't know,' Magda says. 'Seems like that's just how it is with you and me. We're like islands on the moon.'

'There's no water on the moon,' says Annemarie.

'That's what I mean. A person could walk from one to the other if they just decided to do it.'

It's dark. Annemarie is staring out the window when the lights in the parking lot come on all together with a soft blink. From her bed she can only see the tops of the cars glowing quietly in the pink light like some strange crop of luminous mushrooms. Enough time passes, she thinks, and it's tomorrow. Buddy or no Buddy, this baby is going to come. For the first time she lets herself imagine holding a newborn against her stomach, its helplessness and rage pulling on her heart like the greatest tragedy there ever was.

There won't be just one baby, either, but two: her own, and her mother's second daughter. Two more kids with dark, curly hair. Annemarie can see them kneeling in the gravel, their heads identically bent forward on pale, slender necks, driving trucks over the moonlike surface of Island Breezes. Getting trikes for their birthdays, skinning their knees, starting school. Once in a while going down with Magda to the Air Force Base, most likely, to fend off nuclear war.

Magda is still lying on her side, facing Annemarie, but she has drawn the covers up and her eyes are closed. The top of the sheet is bunched into her two hands like a bride's bouquet. The belly underneath pokes forward, begging as the unborn do for attention, some reassurance from the outside world, the flat of a palm. Because she can't help it, Annemarie reaches across and lays a hand on her little sister.

ALICE MUNRO

MY MOTHER'S DREAM

DURING THE NIGHT – or during the time she had been asleep – there had been a heavy fall of snow.

My mother looked out from a big arched window such as you find in a mansion or an old-fashioned public building. She looked down on lawns and shrubs, hedges, flower gardens, trees, all covered by snow that lay in heaps and cushions, not levelled or disturbed by wind. The white of it did not hurt your eyes as it does in sunlight. The white was the white of snow under a clear sky just before dawn. Everything was still; it was like 'O Little Town of Bethlehem' except that the stars had gone out.

Yet something was wrong. There was a mistake in this scene. All the trees, all the shrubs and plants, were out in full summer leaf. The grass that showed underneath them, in spots sheltered from the snow, was fresh and green. Snow had settled overnight on the luxury of summer. A change of season unexplainable, unexpected. Also, everybody had gone away – though she couldn't think who 'everybody' was – and my mother was alone in the high spacious house amongst its rather formal trees and gardens.

She thought that whatever had happened would soon be made known to her. Nobody came, however. The telephone did not ring; the latch of the garden gate was not lifted. She could not hear any traffic, and she did not even know which way the street was – or the road, if she was out in the country. She had to get out of the house, where the air was so heavy and settled.

When she got outside she remembered. She remembered that she had left a baby out there somewhere, before the snow had fallen. Quite a while before the snow had fallen. This memory, this certainty, came over her with horror. It was as if she was awakening from a dream. Within her dream she awakened from a dream, to a knowledge of her responsibility and mistake. She had left her baby out overnight, she had forgotten about it. Left it exposed somewhere as if it was a doll she tired of. And perhaps it was not last night but a week or a month ago that she had done this. For a whole season or for many seasons she had left her baby out. She had been occupied in other ways. She might even have travelled away from here and just returned, forgetting what she was returning to.

She went around looking under hedges and broad-leaved plants. She foresaw how the baby would be shrivelled up. It would be dead, shrivelled and brown, its head like a nut, and on its tiny shut-up face there would be an expression not of distress but of bereavement, an old patient grief. There would not be any accusation of her, its mother – just the look of patience and helplessness with which it waited for its rescue or its fate.

The sorrow that came to my mother was the sorrow of the baby's waiting and not knowing it waited for her, its only hope, when she had forgotten all about it. So small and new a baby that could not even turn away from the snow. She could hardly breathe for her sorrow. There would never be any room in her for anything else. No room for anything but the realization of what she had done.

What a reprieve, then, to find her baby lying in its crib. Lying on its stomach, its head turned to one side, its skin pale and sweet as snowdrops and the down on its head reddish like the dawn. Red hair like her own, on her perfectly safe and unmistakable baby. The joy to find herself forgiven.

The snow and the leafy gardens and the strange house had all withdrawn. The only remnant of the whiteness was the blanket in the crib. A baby blanket of light white wool, crumpled halfway down the baby's back. In the heat, the real summer heat, the baby was wearing only a diaper and a pair of plastic pants to keep the sheet dry. The plastic pants had a pattern of butterflies.

My mother, still thinking no doubt about the snow and the cold that usually accompanies snow, pulled the blanket up to cover the baby's bare back and shoulders, its red-downed head.

It is early morning when this happens in the real world. The world of July 1945. At a time when, on any other morning, it would be demanding its first feeding of the day, the baby sleeps on. The mother, though standing on her feet and with her eyes open, is still too far deep in sleep in her head to wonder about this. Baby and mother are worn out by a long battle, and the mother has forgotten even that at the moment. Some circuits are closed down; the most unrelenting quiet has settled on her brain and her baby's. The mother – my mother – makes no sense of the daylight which is increasing every moment. She doesn't understand that the sun is coming up as she stands there. No memory of the day before, or of what happened around midnight, comes up to jolt her. She pulls the blanket up over her baby's head, over its mild, satisfied, sleeping profile. She pads back to her own room and falls down on the bed and is again, at once, unconscious.

The house in which this happens is nothing like the house in the dream. It is a one-and-a-half-story white wooden house, cramped but respectable, with a porch that comes to within a few feet of the sidewalk, and a bay window in the dining-room looking out on a small hedged yard. It is on a backstreet in a small town that is indistinguishable – to an outsider – from a lot of other small towns to be found ten or fifteen miles apart in the once thickly populated farmland near Lake Huron. My father and his sisters grew up in this house, and the sisters and mother were still living here when my mother joined them – and I joined them too, being large and lively inside her – after my father was killed in the final weeks of the war in Europe.

My mother – Jill – is standing beside the dining-room table in the bright late afternoon. The house is full of people who have been invited back there after the memorial service in the church. They are drinking tea or coffee and managing to hold in their fingers the dinky sandwiches, or slices of banana bread, nut loaf, pound cake. The custard tarts or raisin tarts with their crumbly pastry are supposed to be eaten with a dessert fork off one of the small china plates that were painted with violets by Jill's mother-in-law when she was a bride. Jill picks everything up with her fingers. Pastry crumbs have fallen, a raisin has fallen, and been smeared into the green velvet of her dress. It's too hot a dress for the day, and it's not a maternity dress at all but a loose sort of robe made for recitals, occasions when she plays her violin in public. The hem rides up in front, due to me. But it's the only thing she owns that is large enough and good enough for her to wear at her husband's memorial service.

What is this eating all about? People can't help but notice. 'Eating for two,' Ailsa says to a group of her guests, so that they won't get the better of her by anything they say or don't say about her sister-in-law.

Jill has been queasy all day, until suddenly in the church, when she was thinking how bad the organ was, she realized

80

that she was, all of a sudden, as hungry as a wolf. All through 'O Valiant Hearts' she was thinking of a fat hamburger dripping with meat juice and melted mayonnaise, and now she is trying to find what concoction of walnuts and raisins and brown sugar, what tooth-jabbing sweetness of coconut icing or soothing mouthful of banana bread or dollop of custard, will do as a substitute. Nothing will, of course, but she keeps on going. When her real hunger is satisfied her imaginary hunger is still working, and even more an irritability amounting almost to panic that makes her stuff into her mouth what she can hardly taste any longer. She couldn't describe this irritability except to say it has something to do with furriness and tightness. The barberry hedge outside the window, thick and bristling in the sunlight, the feel of the velvet dress clinging to her damp armpits, the nosegays of curls – the same color as the raisins in the tarts – bunched on her sister-in-law Ailsa's head, even the painted violets that look like scabs you could pick off the plate, all these things seem particularly horrid and oppressive to her though she knows they are quite ordinary. They seem to carry some message about her new and unexpected life.

Why unexpected? She has known for some time about me and she also knew that George Kirkham might be killed. He was in the air force, after all. (And around her in the Kirkhams' house this afternoon people are saying – though not to her, his widow, or to his sisters – that he was just the sort you always knew would be killed. They mean because he was good-looking and high-spirited and the pride of his family, the one on whom all the hopes had been pinned.) She knew this, but she went ahead with her ordinary life, lugging her violin onto the streetcar on dark winter mornings, riding to the Conservatory where she practiced hour after hour within sound of others but alone in a dingy room with the radiator racket for company, the skin of her hands blotchy at first with the cold, then parched in the dry indoor heat. She went on living in a rented room with an ill-fitting window that let in flies in summer and a windowsill sprinkle of snow in winter, and dreaming – when she wasn't sick – of sausages and meat pies and dark chunks of chocolate. At the Conservatory people treated her pregnancy tactfully, as if it was a tumor. It didn't show for a long time anyway, as first pregnancies generally don't on a big girl with a broad pelvis. Even with me turning somersaults she played in public. Majestically thickened, with her long red hair lying in a bush around her shoulders, her face broad and glowing, her expression full of somber concentration, she played a solo in her most important recital so far. The Mendelssohn Violin Concerto.

She paid some attention to the world – she knew the war was ending. She thought that George might be back soon after I was born. She knew that she wouldn't be able to go on living in her room then – she'd have to live somewhere with him. And she knew that I'd be there, but she thought of my birth as bringing something to an end rather than starting something. It would bring an end to the kicking in the permanent sore spot on one side of her belly and the ache in her genitals when she stands up and the blood rushes into them (as if she'd had a burning poultice laid there). Her nipples will no longer be large and dark and nubbly, and she won't have to wind bandages around her legs with their swollen veins before she gets out of bed every morning. She won't have to urinate every half hour or so, and her feet will shrink back into their ordinary shoes. She thinks that once I'm out I won't give her so much trouble.

After she knew that George would not be coming back she thought about keeping me for a while in that same room. She got a book about babies. She bought the basic things that I would need. There was an old woman in the building who could look after me while she practiced. She would get a war widow's pension and in six more months she would graduate from the Conservatory.

Then Ailsa came down on the train and collected her. Ailsa said, 'We couldn't leave you stuck down here all by yourself. Everybody wonders why you didn't come up when George went overseas. It's time you came now.'

'My family's crackers,' George had told Jill. 'Iona's a nervous wreck and Ailsa should have been a sergeant major. And my mother's senile.'

He also said, 'Ailsa got the brains, but she had to quit school and go and work in the Post Office when my dad died. I got the looks and there wasn't anything left for poor old Iona but the bad skin and the bad nerves.'

Jill met his sisters for the first time when they came to Toronto to see George off. They hadn't been at the wedding, which had taken place two weeks before. Nobody was there but George and Jill and the minister and the minister's wife and a neighbor called in to be the second witness. I was there as well, already tucked up inside Jill, but I was not the reason for the wedding and at the time nobody knew of my existence. Afterwards George insisted that he and Jill take some poker-faced wedding pictures of themselves in one of those do-it-yourself picture booths. He was in relentless high spirits. 'That'll fix them,' he said, when he looked at the pictures. Jill wondered if there was anybody special he meant to fix. Ailsa? Or the pretty girls, the cute and perky girls, who had run after him, writing him sentimental letters and knitting him argyle socks? He wore the socks when he could, he pocketed the presents, and he read the letters out in bars for a joke.

83

Jill had not had any breakfast before the wedding, and in the midst of it she was thinking of pancakes and bacon.

The two sisters were more normal-looking than she had expected. Though it was true about George getting the looks. He had a silky wave to his dark-blond hair and a hard gleeful glint in his eyes and a clean-cut enviable set of features. His only drawback was that he was not very tall. Just tall enough to look Jill in the eye. And to be an air force pilot.

'They don't want tall guys for pilots,' he said. 'I beat them out there. The beanpole bastards. Lots of guys in the movies are short. They stand on boxes for the kissing.'

(At the movies, George could be boisterous. He might hiss the kissing. He didn't go in for it much in real life either. Let's get to the action, he said.)

The sisters were short, too. They were named after places in Scotland, where their parents had gone on their honeymoon before the family lost its money. Ailsa was twelve years older than George, and Iona was nine years older. In the crowd at Union Station they looked dumpy and bewildered. Both of them wore new hats and suits, as if they were the ones who had recently been married. And both were upset because Iona had left her good gloves on the train. It was true that Iona had bad skin, though it wasn't broken out at present and perhaps her acne days were over. It was lumpy with old scars and dingy under the pink powder. Her hair slipped out in droopy tendrils from under her hat and her eyes were teary, either because of Ailsa's scolding or because her brother was going away to war. Ailsa's hair was arranged in bunches of tight permanented curls, with her hat riding on top. She had shrewd pale eyes behind sparkle-rimmed glasses, and round pink cheeks, and a dimpled chin. Both she and Iona had tidy figures – high breasts and small waists and flaring hips – but on Iona this figure looked like something she had picked up by mistake and was trying to hide by stooping her shoulders and crossing her arms. Ailsa managed her curves assertively not provocatively, as if she was made of some sturdy ceramic. And both of them had George's dark-blond coloring, but without his gleam. They didn't seem to share his sense of humor either.

'Well I'm off,' George said. 'I'm off to die a hero on the field at Passchendaele.' And Iona said, 'Oh don't say that. Don't talk like that.' Ailsa twitched her raspberry mouth.

'I can see the lost-and-found sign from here,' she said. 'But I don't know if that's just for things you lose in the station or is it for things that they find in the trains? Passchendaele was in the First World War.'

'Was it? You sure? I'm too late?' said George, beating his hand on his chest.

And he was burned up a few months later in a training flight over the Irish Sea.

Ailsa smiles all the time. She says, 'Well of course I am proud. I am. But I'm not the only one to lose somebody. He did what he had to do.' Some people find her briskness a bit shocking. But others say, 'Poor Ailsa.' All that concentrating on George, and saving to send him to law school, and then he flouted her – he signed up; he went off and got himself killed. He couldn't wait.

His sisters sacrificed their own schooling. Even getting their teeth straightened – they sacrificed that. Iona did go to nursing school, but as it turned out getting her teeth fixed would have served her better. Now she and Ailsa have ended up with a hero. Everybody grants it – a hero. The younger people present think it's something to have a hero in the family. They think the importance of this moment will last, that it will stay with Ailsa and Iona forever. 'O Valiant Hearts' will soar around them forever. Older people, those who remember the previous war, know that all they've ended up with is a name on the cenotaph. Because the widow, the girl feeding her face, will get the pension.

Ailsa is in a hectic mood partly because she has been up two nights in a row, cleaning. Not that the house wasn't decently clean before. Nevertheless she felt the need to wash every dish, pot, and ornament, polish the glass on every picture, pull out the fridge and scrub behind it, wash the cellar steps off, and pour bleach in the garbage can. The very lighting fixture overhead, over the dining-room table, had to be taken apart, and every piece on it dunked in soapy water, rinsed, and rubbed dry and reassembled. And because of her work at the Post Office Ailsa couldn't start this till after supper. She is the postmistress now, she could have given herself a day off, but being Ailsa she would never do that.

Now she's hot under her rouge, twitchy in her dark-blue lace-collared crepe dress. She can't stay still. She refills the serving plates and passes them around, deplores the fact that people's tea may have got cold, hurries to make a fresh pot. Mindful of her guests' comfort, asking after their rheumatism or minor ailments, smiling in the face of her tragedy, repeating over and over again that hers is a common loss, that she must not complain when so many others are in the same boat, that George would not want his friends to grieve but to be thankful that all together we have ended the war. All in a high and emphatic voice of cheerful reproof that people are used to from the Post Office. So that they are left with an uncertain feeling of perhaps having said the wrong thing, just as in the Post Office they may be made to understand that their handwriting cannot help but be a trial or their packages are done up sloppily.

Ailsa is aware that her voice is too high and that she is smiling too much and that she has poured out tea for people who said they didn't want any more. In the kitchen, while warming the teapot, she says, 'I don't know what's the matter with me. I'm all wound up.'

The person she says this to is Dr Shantz, her neighbor across the backyard.

'It'll soon be over,' he says. 'Would you like a bromide?'

His voice undergoes a change as the door from the dining-room opens. The word 'bromide' comes out firm and pro-fessional.

Ailsa's voice changes too, from forlorn to valiant. She says, 'Oh, no thank you. I'll just try and keep going on my own.'

Iona's job is supposed to be to watch over their mother, to see that she doesn't spill her tea – which she may do not out of clumsiness but forgetfulness – and that she is taken away if she starts to sniffle and cry. But in fact Mrs Kirkham's manners are gracious most of the time and she puts people at ease more readily than Ailsa does. For a quarter of an hour at a time she understands the situation – or she seems to – and she speaks bravely and cogently about how she will always miss her son but is grateful she still has her daughters: Ailsa so efficient and reliable, a wonder as she's always been, and Iona the soul of kindness. She even remembers to speak of her new daughter-in-law but perhaps gives a hint of being out of line when she mentions what most women of her age don't mention at a social gathering, and with men listening. Looking at Jill and me, she says, 'And we all have a comfort to come.'

Then passing from room to room or guest to guest, she forgets entirely, she looks around her own house and says, 'Why are we here? What a lot of people – what are we celebrating?' And catching on to the fact that it all has something to do with George, she says, 'Is it George's wedding?' Along with her up-to-date information she has lost some of her mild discretion. 'It's not your wedding, is it?' she says to Iona. 'No. I didn't think so. You never had a boyfriend, did you?' A let's-face-facts, devil-take-the-hindmost note has come into her voice. When she spots Jill she laughs.

'That's not the bride, is it? Oh-oh. Now we understand.'

But the truth comes back to her as suddenly as it went away.

'Is there news?' she says. 'News about George?' And it's then that the weeping starts that Ailsa was afraid of.

'Get her out of the way if she starts making a spectacle,' Ailsa had said.

Iona isn't able to get her mother out of the way – she has never been able to exert authority over anybody in her life – but Dr Shantz's wife catches the old woman's arm.

'George is dead?' says Mrs Kirkham fearfully, and Mrs Shantz says, 'Yes he is. But you know his wife is having a baby.'

Mrs Kirkham leans against her; she crumples and says softly, 'Could I have my tea?'

Everywhere my mother turns in that house, it seems she sees a picture of my father. The last and official one, of him in his uniform, sits on an embroidered runner on the closed sewing machine in the bay of the dining-room window. Iona put flowers around it, but Ailsa took them away. She said it made him look too much like a Catholic saint. Hanging above the stairs there is one of him at six years old, out on the sidewalk, with his knee in his wagon, and in the room where Jill sleeps there's one of him beside his bicycle, with his *Free Press* newspaper sack. Mrs Kirkham's room has the one of him dressed for the grade-eight operetta, with a gold

88

cardboard crown on his head. Being unable to carry a tune, he couldn't have a leading role, but he was of course picked for the best background role, that of the king.

The hand-tinted studio photo over the buffet shows him at the age of three, a blurred blond tot dragging a rag doll by one leg. Ailsa thought of taking that down because it might seem tear-jerking, but she left it up rather than show a bright patch on the wallpaper. And no one said anything about it but Mrs Shantz, who paused and said what she had said sometimes before, and not tearfully but with a faintly amused appreciation.

'Ah – Christopher Robin.'

People were used to not paying much attention to what Mrs Shantz said.

In all of his pictures George looks bright as a dollar. There's always a sunny dip of hair over his brow, unless he's wearing his officer's hat or his crown. And even when he was little more than an infant he looked as if he knew himself to be a capering, calculating, charming sort of fellow. The sort who never let people alone, who whipped them up to laugh. At his own expense occasionally, but usually at other people's. Jill recalls when she looks at him how he drank but never seemed drunk and how he occupied himself getting other drunk people to confess to him their fears, prevarications, virginity, or two-timing, which he would then turn into jokes or humiliating nicknames that his victims pretended to enjoy. For he had legions of followers and friends, who maybe latched on to him out of fear – or maybe just because, as was always said of him, he livened things up. Wherever he was was the center of the room, and the air around him crackled with risk and merriment.

What was Jill to make of such a lover? She was nineteen when she met him, and nobody had ever claimed her before.

She couldn't understand what attracted him, and she could see that nobody else could understand it, either. She was a puzzle to most people of her own age, but a dull puzzle. A girl whose life was given over to the study of the violin and who had no other interests.

That was not quite true. She would snuggle under her shabby quilts and imagine a lover. But he was never a shining cutup like George. She thought of some warm and bearlike fellow, or of a musician a decade older than herself and already legendary, with a fierce potency. Her notions of love were operatic, though that was not the sort of music she most admired. But George made jokes when he made love; he pranced around her room when he had finished; he made rude and infantile noises. His brisk performances brought her little of the pleasure she knew from her assaults on herself, but she was not exactly disappointed.

Dazed at the speed of things was more like it. And expecting to be happy – grateful and happy – when her mind caught up with physical and social reality. George's attentions, and her marriage – those were all like a brilliant extension of her life. Lighted rooms showing up full of a bewildering sort of splendor. Then came the bomb or the hurricane, the not unlikely stroke of disaster, and the whole extension was gone. Blown up and vanished, leaving her with the same space and options she'd had before. She had lost something, certainly. But not something she had really got hold of, or understood as more than a hypothetical layout of the future.

She has had enough to eat, now. Her legs ache from standing so long. Mrs Shantz is beside her, saying, 'Have you had a chance to meet any of George's local friends?'

She means the young people keeping to themselves in the hall doorway. A couple of nice-looking girls, a young man still wearing a naval uniform, others. Looking at them, Jill thinks clearly that no one is really sorry. Ailsa perhaps, but Ailsa has her own reasons. No one is really sorry George is dead. Not even the girl who was crying in church and looks as if she will cry some more. Now that girl can remember that she was in love with George and think that he was in love with her – in spite of all – and never be afraid of what he may do or say to prove her wrong. And none of them will have to wonder, when a group of people clustered around George has started laughing, whom they are laughing at or what George is telling them. Nobody will have to strain to keep up with him or figure out how to stay in his good graces anymore.

It doesn't occur to her that if he had lived George might have become a different person, because she doesn't think of becoming a different person herself.

She says, 'No,' with a lack of enthusiasm that causes Mrs Shantz to say, 'I know. It's hard meeting new people. Particularly – if I was you I would rather go and lie down.'

Jill was almost sure she was going to say 'go and have a drink.' But there's nothing being offered here, only tea and coffee. Jill hardly drinks anyway. She can recognize the smell on someone's breath, though, and she thought she smelled it on Mrs Shantz.

'Why don't you?' says Mrs Shantz. 'These things are a great strain. I'll tell Ailsa. Go on now.'

Mrs Shantz is a small woman with fine gray hair, bright eyes, and a wrinkled, pointed face. Every winter she spends a month by herself in Florida. She has money. The house that she and her husband built for themselves, behind the Kirkhams' house, is long and low and blindingly white, with curved corners and expanses of glass bricks. Dr Shantz is twenty or twenty-five years younger than she is – a thickset, fresh, and amiable-looking man with a high smooth fore-head and fair curly hair. They have no children. It is believed that she has some, from a first marriage, but they don't come to visit her. In fact the story is that Dr Shantz was her son's friend, brought home from college, and that he fell in love with his friend's mother, she fell in love with her son's friend, there was a divorce, and here they are married, living in lux-urious, close-mouthed exile.

Jill did smell whiskey. Mrs Shantz carries a flask whenever she goes to a gathering of which – as she says – she can have no reasonable hopes. Drink does not make her fall about or garble her words or pick fights or throw her arms about people. The truth may be that she's always a little bit drunk but never really drunk. She is used to letting the alcohol enter her body in a reasonable, reassuring way, so that her brain cells never get soaked or quite dried out. The only giveaway is the smell (which many people in this dry town attribute to some medicine she has to take or even to an ointment that she has to rub on her chest). That, and perhaps a deliberate-ness about her speech, the way she seems to clear a space around each word. She says things of course which a woman brought up around here would not say. She tells things on herself. She tells about being mistaken every once in a while for her husband's mother. She says most people go into a tailspin when they discover their mistake, they're so embar-rassed. But some women – a waitress, maybe – will fasten on Mrs Shantz quite a dirty look, as if to say, What's he doing wasted on you?

And Mrs Shantz just says to them, 'I know. It isn't fair. But life isn't fair and you might as well get used to it.'

There isn't any way this afternoon that she can space her sips properly. The kitchen and even the poky pantry behind it are places where women can be coming and going at any time. She has to go upstairs to the bathroom, and that not too often. When she does that late in the afternoon, a little while after Jill has disappeared, she finds the bathroom door locked. She thinks of nipping into one of the bedrooms and is wondering which one is empty, which occupied by Jill. Then she hears Jill's voice coming from the bathroom, saying, 'Just a minute,' or something like that. Something quite ordinary, but the tone of voice is strained and frightened.

Mrs Shantz takes a quick swallow right there in the hall, seizing the excuse of emergency.

'Jill? Are you all right? Can you let me in?'

Jill is on her hands and knees, trying to mop up the puddle on the bathroom floor. She has read about the water breaking – just as she has read about contractions, show, transition stage, placenta – but just the same the escape of warm fluid surprised her. She has to use toilet paper, because Ailsa took all the regular towels away and put out the smooth scraps of embroidered linen called guest towels.

She holds on to the rim of the tub to pull herself up. She unbolts the door and that's when the first pain astonishes her. She is not to have a single mild pain, or any harbingers or orchestrated first stage of labor; it's all to be an unsparing onslaught and ripping headlong delivery.

'Easy,' says Mrs Shantz, supporting her as well as she can. 'Just tell me which room is yours, we'll get you lying down.'

Before they even reach the bed Jill's fingers dig into Mrs Shantz's thin arm to leave it black and blue.

'Oh, this is fast,' Mrs Shantz says. 'This is a real mover and shaker for a first baby. I'm going to get my husband.'

In that way I was born right in the house, about ten days early if Jill's calculations were to be relied on. Ailsa had barely time to get the company cleared out before the place was

93

filled with Jill's noise, her disbelieving cries and the great shameless grunts that followed.

Even if a mother had been taken by surprise and had given birth at home, it was usual by that time to move her and the baby into the hospital afterwards. But there was some sort of summer flu in town, and the hospital had filled up with the worst cases, so Dr Shantz decided that Jill and I would be better off at home. Iona after all had finished part of her nurse's training, and she could take her two-week holiday now, to look after us.

Jill really knew nothing about living in a family. She had grown up in an orphanage. From the age of six to sixteen she had slept in a dormitory. Lights turned on and off at a specified time, furnace never operating before or beyond a specified date. A long oilcloth-covered table where they ate and did their homework, a factory across the street. George had liked the sound of that. It would make a girl tough, he said. It would make her self-possessed, hard and solitary. It would make her the sort who would not expect any romantic nonsense. But the place had not been run in such a heartless way as perhaps he thought, and the people who ran it had not been ungenerous. Jill was taken to a concert, with some others, when she was twelve years old, and there she decided that she must learn to play the violin. She had already fooled around with the piano at the orphanage. Somebody took enough interest to get her a second-hand, very second-rate violin, and a few lessons, and this led, finally, to a scholarship at the Conservatory. There was a recital for patrons and directors, a party with best dresses, fruit punch, speeches, and cakes. Jill had to make a little speech herself, expressing gratitude, but the truth was that she took all this pretty much for granted. She was sure that she and some violin were naturally, fatefully connected, and would have come together without human help.

In the dormitory she had friends, but they went off early to factories and offices and she forgot about them. At the high school that the orphans were sent to, a teacher had a talk with her. The words 'normal' and 'well rounded' came up in the talk. The teacher seemed to think that music was an escape from something or a substitute for something. For sisters and brothers and friends and dates. She suggested that Jill spread her energy around instead of concentrating on one thing. Loosen up, play volleyball, join the school orchestra if music was what she wanted.

Jill started to avoid that particular teacher, climbing the stairs or going round the block so as not to have to speak to her. Just as she stopped reading any page from which the words 'well rounded' or the word 'popular' leapt out at her.

At the Conservatory it was easier. There she met people quite as un-well-rounded, as hard driven, as herself. She formed a few rather absentminded and competitive friend-ships. One of her friends had an older brother who was in the air force, and this brother happened to be a victim and worshipper of George Kirkham's. He and George dropped in on a family Sunday-night supper, at which Jill was a guest. They were on their way to get drunk somewhere else. And that was how George met Jill. My father met my mother.

There had to be somebody at home all the time, to watch Mrs Kirkham. So Iona worked the night shift at the bakery. She decorated cakes – even the fanciest wedding cakes – and she got the first round of bread loaves in the oven at five o'clock. Her hands, which shook so badly that she could not serve anybody a teacup, were strong and clever and patient, even inspired, at any solitary job.

One morning after Ailsa had gone off to work – this was during the short time that Jill was in the house before I was born – Iona hissed from the bedroom as Jill was going by. As if there was a secret. But who was there now in the house to keep a secret from? It couldn't be Mrs Kirkham.

Iona had to struggle to get a stuck drawer of her bureau open. 'Darn,' she said, and giggled. 'Darn it. There.'

The drawer was full of baby clothes – not plain necessary shirts and nightgowns such as Jill had bought at a shop that sold seconds, factory rejects, in Toronto, but knitted bonnets, sweaters and bootees and soakers, handmade tiny gowns. All possible pastel colors or combinations of colors – no blue or pink prejudice – with crocheted trimming and minute embroidered flowers and birds and lambs. The sort of stuff that Jill had barely known existed. She would have known, if she had done any thorough research in baby departments or peering into baby carriages, but she hadn't.

'Of course I don't know what you've got,' Iona said. 'You may have got so many things already, or maybe you don't like homemade, I don't know –' Her giggling was a kind of punctuation of speech and it was also an extension of her tone of apology. Everything she said, every look and gesture, seemed to be clogged up, overlaid with a sticky honey or snuffled mucus of apology, and Jill did not know how to deal with this.

'It's really nice,' she said flatly.

'Oh no, I didn't know if you'd even want it. I didn't know if you'd like it at all.'

'It's lovely.'

'I didn't do it all, I bought some of it. I went to the church bazaar and the Hospital Auxiliary, their bazaar, I just thought it would be nice, but if you don't like it or maybe you don't need it I can just put it in the Missionary Bale.'

96

'I do need it,' Jill said. 'I haven't got anything like this at all.'

'Haven't you really? What I did isn't so good, but maybe what the church ladies did or the Auxiliary, maybe you'd think that was all right.'

Was this what George had meant about Iona's being a nervous wreck? (According to Ailsa, her breakdown at the nursing school had been caused by her being a bit too thin-skinned and the supervisor's being a bit too hard on her.) You might think she was clamoring for reassurance, but whatever reassurance you tried seemed to be not enough, or not to get through to her. Jill felt as if Iona's words and giggles and sniffles and damp looks (no doubt she had damp hands as well) were things crawling on her – on Jill – mites trying to get under her skin.

But this was something she got used to, in time. Or Iona toned it down. Both she and Iona felt relief – it was as if a teacher had gone out of the room – when the door closed behind Ailsa in the morning. They took to having a second cup of coffee, while Mrs Kirkham washed the dishes. She did this job very slowly – looking around for the drawer or shelf where each item should go – and with some lapses. But with rituals, too, which she never omitted, such as scattering the coffee grounds on a bush by the kitchen door.

'She thinks the coffee makes it grow,' Iona whispered. 'Even if she puts it on the leaves not the ground. Every day we have to take the hose and rinse it off.'

Jill thought that Iona sounded like the girls who were most picked on at the orphanage. They were always eager to pick on somebody else. But once you got Iona past her strung-out apologies or barricades of humble accusations ('Of course I'm the last person they'd consult about anything down at the shop,' 'Of course Ailsa wouldn't listen to my opinion,' 'Of course George never made any secret about how he despised me') you might get her to talk about fairly interesting things. She told Jill about the house that had been their grandfather's and was now the center wing of the hospital, about the specific shady deals that had lost their father his job, and about a romance that was going on between two married people at the bakery. She also mentioned the supposed previous history of the Shantzes, and even the fact that Ailsa was soft on Dr Shantz. The shock treatment Iona had had after her nervous breakdown seemed perhaps to have blown a hole in her discretion, and the voice that came through this hole – once the disguising rubbish had been cleared away – was baleful and sly.

And Jill might as well spend her time chatting – her fingers had got too puffy now to try to play the violin.

And then I was born and everything changed, especially for Iona.

Jill had to stay in bed for a week, and even after she got up she moved like a stiff old woman and breathed warily each time she lowered herself into a chair. She was all painfully stitched together, and her stomach and breasts were bound tight as a mummy's – that was the custom then. Her milk came in plentifully; it was leaking through the binding and onto the sheets. Iona loosened the binding and tried to connect the nipple to my mouth. But I would not take it. I refused to take my mother's breast. I screamed blue murder. The big stiff breast might just as well have been a snouted beast rummaging in my face. Iona held me, she gave me a little warm boiled water, and I quieted down. I was losing weight, though. I couldn't live on water. So Iona mixed up a formula and took me out of Jill's arms where I stiffened and wailed. Iona rocked and soothed me and touched my cheek with the rubber nipple and that turned out to be what I preferred. I drank the formula greedily and kept it down. Iona's arms and the nipple that she was in charge of became my chosen home. Jill's breasts had to be bound even tighter, and she had to forgo liquids (remember, this was in the hot weather) and endure the ache until her milk dried up.

'What a monkey, what a monkey,' crooned Iona. 'You are a monkey, you don't want your mommy's good milk.'

I soon got fatter and stronger. I could cry louder. I cried if anybody but Iona tried to hold me. I rejected Ailsa and Dr Shantz with his thoughtfully warmed hands, but of course it was my aversion to Jill that got the most attention.

Once Jill was out of bed Iona got her sitting in the chair where she herself usually sat to feed me; she put her own blouse around Jill's shoulders and the bottle in Jill's hand.

No use, I was not fooled. I batted my cheek against the bottle and straightened my legs and hardened my abdomen into a ball. I would not accept the substitution. I cried. I would not give in.

My cries were still thin new-baby cries, but they were a disturbance in the house, and Iona was the only person who had the power to stop them. Touched or spoken to by a non-Iona, I cried. Put down to sleep, not rocked by Iona, I cried myself into exhaustion and slept for ten minutes and woke ready to go at it again. I had no good times or fussy times. I had the Iona-times and the Iona-desertion-times, which might become – oh, worse and worse – the other-people-times, mostly Jill-times.

How could Iona go back to work, then, once her two weeks were up? She couldn't. There wasn't any question of it. The bakery had to get someone else. Iona had gone from being the most negligible to being the most important person in the house; she was the one who stood between those who lived there and constant discordance, unanswerable complaint. She had to be up at all hours to keep the household in any sort of ease. Dr Shantz was concerned; even Ailsa was concerned.

'Iona, don't wear yourself out.'

And yet a wonderful change had taken place. Iona was pale but her skin glowed, as if she had finally passed out of adolescence. She could look anybody in the eye. And there was no more trembling, hardly any giggling, no sly cringing in her voice, which had grown as bossy as Ailsa's and more joyful. (Never more joyful than when she was scolding me for my attitude to Jill.)

'Iona's in seventh heaven – she just adores that baby,' Ailsa told people. But in fact Iona's behavior seemed too brisk for adoration. She did not care how much noise she made, quelling mine. She tore up the stairs calling breathlessly, 'I'm coming, I'm coming, hold your horses.' She would walk around with me carelessly plastered to her shoulder, held with one hand, while the other hand accomplished some task connected with my maintenance. She ruled in the kitchen, commandeering the stove for the sterilizer, the table for the mixing of the formula, the sink for the baby wash. She swore cheerfully, even in Ailsa's presence, when she had misplaced or spilled something.

She knew herself to be the only person who didn't wince, who didn't feel the distant threat of annihilation, when I sent up my first signal wail. Instead, she was the one whose heart jumped into double time, who felt like dancing, just from the sense of power she had, and gratitude.

Once her bindings were off and she'd seen the flatness of her stomach, Jill took a look at her hands. The puffiness seemed to be all gone. She went downstairs and got her violin out of the closet and took off its cover. She was ready to try some scales.

This was on a Sunday afternoon. Iona had lain down for a nap, one ear always open to hear my cry. Mrs Kirkham too was lying down. Ailsa was painting her fingernails in the kitchen. Jill began to tune the violin.

My father and my father's family had no real interest in music. They didn't quite know this. They thought that the intolerance or even hostility they felt towards a certain type of music (this showed even in the way they pronounced the word 'classical') was based on a simple strength of character, an integrity and a determination not to be fooled. As if music that departed from a simple tune was trying to put something over on you, and everybody knew this, deep down, but some people – out of pretentiousness, from want of simplicity and honesty – would never admit that it was so. And out of this artificiality and spineless tolerance came the whole world of symphony orchestras, opera, and ballet, concerts that put people to sleep.

Most of the people in this town felt the same way. But because she hadn't grown up here Jill did not understand the depth of this feeling, the taken-for-granted extent of it. My father had never made a parade of it, or a virtue of it, because he didn't go in for virtues. He had liked the idea of Jill's being a musician – not because of the music but because it made her an odd choice, as did her clothes and her way of living and her wild hair. Choosing her, he showed people what he thought of them. Showed those girls who had hoped to get their hooks in him. Showed Ailsa.

Jill had closed the curtained glass doors of the living-room and she tuned up quite softly. Perhaps no sound escaped. Or if Ailsa heard something in the kitchen, she might have thought it was a sound from outdoors, a radio in the neighborhood.

Now Jill began to play her scales. It was true that her fingers were no longer puffy, but they felt stiff. Her whole body felt stiff, her stance was not quite natural, she felt the instrument clamped onto her in a distrustful way. But no matter, she would get into her scales. She was sure that she had felt this way before, after she'd had flu, or when she was very tired, having overstrained herself practicing, or even for no reason at all.

I woke without a whimper of discontent. No warning, no buildup. Just a shriek, a waterfall of shrieks descended on the house, a cry unlike any cry I'd managed before. The letting loose of a new flood of unsuspected anguish, a grief that punished the world with its waves full of stones, the volley of woe sent down from the windows of the torture chamber.

Iona was up at once, alarmed for the first time at any noise made by me, crying, 'What is it, what is it?'

And Ailsa, rushing around to shut the windows, was calling out, 'It's the fiddle, it's the fiddle.' She threw open the doors of the living-room.

'Jill. Jill. This is awful. This is just awful. Don't you hear your baby?'

She had to wrench out the screen under the living-room window, so that she could get it down. She had been sitting in her kimono to do her nails, and now a boy going by on a bicycle looked in and saw her kimono open over her slip.

'My God,' she said. She hardly ever lost control of herself to this extent. 'Will you put that thing away.'

Jill set her violin down.

Ailsa ran out into the hall and called up to Iona.

'It's Sunday. Can't you get it to stop?'

Jill walked speechlessly and deliberately out to the kitchen, and there was Mrs Kirkham in her stocking feet, clinging to the counter.

'What's the matter with Ailsa?' she said. 'What did Iona do?'

Jill went out and sat down on the back step. She looked across at the glaring, sunlit back wall of the Shantzes' white house. All around were other hot backyards and hot walls of other houses. Inside them people well known to each other by sight and by name and by history. And if you walked three blocks east from here or five blocks west, six blocks south or ten blocks north, you would come to walls of summer crops already sprung high out of the earth, fenced fields of hay and wheat and corn. The fullness of the country. Nowhere to breathe for the reek of thrusting crops and barnyards and jostling munching animals. Woodlots at a distance beckoning like pools of shade, of peace and shelter, but in reality they were boiling up with bugs.

How can I describe what music is to Jill? Forget about landscapes and visions and dialogues. It is more of a problem, I would say, that she has to work out strictly and daringly, and that she has taken on as her responsibility in life. Suppose then that the tools that serve her for working on this problem are taken away. The problem is still there in its grandeur and other people sustain it, but it is removed from her. For her, just the back step and the glaring wall and my crying. My crying is a knife to cut out of her life all that isn't useful. To me.

'Come in,' says Ailsa through the screen door. 'Come on in. I shouldn't have yelled at you. Come in, people will see.'

By evening the whole episode could be passed off lightly. 'You must've heard the caterwauling over here today,' said Ailsa to the Shantzes. They had asked her over to sit on their patio, while Iona settled me to sleep.

'Baby isn't a fan of the fiddle apparently. Doesn't take after Mommy.'

Even Mrs Shantz laughed.

'An acquired taste.'

Jill heard them. At least she heard the laughing, and guessed what it was about. She was lying on her bed reading *The Bridge of San Luis Rey*, which she had helped herself to from the bookcase, without understanding that she should ask Ailsa's permission. Every so often the story blanked out on her and she heard those laughing voices over in the Shantzes' yard, then the next-door patter of Iona's adoration, and she broke out in a sullen sweat. In a fairy tale she would have risen off the bed with the strength of a young giantess and gone through the house breaking furniture and necks.

When I was almost six weeks old, Ailsa and Iona were supposed to take their mother on an annual overnight visit to Guelph, to stay with some cousins. Iona wanted to take me along. But Ailsa brought in Dr Shantz to convince her that it was not a good idea to take a small baby on such a trip in hot weather. Then Iona wanted to stay at home.

'I can't drive and look after Mother both,' said Ailsa.

She said that Iona was getting too wrapped up in me, and that a day and a half looking after her own baby was not going to be too much for Jill.

'Is it, Jill?'

Jill said no.

Iona tried to pretend it wasn't that she wanted to stay with me. She said that driving on a hot day made her carsick.

'You don't drive, you just have to sit there,' Ailsa said. 'What about me? I'm not doing it for fun. I'm doing it because they expect us.'

Iona had to sit in the back, which she said made her car-sickness worse. Ailsa said it wouldn't look right to put their mother there. Mrs Kirkham said she didn't mind. Ailsa said no. Iona rolled down the window as Ailsa started the car. She fixed her eyes on the window of the upstairs room where she had put me down to sleep after my morning bath and bottle. Ailsa waved to Jill, who stood at the front door.

'Good-bye little mother,' she called, in a cheerful, challenging voice that reminded Jill somehow of George. The prospect of getting away from the house and the new threat of disruption that was lodged in it seemed to have lifted Ailsa's spirits. And perhaps it also felt good to her – felt reassuring – to have Iona back in her proper place.

It was about ten o'clock in the morning when they left, and the day ahead was to be the longest and the worst in Jill's experience. Not even the day of my birth, her nightmare labor, could compare to it. Before the car could have reached the next town, I woke in distress, as if I could feel Iona's being removed from me. Iona had fed me such a short time before that Jill did not think I could possibly be hungry. But she discovered that I was wet, and though she had read that babies did not need to be changed every time they were found wet and that wasn't usually what made them cry, she decided to change me. It wasn't the first time she had done this, but she had never done it easily, and in fact Iona had taken over more often than not and got the job finished. I made it as hard as I could – I flailed my arms and legs, arched my back, tried my best to turn over, and of course kept up my noise. Jill's hands shook, she had trouble driving the pins through the cloth. She pretended to be calm, she tried talking to me, trying to imitate Iona's baby talk and fond cajoling, but it was no use, such stumbling insincerity enraged me further. She picked me up once she had my diaper pinned, she tried to mold me to her chest and shoulder, but I stiffened as if her body was made of red-hot needles. She sat down, she rocked me. She stood up, she bounced me. She sang to me the sweet words of a lullaby that were filled and trembling with her exasperation, her anger, and something that could readily define itself as loathing.

We were monsters to each other. Jill and I.

At last she put me down, more gently than she would have liked to do, and I quieted, in my relief it seemed at getting away from her. She tiptoed from the room. And it wasn't long before I started up again.

So it continued. I didn't cry nonstop. I would take breaks of two or five or ten or twenty minutes. When the time came for her to offer me the bottle I accepted it, I lay in her arm stiffly and snuffled warningly as I drank. Once half the milk was down I returned to the assault. I finished the bottle eventually, almost absentmindedly, between wails. I dropped off to sleep and she put me down. She crept down the stairs; she stood in the hall as if she had to judge a safe way to go. She was sweating from her ordeal and from the heat of the day. She moved through the precious brittle silence into the kitchen and dared to put the coffeepot on the stove.

Before the coffee was perked I sent a meat cleaver cry down on her head.

She realized that she had forgotten something. She hadn't burped me after the bottle. She went determinedly upstairs and picked me up and walked with me patting and rubbing my angry back, and in a while I burped, but I didn't stop crying and she gave up; she laid me down.

What is it about an infant's crying that makes it so powerful, able to break down the order you depend on, inside and outside of yourself? It is like a storm — insistent, theatrical, yet in a way pure and uncontrived. It is reproachful rather than supplicating – it comes out of a rage that can't be dealt with, a birthright rage free of love and pity, ready to crush your brains inside your skull.

All Jill can do is walk around. Up and down the living-room rug, round and round the dining-room table, out to the kitchen where the clock tells her how slowly, slowly time is passing. She can't stay still to take more than a sip of her coffee. When she gets hungry she can't stop to make a sandwich but eats cornflakes out of her hands, leaving a trail all over the house. Eating and drinking, doing any ordinary thing at all, seem as risky as doing such things in a little boat out in the middle of a tempest or in a house whose beams are buckling in an awful wind. You can't take your attention from the tempest or it will rip open your last defenses. You try for sanity's sake to fix on some calm detail of your surroundings, but the wind's cries – my cries – are able to inhabit a cushion or a figure in the rug or a tiny whirlpool in the window glass. I don't allow escape.

The house is shut up like a box. Some of Ailsa's sense of shame has rubbed off on Jill, or else she's been able to manufacture some shame of her own. A mother who can't appease her own baby – what is more shameful? She keeps the doors and windows shut. And she doesn't turn the portable floor fan on because in fact she's forgotten about it. She doesn't think anymore in terms of practical relief. She doesn't think that this Sunday is one of the hottest days of the summer and maybe that is what is the matter with me. An experienced or instinctive mother would surely have given me an airing instead of granting me the powers of a demon. Prickly heat would have been what came to her mind, instead of rank despair.

Sometime in the afternoon, Jill makes a stupid or just desperate decision. She doesn't walk out of the house and leave me. Stuck in the prison of my making, she thinks of a space of her own, an escape within. She gets out her violin, which she has not touched since the day of the scales, the attempt that Ailsa and Iona have turned into a family joke. Her playing can't wake me up because I'm wide awake already, and how can it make me any angrier than I am?

In a way she does me honor. No more counterfeit soothing, no more pretend lullabies or concern for tummy-ache, no petsy-wetsy whatsamatter. Instead she will play Mendelssohn's Violin Concerto, the piece she played at her recital and must play again at her examination to get her graduating diploma.

The Mendelssohn is her choice – rather than the Beethoven Violin Concerto which she more passionately admires – because she believes the Mendelssohn will get her higher marks. She thinks she can master – has mastered – it more fully; she is confident that she can show off and impress the examiners without the least fear of catastrophe. This is not a work that will trouble her all her life, she has decided; it is not something she will struggle with and try to prove herself at forever.

She will just play it.

She tunes up, she does a few scales, she attempts to banish me from her hearing. She knows she's stiff, but this time she's prepared for that. She expects her problems to lessen as she gets into the music.

She starts to play it, she goes on playing, she goes on and on, she plays right through to the end. And her playing is terrible. It's a torment. She hangs on, she thinks this must change, she can change it, but she can't. Everything is off, she plays as badly as Jack Benny does in one of his resolute parodies. The violin is bewitched, it hates her. It gives her back a stubborn distortion of everything she intends. Nothing could be worse than this – it's worse than if she looked in the mirror and saw her reliable face caved in, sick and leering. A trick played on her that she couldn't believe, and would try to disprove by looking away and looking back, away and back, over and over again. That is how she goes on playing, trying to undo the trick. But not succeeding. She gets worse, if anything; sweat pours down her face and arms and the sides of her body, and her hand slips – there is simply no bottom to how badly she can play.

Finished. She is finished altogether. The piece that she mastered months ago and perfected since, so that nothing in it remained formidable or even tricky, has completely defeated her. It has shown her to herself as somebody emptied out, vandalized. Robbed overnight.

She doesn't give up. She does the worst thing. In this state of desperation she starts in again; she will try the Beethoven. And of course it's no good, it's worse and worse, and she seems to be howling, heaving inside. She sets the bow and the violin down on the living-room sofa, then picks them up and shoves them underneath it, getting them out of sight because she has a picture of herself smashing and wrecking them against a chair back, in a sickening dramatic display.

I haven't given up in all this time. Naturally I wouldn't, against such competition.

Jill lies down on the hard sky-blue brocade sofa where nobody ever lies or even sits, unless there's company, and she actually falls asleep. She wakes up after who knows how long with her hot face pushed down into the brocade, its pattern marked on her cheek, her mouth drooling a little and staining the sky-blue material. My racket still or again going on rising and falling like a hammering headache. And she has got a headache, too. She gets up and pushes her way – that's what it feels like – through the hot air to the kitchen cupboard where Ailsa keeps the 222's. The thick air makes her think of sewage. And why not? While she slept I dirtied my diaper, and its ripe smell has had time to fill the house.

222's. Warm another bottle. Climb the stairs. She changes the diaper without lifting me from the crib. The sheet as well as the diaper is a mess. The 222's are not working yet and her headache increases in fierceness as she bends over. Haul the mess out, wash off my scalded parts, pin on a clean diaper, and take the dirty diaper and sheet into the bathroom to be scrubbed off in the toilet. Put them in the pail of disinfectant which is already full to the brim because the usual baby wash has not been done today. Then get to me with the bottle. I quiet again enough to suck. It's a wonder I have the energy left to do that, but I do. The feeding is more than an hour late, and I have real hunger to add to – but maybe also subvert – my store of grievance. I suck away, I finish the bottle, and then worn out I go to sleep, and this time actually stay asleep.

Jill's headache dulls. Groggily she washes out my diapers and shirts and gowns and sheets. Scrubs them and rinses them and even boils the diapers to defeat the diaper rash to which I am prone. She wrings them all out by hand. She hangs them up indoors because the next day is Sunday, and Ailsa, when she returns, will not want to see anything hanging outdoors on Sunday. Jill would just as soon not have to appear outside, anyway, especially now with evening thickening and people sitting out, taking advantage of the cool. She dreads being seen by the neighbors – even being greeted by the friendly Shantzes – after what they must have listened to today.

And such a long time it takes for today to be over. For the

long reach of sunlight and stretched shadows to give out and the monumental heat to stir a little, opening sweet cool cracks. Then all of a sudden the stars are out in clusters and the trees are enlarging themselves like clouds, shaking down peace. But not for long and not for Jill. Well before midnight comes a thin cry – you could not call it tentative, but thin at least, experimental, as if in spite of the day's practice I have lost the knack. Or as if I actually wonder if it's worth it. A little rest then, a false respite or giving up. But after that a thoroughgoing, an anguished, unforgiving resumption. Just when Jill had started to make more coffee, to deal with the remnants of her headache. Thinking that this time she might sit by the table and drink it.

Now she turns the burner off.

It's almost time for the last bottle of the day. If the feeding before had not been delayed, I'd be ready now. Perhaps I am ready? While it's warming, Jill thinks she'll dose herself with a couple more 222's. Then she thinks maybe that won't do; she needs something stronger. In the bathroom cupboard she finds only Pepto-Bismol, laxatives, foot powder, prescriptions she wouldn't touch. But she knows that Ailsa takes something strong for her menstrual cramps, and she goes into Ailsa's room and looks through her bureau drawers until she finds a bottle of pain pills lying, logically, on top of a pile of sanitary pads. These are prescription pills, too, but the label says clearly what they're for. She removes two of them and goes back to the kitchen and finds the water in the pan around the milk boiling, the milk too hot.

She holds the bottle under the tap to cool it – my cries coming down at her like the clamor of birds of prey over a gurgling river – and she looks at the pills waiting on the counter and she thinks, *Yes*. She gets out a knife and shaves a few grains off one of the pills, takes the nipple off the bottle, picks up the shaved grains on the blade of the knife, and sprinkles them – just a sprinkle of white dust – over the milk. Then she swallows one and seven-eighths or maybe one and eleven-twelfths or even one and fifteen-sixteenths of a pill herself, and takes the bottle upstairs. She lifts up my immediately rigid body and gets the nipple into my accusing mouth. The milk is still a little too warm for my liking and at first I spit it back at her. Then in a while I decide that it will do, and I swallow it all down.

Iona is screaming. Jill wakes up to a house full of hurtful sunlight and Iona's screaming.

The plan was that Ailsa and Iona and their mother would visit with their relatives in Guelph until the late afternoon, avoiding driving during the hot part of the day. But after breakfast Iona began to make a fuss. She wanted to get home to the baby, she said she had hardly slept all night for worrying. It was embarrassing to keep on arguing with her in front of the relatives, so Ailsa gave in and they arrived home late in the morning and opened the door of the still house.

Ailsa said, 'Phew. Is this what it always smells like in here, only we're so used to it we don't notice?'

Iona ducked past her and ran up the stairs.

Now she's screaming.

Dead. Dead. Murderer.

She knows nothing about the pills. So why does she scream 'Murderer'? It's the blanket. She sees the blanket pulled up right over my head. Suffocation. Not poison. It has not taken her any time, not half a second, to get from 'dead' to 'murderer.' It's an immediate flying leap. She grabs me from the crib, with the death blanket twisted round me, and holding the blanketed bundle squeezed against her body she runs screaming out of the room and into Jill's room.

Jill is struggling up, dopily, after twelve or thirteen hours of sleep.

'You've killed my baby,' Iona is screaming at her.

Jill doesn't correct her – she doesn't say, *Mine*. Iona holds me out accusingly to show me to Jill, but before Jill can get any kind of a look at me I have been snatched back. Iona groans and doubles up as if she's been shot in the stomach. Still holding on to me she stumbles down the stairs, bumping into Ailsa who is on her way up. Ailsa is almost knocked off her feet; she hangs on to the banister and Iona takes no notice; she seems to be trying to squeeze the bundle of me into a new terrifying hole in the middle of her body. Words come out of her between fresh groans of recognition.

Baby. Love my. Darling. Ooh. Oh. Get the. Suffocated. Blanket. Baby. Police.

Jill has slept with no covers over her and without changing into a nightdress. She is still in yesterday's shorts and halter, and she's not sure if she's waking from a night's sleep or a nap. She isn't sure where she is or what day it is. And what did Iona say? Groping her way up out of a vat of warm wool, Jill sees rather than hears Iona's cries, and they're like red flashes, hot veins in the inside of her eyelids. She clings to the luxury of not having to understand, but then she knows she has understood. She knows it's about me.

But Jill thinks that Iona has made a mistake. Iona has got into the wrong part of the dream. That part is all over.

The baby is all right. Jill took care of the baby. She went out and found the baby and covered it up. All right.

In the downstairs hall, Iona makes an effort and shouts some words all together. 'She pulled the blanket all the way over its head, she smothered it.'

Ailsa comes downstairs hanging on to the banister.

'Put it down,' she says. 'Put it down.'

Iona squeezes me and groans. Then she holds me out to Ailsa and says, 'Look. Look.'

Ailsa whips her head aside. 'I won't,' she says. 'I won't look.' Iona comes close to push me into her face – I am still all wrapped up in my blanket, but Ailsa doesn't know that and Iona doesn't notice or doesn't care.

Now it's Ailsa screaming. She runs to the other side of the dining-room table screaming, 'Put it down. Put it down. I'm not going to look at a corpse.'

Mrs Kirkham comes in from the kitchen, saying, 'Girls, oh, girls. What's the trouble between you? I can't have this, you know.'

'Look,' says Iona, forgetting Ailsa and coming around the table to show me to her mother.

Ailsa gets to the hall phone and gives the operator Dr Shantz's number.

'Oh, a baby,' says Mrs Kirkham, twitching the blanket aside.

'She smothered it,' Iona says.

'Oh, no,' says Mrs Kirkham.

Ailsa is talking to Dr Shantz on the phone, telling him in a shaky voice to get over here at once. She turns from the phone and looks at Iona, gulps to steady herself, and says, 'Now you. You pipe down.'

Iona gives a high-pitched defiant yelp and runs away from her, across the hall into the living-room. She is still hanging on to me.

Jill has come to the top of the stairs. Ailsa spots her.

She says, 'Come on down here.'

She has no idea what she's going to do to Jill, or say to her, once she gets her down. She looks as if she wants to slap her. 'It's no good now getting hysterical,' she says.

Jill's halter is twisted partway round so that most of one breast has got loose.

'Fix yourself up,' says Ailsa. 'Did you sleep in your clothes? You look drunk.'

Jill seems to herself to be walking still in the snowy light of her dream. But the dream has been invaded by these frantic people.

Ailsa is able to think now about some things that have to be done. Whatever has happened, there has got to be no question of such a thing as a murder. Babies do die, for no reason, in their sleep. She has heard of that. No question of the police. No autopsy — a sad quiet little funeral. The obstacle to this is Iona. Dr Shantz can give Iona a needle now; the needle will put her to sleep. But he can't go on giving her a needle every day.

The thing is to get Iona into Morrisville. This is the Hospital for the Insane, which used to be called the Asylum and in the future will be called the Psychiatric Hospital, then the Mental Health Unit. But most people just call it Morrisville, after the village nearby.

Going to Morrisville, they say. They took her off to Morrisville. Carry on like that and you're going to end up in Morrisville.

Iona has been there before and she can go there again. Dr Shantz can get her in and keep her in until it's judged she's ready to come out. Affected by the baby's death. Delusions. Once that is established she won't pose a threat. Nobody will pay any attention to what she says. She will have had a breakdown. In fact it looks as if that may be the truth — it looks as if she might be halfway to a breakdown already, with that yelping and running around. It might be permanent. But probably not. There's all kinds of treatment nowadays.

Drugs to calm her down, and shock if it's better to blot out some memories, and an operation they do, if they have to, on people who are obstinately confused and miserable. They don't do that at Morrisville – they have to send you to the city.

For all this – which has gone through her mind in an instant – Ailsa will have to count on Dr Shantz. Some obliging lack of curiosity on his part and a willingness to see things her way. But that should not be hard for anybody who knows what she has been through. The investment she has made in this family's respectability and the blows she's had to take, from her father's shabby career and her mother's mixed-up wits to Iona's collapse at nursing school and George's going off to get killed. Does Ailsa deserve a public scandal on top of this – a story in the papers, a trial, maybe even a sister-in-law in jail?

Dr Shantz would not think so. And not just because he can tote up these reasons from what he has observed as a friendly neighbor. Not just because he can appreciate that people who have to do without respectability must sooner or later feel the cold.

The reasons he has for helping Ailsa are all in his voice as he comes running in the back door now, through the kitchen, calling her name.

Jill at the bottom of the stairs has just said, 'The baby's all right.'

And Ailsa has said, 'You keep quiet until I tell you what to say.'

Mrs Kirkham stands in the doorway between the kitchen and the hall, square in Dr Shantz's path.

'Oh, I'm glad to see you,' she says. 'Ailsa and Iona are all upset with each other. Iona found a baby at the door and now she says it's dead.'

Dr Shantz picks Mrs Kirkham up and puts her aside. He says again, 'Ailsa?' and reaches out his arms, but ends up just setting his hands down hard on her shoulders.

Iona comes out of the living-room empty-handed.

Jill says, 'What did you do with the baby?'

'Hid it,' Iona says saucily, and makes a face at her – the kind of face a terminally frightened person can make, pretending to be vicious.

'Dr Shantz is going to give you a needle,' Ailsa says. 'That'll put paid to you.'

Now there is an absurd scene of Iona running around, throwing herself at the front door – Ailsa jumps to block her – and then at the stairs, which is where Dr Shantz gets hold of her and straddles her, pinning her arms and saying, 'Now, now, now, Iona. Take it easy. You'll be okay in a little while.' And Iona yells and whimpers and subsides. The noises she makes, and her darting about, her efforts at escape, all seem like playacting. As if – in spite of being quite literally at her wit's end – she finds the effort of standing up to Ailsa and Dr Shantz so nearly impossible that she can only try to manage it by this sort of parody. Which makes it clear – and maybe this is what she really intends – that she is not standing up to them at all but falling apart. Falling apart as embarrassingly and inconveniently as possible with Ailsa shouting at her, 'You ought to be disgusted with yourself.'

Administering the needle, Dr Shantz says, 'That-a-girl Iona. There now.'

Over his shoulder he says to Ailsa, 'Look after your mother. Get her to sit down.'

Mrs Kirkham is wiping tears with her fingers. 'I'm all right dear,' she says to Ailsa. 'I just wish you girls wouldn't fight. You should have told me Iona had a baby. You should have let her keep it.'

Mrs Shantz, wearing a Japanese kimono over her summer pajamas, comes into the house by the kitchen door.

'Is everybody all right?' she calls.

She sees the knife lying on the kitchen counter and thinks it prudent to pick it up and put it in a drawer. When people are making a scene the last thing you want is a knife ready to hand.

In the midst of this Jill thinks she has heard a faint cry. She has climbed clumsily over the banister to get around Iona and Dr Shantz – she ran partway up the stairs again when Iona came running in that direction – and has lowered herself to the floor. She goes through the double doors into the living-room where at first she sees no sign of me. But the faint cry comes again and she follows the sound to the sofa and looks underneath it.

That's where I am, pushed in beside the violin.

During that short trip from the hall to the living-room, Jill has remembered everything, and it seems as if her breath stops and horror crowds in at her mouth, then a flash of joy sets her life going again, when just as in the dream she comes upon a live baby, not a little desiccated nutmeg-headed corpse. She holds me. I don't stiffen or kick or arch my back. I am still pretty sleepy from the sedative in my milk which knocked me out for the night and half a day and which, in a larger quantity – maybe not so much larger, at that – would have really finished me off.

It wasn't the blanket at all. Anybody who took a serious look at that blanket could see that it was so light and loosely woven that it could not prevent my getting all the air I needed. You could breathe through it just as easily as through a fishnet.

Exhaustion might have played a part. A whole day's howling, such a furious feat of self-expression, might have worn me out. That, and the white dust that fell on my milk, had knocked me into a deep and steadfast sleep with breathing so slight that Iona had not been able to detect it. You would think she would notice that I was not cold and you would think that all that moaning and crying out and running around would have brought me up to consciousness in a hurry. I don't know why that didn't happen. I think she didn't notice because of her panic and the state she was in even before she found me, but I don't know why I didn't cry sooner. Or maybe I did cry and in the commotion nobody heard me. Or maybe Iona did hear me and took a look at me and stuffed me under the sofa because by that time everything had been spoiled.

Then Jill heard. Jill was the one.

Iona was carried to that same sofa. Ailsa slipped off her shoes to save the brocade, and Mrs Shantz went upstairs to get a light quilt to put over her.

'I know she doesn't need it for warmth,' she said. 'But I think when she wakes up she'll feel better to have a quilt over her.'

Before this, of course, everybody had gathered round to take note of my being alive. Ailsa was blaming herself for not having discovered that right away. She hated to admit that she had been afraid to look at a dead baby.

'Iona's nerves must be contagious,' she said. 'I absolutely should have known.'

She looked at Jill as if she was going to tell her to go and put a blouse on over her halter. Then she recalled how roughly she had spoken to her, and for no reason as it turned out, so she didn't say anything. She did not even try to convince her mother that Iona had not had a baby, though she said in an undertone, to Mrs Shantz, 'Well, that could start the rumor of the century.'

'I'm so glad nothing terrible happened,' Mrs Kirkham said. 'I thought for a minute Iona had done away with it. Ailsa, you must try not to blame your sister.'

'No Momma,' said Ailsa. 'Let's go sit down in the kitchen.'

There was one bottle of formula made up that by rights I should have demanded and drunk earlier that morning. Jill put it on to warm, holding me in the crook of her arm all the time.

She had looked at once for the knife, when she came into the kitchen, and seen in wonderment that it wasn't there. But she could make out the faintest dust on the counter – or she thought she could. She wiped it with her free hand before she turned the tap on to get the water to heat the bottle.

Mrs Shantz busied herself making coffee. While it was perking she put the sterilizer on the stove and washed out yesterday's bottles. She was being tactful and competent, just managing to hide the fact that there was something about this whole debacle and disarray of feelings that buoyed her up.

'I guess Iona did have an obsession about the baby,' she said. 'Something like this was bound to happen.'

Turning from the stove to address the last of these words to her husband and Ailsa, she saw that Dr Shantz was pulling Ailsa's hands down from where she held them, on either side of her head. Too speedily and guiltily he took his own hands away. If he had not done that, it would have looked like ordinary comfort he was administering. As a doctor is certainly entitled to do.

'You know Ailsa, I think your mother ought to lie down too,' said Mrs Shantz thoughtfully and without a break. 'I think I'll go and persuade her. If she can get to sleep this may all pass right out of her head. Out of Iona's too, if we're lucky.'

Mrs Kirkham had wandered out of the kitchen almost as soon as she got there. Mrs Shantz found her in the living-room looking at Iona, and fiddling with the quilt to make sure she was well covered. Mrs Kirkham did not really want to lie down. She wanted to have things explained to her – she knew that her own explanations were somehow out of kilter. And she wanted to have people talk to her as they used to do, not in the peculiarly gentle and self-satisfied way they did now. But because of her customary politeness and her knowledge that the power she had in the household was negligible, she allowed Mrs Shantz to take her upstairs.

Jill was reading the instructions for making baby formula. They were printed on the side of the corn syrup tin. When she heard the footsteps going up the stairs she thought that there was something she had better do while she had the chance. She carried me into the living-room and laid me down on a chair.

'There now,' she whispered confidentially. 'You stay still.'

She knelt down and nudged and gently tugged the violin out of its hiding place. She found its cover and case and got it properly stowed away. I stayed still – not yet being quite able to turn over – and I stayed quiet.

Left alone by themselves, alone in the kitchen, Dr Shantz and Ailsa probably did not seize this chance to embrace, but only looked at each other. With their knowledge, and without promises or despair.

Iona admitted that she hadn't felt for a pulse. And she never claimed that I was cold. She said I felt stiff. Then she said not stiff but heavy. So heavy, she said, she instantly thought I could not be alive. A lump, a dead weight.

I think there is something to this. I don't believe that I was dead, or that I came back from the dead, but I do think that

I was at a distance, from which I might or might not have come back. I think that the outcome was not certain and that will was involved. It was up to me, I mean, to go one way or the other.

And Iona's love, which was certainly the most whole-hearted love I will ever receive, didn't decide me. Her cries and her crushing me into her body didn't work, were not finally persuasive. Because it wasn't Iona I had to settle for. (Could I have known that – could I even have known that it wasn't Iona, in the end, who would do me the most good?) It was Jill. I had to settle for Jill and for what I could get from her, even if it might look like half a loaf.

To me it seems that it was only then that I became female. I know that the matter was decided long before I was born and was plain to everybody else since the beginning of my life, but I believe that it was only at the moment when I decided to come back, when I gave up the fight against my mother (which must have been a fight for something like her total surrender) and when in fact I chose survival over victory (death would have been victory), that I took on my female nature.

And to some extent Jill took on hers. Sobered and grateful, not even able to risk thinking about what she'd just escaped, she took on loving me, because the alternative to loving was disaster.

Dr Shantz suspected something, but he let it go. He asked Jill how I had been the day before. Fussy? She said yes, very fussy. He said that premature babies, even slightly premature babies, were susceptible to shocks and you had to be careful with them. He recommended that I always be put to sleep on my back.

Iona did not have to have shock treatment. Dr Shantz gave

122

her pills. He said that she had overstrained herself looking after me. The woman who had taken over her job at the bakery wanted to give it up – she did not like working nights. So Iona went back there.

That's what I remember best about my summer visits to my aunts, when I was six or seven years old. Being taken down to the bakery at the strange, usually forbidden hour of midnight and watching Iona put on her white hat and apron, watching her knead the great white mass of dough that shifted and bubbled like something alive. Then cutting out cookies and feeding me the leftover bits and on special occasions sculpting a wedding cake. How bright and white that big kitchen was, with night filling every window. I scraped the wedding icing from the bowl – the melting stabbing irresistible sugar.

Ailsa thought I should not be up so late, or eat so much sweet stuff. But she didn't do anything about it. She said she wondered what my mother would say – as if Jill was the person who swung the weight, not herself. Ailsa had some rules that I didn't have to observe at home – hang up that jacket, rinse that glass before you dry it, else it'll have spots – but I never saw the harsh, hounding person Jill remembered.

Nothing slighting was ever said then, about Jill's music. After all, she made our living at it. She had not been finally defeated by the Mendelssohn. She got her diploma; she graduated from the Conservatory. She cut her hair and got thin. She was able to rent a duplex near High Park in Toronto, and hire a woman to look after me part of the time, because she had her war widow's pension. And then she found a job with a radio orchestra. She was to be proud that all her working life she was employed as a musician and never had to fall back on teaching. She said that she knew that she was not a great violinist, she had no marvellous gift or destiny, but at least she could make her living doing what she wanted to do. Even after she married my stepfather, after we moved with him to Edmonton (he was a geologist), she went on playing in the symphony orchestra there. She played up until a week before each of my half sisters was born. She was lucky, she said – her husband never objected.

Iona did have a couple of further setbacks, the more serious one when I was about twelve. She was taken to Morrisville for several weeks. I think she was given insulin there – she returned fat and loquacious. I came back to visit while she was away, and Jill came with me, bringing my first little sister who had been born shortly before. I understood from the talk between my mother and Ailsa that it would not have been advisable to bring a baby into the house if Iona was there; it might have 'set her off.' I don't know if the episode that sent her to Morrisville had anything to do with a baby.

I felt left out of things on that visit. Both Jill and Ailsa had taken up smoking, and they would sit up late at night, drinking coffee and smoking cigarettes at the kitchen table, while they waited for the baby's one o'clock feeding. (My mother fed this baby from her breasts – I was glad to hear that no such intimate body-heated meals had been served to me.) I remember coming downstairs sulkily because I couldn't sleep, then turning talkative, full of giddy bravado, trying to break into their conversation. I understood that they were talking over things they didn't want me to hear about. They had become, unaccountably, good friends.

I grabbed for a cigarette, and my mother said, 'Go on now, leave those alone. We're talking.' Ailsa told me to get something to drink out of the fridge, a Coke or a ginger ale. So I did, and instead of taking it upstairs I went outside.

I sat on the back step, but the women's voices immediately

went too low for me to make out any of their soft regretting or reassuring. So I went prowling around the backyard, beyond the patch of light thrown through the screen door.

The long white house with the glass-brick corners was occupied by new people now. The Shantzes had moved away, to live year-round in Florida. They sent my aunts oranges, which Ailsa said would make you forever disgusted with the kind of oranges you could buy in Canada. The new people had put in a swimming pool, which was used mostly by the two pretty teenage daughters – girls who would look right through me when they met me on the street – and by the daughters' boyfriends. Some bushes had grown up fairly high between my aunts' yard and theirs, but it was still possible for me to watch them running around the pool and pushing each other in, with great shrieks and splashes. I despised their antics because I took life seriously and had a much more lofty and tender notion of romance. But I would have liked to get their attention just the same. I would have liked for one of them to see my pale pajamas moving in the dark, and to scream out in earnest, thinking that I was a ghost.

ELIZABETH BOWEN

COMING HOME

ALL THE WAY home from school Rosalind's cheeks burnt, she felt something throbbing in her ears. It was sometimes terrible to live so far away. Before her body had turned the first corner her mind had many times wrenched open their gate, many times rushed up their path through the damp smells of the garden, waving the essay-book, and seen Darlingest coming to the window. Nothing like this had ever happened before to either her or Darlingest; it was the supreme moment that all these years they had been approaching, of which those dim, improbable future years would be spent in retrospect.

Rosalind's essay had been read aloud and everybody had praised it. Everybody had been there, the big girls sitting along the sides of the room had turned and looked at her, raising their eyebrows and smiling. For an infinity of time the room had held nothing but the rising and falling of Miss Wilfred's beautiful voice doing the service of Rosalind's brain. When the voice dropped to silence and the room was once more unbearably crowded, Rosalind had looked at the clock and seen that her essay had taken four and a half minutes to read. She found that her mouth was dry and her eyes ached from staring at a small fixed spot in the heart of whirling circles, and her knotted hands were damp and trembling. Somebody behind her gently poked the small of her back. Everybody in the room was thinking about Rosalind;

she felt their admiration and attention lapping up against her in small waves. A long way off somebody spoke her name repeatedly, she stood up stupidly and everybody laughed. Miss Wilfred was trying to pass her back the red exercise-book. Rosalind sat down thinking to herself how dazed she was, dazed with glory. She was beginning already to feel about for words for Darlingest.

She had understood some time ago that nothing became real for her until she had had time to live it over again. An actual occurrence was nothing but the blankness of a shock, then the knowledge that something had happened; after-wards one could creep back and look into one's mind and find new things in it, clear and solid. It was like waiting out-side the hen-house till the hen came off the nest and then going in to look for the egg. She would not touch this egg until she was with Darlingest, then they would go and look for it together. Suddenly and vividly this afternoon would be real for her. 'I won't think about it yet,' she said, 'for fear I'd spoil it.'

The houses grew scarcer and the roads greener, and Rosa-lind relaxed a little; she was nearly home. She looked at the syringa bushes by the gate, and it was as if a cold wing had brushed against her. Supposing Darlingest were out . . . ?

She slowed down her running steps to a walk. From here she would be able to call to Darlingest. But if she didn't answer there would be still a tortuous hope; she might be at the back of the house. She decided to pretend it didn't matter, one way or the other; she had done this before, and it rather took the wind out of Somebody's sails, she felt. She hitched up her essay-book under her arm, approached the gate, turned carefully to shut it, and walked slowly up the path looking carefully down at her feet, not up at all at the drawing-room window. Darlingest would think she was playing a game. Why didn't she hear her tapping on the glass with her thimble?

As soon as she entered the hall she knew that the house was empty. Clocks ticked very loudly; upstairs and downstairs the doors were a little open, letting through pale strips of light. Only the kitchen door was shut, down the end of the passage, and she could hear Emma moving about behind it. There was a spectral shimmer of light in the white panelling. On the table was a bowl of primroses, Darlingest must have put them there that morning. The hall was chilly; she could not think why the primroses gave her such a feeling of horror, then she remembered the wreath of primroses, and the scent of it, lying on the raw new earth of that grave ... The pair of grey gloves were gone from the bowl of visiting-cards. Darlingest had spent the morning doing those deathly primroses, and then taken up her grey gloves and gone out, at the end of the afternoon, just when she knew her little girl would be coming in. A quarter-past four. It was unforgivable of Darlingest: she had been a mother for more than twelve years, the mother exclusively of Rosalind, and still, it seemed, she knew no better than to do a thing like that. Other people's mothers had terrible little babies: they ran quickly in and out to go to them, or they had smoky husbands who came in and sat, with big feet. There was something distracted about other people's mothers. But Darlingest, so exclusively one's own ...

Darlingest could never have really believed in her. She could never have really believed that Rosalind would do anything wonderful at school, or she would have been more careful to be in to hear about it. Rosalind flung herself into the drawing-room; it was honey-coloured and lovely in the pale spring light, another little clock was ticking in the corner, there were more bowls of primroses and black-eyed,

lowering anemones. The tarnished mirror on the wall distorted and reproved her angry face in its mild mauveness.
Tea was spread on the table by the window, tea for two that
the two might never . . . Her work and an open book lay on
the tumbled cushions of the window-seat. All the afternoon
she had sat there waiting and working, and now – poor little
Darlingest, perhaps she had gone out because she was lonely.

People who went out sometimes never came back again.
Here she was, being angry with Darlingest, and all the time
. . . Well, she had drawn on those grey gloves and gone out
wandering along the roads, vague and beautiful, because she
was lonely, and then?

Ask Emma? No, she wouldn't; fancy having to ask *her*!

'Yes, your mother'll be in soon, Miss Rosie. Now run and
get your things off, there's a good girl –' Oh no, intolerable.

The whole house was full of the scent and horror of the
primroses. Rosalind dropped the exercise-book on the floor,
looked at it, hesitated, and putting her hands over her
mouth, went upstairs, choking back her sobs. She heard the
handle of the kitchen door turn; Emma was coming out.
O God! Now she was on the floor by Darlingest's bed, with
the branches swaying and brushing outside the window,
smothering her face in the eiderdown, smelling and tasting
the wet satin. Down in the hall she heard Emma call her,
mutter something, and slam back into the kitchen.

How could she ever have left Darlingest? She might have
known, she might have known. The sense of insecurity had
been growing on her year by year. A person might be part of
you, almost part of your body, and yet once you went away
from them they might utterly cease to be. That sea of horror
ebbing and flowing round the edges of the world, whose tides
were charted in the newspapers, might sweep out a long wave
over them and they would be gone. There was no security.

Safety and happiness were a game that grown-up people played with children to keep them from understanding, possibly to keep themselves from thinking. But they did think, that was what made grown-up people – queer. Anything might happen, there was no security. And now Darlingest –

This was her dressing-table, with the long beads straggling over it, the little coloured glass barrels and bottles had bright flames in the centre. In front of the looking-glass, filmed faintly over with a cloud of powder, Darlingest had put her hat on – for the last time. Supposing all that had ever been reflected in it were imprisoned somewhere in the back of a looking-glass. The blue hat with the drooping brim was hanging over the corner of a chair. Rosalind had never been kind about that blue hat, she didn't think it was becoming. And Darlingest had loved it so. She must have gone out wearing the brown one; Rosalind went over to the wardrobe and stood on tip-toe to look on the top shelf. Yes, the brown hat was gone. She would never see Darlingest again, in the brown hat, coming down the road to meet her and not seeing her because she was thinking about something else. Peau d'Espagne crept faintly from among the folds of the dresses; the blue, the gold, the soft furred edges of the tea-gown dripping out of the wardrobe. She heard herself making a high, whining noise at the back of her throat, like a puppy, felt her swollen face distorted by another paroxysm.

'I can't bear it, I can't bear it. What have I done? I did love her, I did so awfully love her.

'Perhaps she was all right when I came in; coming home smiling. Then I stopped loving her, I hated her and was angry. And it happened. She was crossing a road and something happened to her. I was angry and she died. I killed her.

'I don't know that she's dead. I'd better get used to believing it, it will hurt less afterwards. Supposing she does come back this time; it's only for a little. I shall never be able to keep her; now I've found out about this I shall never be happy. Life's nothing but waiting for awfulness to happen and trying to think about something else.

'If she could come back just this once – Darlingest.'

Emma came half-way upstairs; Rosalind flattened herself behind the door.

'Will you begin your tea, Miss Rosie?'

'No. Where's mother?'

'I didn't hear her go out. I have the kettle boiling – will I make your tea?'

'No. *No.*'

Rosalind slammed the door on the angry mutterings, and heard with a sense of desolation Emma go downstairs. The silver clock by Darlingest's bed ticked; it was five o'clock. They had tea at a quarter-past four; Darlingest was never, never late. When they came to tell her about *It*, men would come, and they would tell Emma, and Emma would come up with a frightened, triumphant face and tell her.

She saw the grey-gloved hands spread out in the dust.

A sound at the gate. 'I can't bear it, I can't bear it. Oh, save me, God!'

Steps on the gravel.

Darlingest.

She was at the window, pressing her speechless lips together.

Darlingest came slowly up the path with the long ends of her veil, untied, hanging over her shoulders. A paper parcel was pressed between her arm and her side. She paused, stood smiling down at the daffodils. Then she looked up with a start at the windows, as though she heard somebody calling. Rosalind drew back into the room.

She heard her mother's footsteps cross the stone floor of

the hall, hesitate at the door of the drawing-room, and come over to the foot of the stairs. The voice was calling 'Lindie! Lindie, duckie!' She was coming upstairs.

Rosalind leaned the weight of her body against the dressing-table and dabbed her face with the big powder-puff; the powder clung in paste to her wet lashes and in patches over her nose and cheeks. She was not happy, she was not relieved, she felt no particular feeling about Darling-est, did not even want to see her. Something had slackened down inside her, leaving her a little sick.

'Oh, you're *there*,' said Darlingest from outside, hearing her movements. 'Where did, where were –?'

She was standing in the doorway. Nothing had been for the last time, after all. She had come back. One could never explain to her how wrong she had been. She was holding out her arms; something drew one towards them.

'But, my little *Clown*,' said Darlingest, wiping off the powder. 'But, oh –' She scanned the glazed, blurred face. 'Tell me why,' she said.

'You were late.'

'Yes, it was horrid of me; did you mind? . . . But that was silly, Rosalind; I can't be always in.'

'But you're my mother.'

Darlingest was amused; little trickles of laughter and grati-fication ran out of her. 'You weren't *frightened*, Silly Billy.' Her tone changed to distress. 'Oh, Rosalind, don't be cross.'

'I'm not,' said Rosalind coldly.

'Then come –'

'I was wanting my tea.'

'Rosalind, *don't* be –'

Rosalind walked past her to the door. She was hurting Darlingest, beautifully hurting her. She would never tell her about that essay. Everybody would be talking about it, and when Darlingest heard and asked her about it she would say: 'Oh, that? I didn't think you'd be interested.' That would hurt. She went down into the drawing-room, past the primroses. The grey gloves were back on the table. This was the mauve and golden room that Darlingest had come back to, from under the Shadow of Death, expecting to find her little daughter ... They would have sat together on the window-seat while Rosalind read the essay aloud, leaning their heads closer together as the room grew darker.

That was all spoilt.

Poor Darlingest, up there alone in the bedroom, puzzled, hurt, disappointed, taking off her hat. She hadn't known she was going to be hurt like this when she stood out there on the gravel, smiling at the daffodils. The red essay-book lay spread open on the carpet. There was the paper bag she had been carrying, lying on a table by the door; macaroons, all squashy from being carried the wrong way, disgorging, through a tear in the paper, a little trickle of crumbs.

The pathos of the forgotten macaroons, the silent pain! Rosalind ran upstairs to the bedroom.

Darlingest did not hear her; she had forgotten. She was standing in the middle of the room with her face turned towards the window, looking at something a long way away, smiling and singing to herself and rolling up her veil.

ERNEST J. GAINES

THE SKY IS GRAY

I

GO'N BE COMING in a few minutes. Coming round that bend down there full speed. And I'm go'n get out my hand-kerchief and wave it down, and we go'n get on it and go.

I keep on looking for it, but Mama don't look that way no more. She's looking down the road where we just come from. It's a long old road, and far 's you can see you don't see nothing but gravel. You got dry weeds on both sides, and you got trees on both sides, and fences on both sides, too. And you got cows in the pastures and they standing close together. And when we was coming out here to catch the bus I seen the smoke coming out of the cows's noses.

I look at my mama and I know what she's thinking. I been with Mama so much, just me and her, I know what she's thinking all the time. Right now it's home – Auntie and them. She's thinking if they got enough wood – if she left enough there to keep them warm till we get back. She's thinking if it go'n rain and if any of them go'n have to go out in the rain. She's thinking 'bout the hog – if he go'n get out, and if Ty and Val be able to get him back in. She always worry like that when she leaves the house. She don't worry too much if she leave me there with the smaller ones, 'cause she know I'm go'n look after them and look after Auntie and everything else. I'm the oldest and she say I'm the man.

I look at my mama and I love my mama. She's wearing

that black coat and that black hat and she's looking sad. I love my mama and I want put my arm round her and tell her. But I'm not supposed to do that. She say that's weakness and that's crybaby stuff, and she don't want no crybaby round her. She don't want you to be scared, either. 'Cause Ty's scared of ghosts and she's always whipping him. I'm scared of the dark, too, but I make 'tend I ain't. I make 'tend I ain't 'cause I'm the oldest, and I got to set a good sample for the rest. I can't ever be scared and I can't ever cry. And that's why I never said nothing 'bout my teeth. It's been hurting me and hurting me close to a month now, but I never said it. I didn't say it 'cause I didn't want act like a crybaby, and 'cause I know we didn't have enough money to go have it pulled. But, Lord, it been hurting me. And look like it wouldn't start till at night when you was trying to get yourself little sleep. Then soon 's you shut your eyes – ummm-ummm, Lord, look like it go right down to your heartstring.

'Hurting, hanh?' Ty'd say.

I'd shake my head, but I wouldn't open my mouth for nothing. You open your mouth and let that wind in, and it almost kill you.

I'd just lay there and listen to them snore. Ty there, right 'side me, and Auntie and Val over by the fireplace. Val younger than me and Ty, and he sleeps with Auntie. Mama sleeps round the other side with Louis and Walker.

I'd just lay there and listen to them, and listen to that wind out there, and listen to that fire in the fireplace. Sometimes it'd stop long enough to let me get little rest. Sometimes it just hurt, hurt, hurt. Lord, have mercy.

II

Auntie knowed it was hurting me. I didn't tell nobody but Ty, 'cause we buddies and he ain't go'n tell nobody. But some kind of way Auntie found out. When she asked me, I told her no, nothing was wrong. But she knowed it all the time. She told me to mash up a piece of aspirin and wrap it in some cotton and jugg it down in that hole. I did it, but it didn't do no good. It stopped for a little while, and started right back again. Auntie wanted to tell Mama, but I told her, 'Uh-uh.' 'Cause I knowed we didn't have any money, and it just was go'n make her mad again. So Auntie told Monsieur Bayonne, and Monsieur Bayonne came over to the house and told me to kneel down 'side him on the fireplace. He put his finger in his mouth and made the Sign of the Cross on my jaw. The tip of Monsieur Bayonne's finger is some hard, 'cause he's always playing on that guitar. If we sit outside at night we can always hear Monsieur Bayonne playing on his guitar. Sometimes we leave him out there playing on the guitar.

Monsieur Bayonne made the Sign of the Cross over and over on my jaw, but that didn't do no good. Even when he prayed and told me to pray some, too, that tooth still hurt me.

'How you feeling?' he say.

'Same,' I say.

He kept on praying and making the Sign of the Cross and I kept on praying, too.

'Still hurting?' he says.

'Yes, sir.'

Monsieur Bayonne mashed harder and harder on my jaw. He mashed so hard he almost pushed me over on Ty. But then he stopped.

'What kind of prayers you praying, boy?' he say.

'Baptist,' I say.

'Well, I'll be – no wonder that tooth still killing him. I'm going one way and he pulling the other. Boy, don't you know any Catholic prayers?'

'I know "Hail Mary," ' I say.

'Then you better start saying it.'

'Yes, sir.'

He started mashing on my jaw again, and I could hear him praying at the same time. And, sure enough, after while it stopped hurting me.

Me and Ty went outside where Monsieur Bayonne's two hounds was and we started playing with them. 'Let's go hunting,' Ty say. 'All right,' I say; and we went on back in the pasture. Soon the hounds got on a trail, and me and Ty followed them all 'cross the pasture and then back in the woods, too. And then they cornered this little old rabbit and killed him, and me and Ty made them get back, and we picked up the rabbit and started on back home. But my tooth had started hurting me again. It was hurting me plenty now, but I wouldn't tell Monsieur Bayonne. That night I didn't sleep a bit, and first thing in the morning Auntie told me to go back and let Monsieur Bayonne pray over me some more. Monsieur Bayonne was in his kitchen making coffee when I got there. Soon 's he seen me he knowed what was wrong.

'All right, kneel down there 'side that stove,' he say. 'And this time make sure you pray Catholic. I don't know nothing 'bout that Baptist, and I don't want know nothing 'bout him.'

III

Last night Mama say, 'Tomorrow we going to town.'

'It ain't hurting me no more,' I say. 'I can eat anything on it.'

'Tomorrow we going to town,' she say.

And after she finished eating, she got up and went to bed. She always go to bed early now. 'Fore Daddy went in the Army, she used to stay up late. All of us sitting out on the gallery or round the fire. But now, look like soon 's she finish eating she go to bed.

This morning when I woke up, her and Auntie was standing 'fore the fireplace. She say: 'Enough to get there and get back. Dollar and a half to have it pulled. Twenty-five for me to go, twenty-five for him. Twenty-five for me to come back, twenty-five for him. Fifty cents left. Guess I get little piece of salt meat with that.'

'Sure can use it,' Auntie say. 'White beans and no salt meat ain't white beans.'

'I do the best I can,' Mama say.

They was quiet after that, and I made 'tend I was still asleep.

'James, hit the floor,' Auntie say.

I still made 'tend I was asleep. I didn't want them to know I was listening.

'All right,' Auntie say, shaking me by the shoulder. 'Come on. Today's the day.'

I pushed the cover down to get out, and Ty grabbed it and pulled it back.

'You, too, Ty,' Auntie say.

'I ain't getting no teef pulled,' Ty say.

'Don't mean it ain't time to get up,' Auntie say. 'Hit it, Ty.'

Ty got up grumbling.

'James, you hurry up and get in your clothes and eat your food,' Auntie say. 'What time y'all coming back?' she say to Mama.

'That 'leven o'clock bus,' Mama say. 'Got to get back in that field this evening.'

'Get a move on you, James,' Auntie say.

I went in the kitchen and washed my face, then I ate my breakfast. I was having bread and syrup. The bread was warm and hard and tasted good. And I tried to make it last a long time.

Ty came back there grumbling and mad at me.

'Got to get up,' he say. 'I ain't having no teefes pulled. What I got to be getting up for?'

Ty poured some syrup in his pan and got a piece of bread. He didn't wash his hands, neither his face, and I could see that white stuff in his eyes.

'You the one getting your teef pulled,' he say. 'What I got to get up for. I bet if I was getting a teef pulled, you wouldn't be getting up. Shucks; syrup again. I'm getting tired of this old syrup. Syrup, syrup, syrup. I'm go'n take with the sugar diabetes. I want me some bacon sometime.'

'Go out in the field and work and you can have your bacon,' Auntie say. She stood in the middle door looking at Ty. 'You better be glad you got syrup. Some people ain't got that – hard 's time is.'

'Shucks,' Ty say. 'How can I be strong.'

'I don't know too much 'bout your strength,' Auntie say; 'but I know where you go'n be hot at, you keep that grumbling up. James, get a move on you; your mama waiting.'

I ate my last piece of bread and went in the front room. Mama was standing 'fore the fireplace warming her hands. I put on my coat and my cap, and we left the house.

IV

I look down there again, but it still ain't coming. I almost say, 'It ain't coming yet,' but I keep my mouth shut. 'Cause that's something else she don't like. She don't like for you to say something just for nothing. She can see it ain't coming, I can see it ain't coming, so why say it ain't coming. I don't say it, I turn and look at the river that's back of us. It's so cold the smoke's just raising up from the water. I see a bunch of pool-doos not too far out – just on the other side the lilies. I'm wondering if you can eat pool-doos. I ain't too sure, 'cause I ain't never ate none. But I done ate owls and black-birds, and I done ate redbirds, too. I didn't want kill the redbirds, but she made me kill them. They had two of them back there. One in my trap, one in Ty's trap. Me and Ty was go'n play with them and let them go, but she made me kill them 'cause we needed the food.

'I can't,' I say. 'I can't.'

'Here,' she say. 'Take it.'

'I can't,' I say. 'I can't. I can't kill him, Mama, please.'

'Here,' she say. 'Take this fork, James.'

'Please, Mama, I can't kill him,' I say.

I could tell she was go'n hit me. I jerked back, but I didn't jerk back soon enough.

'Take it,' she say.

I took it and reached in for him, but he kept on hopping to the back.

'I can't, Mama,' I say. The water just kept on running down my face. 'I can't,' I say.

'Get him out of there,' she say.

I reached in for him and he kept on hopping to the back. Then I reached in farther, and he pecked me on the hand.

'I can't, Mama,' I say.

She slapped me again.

I reached in again, but he kept on hopping out my way. Then he hopped to one side and I reached there. The fork got him on the leg and I heard his leg pop. I pulled my hand out 'cause I had hurt him.

'Give it here,' she say, and jerked the fork out my hand.

She reached in and got the little bird right in the neck. I heard the fork go in his neck, and I heard it go in the ground. She brought him out and helt him right in front of me.

'That's one,' she say. She shook him off and gived me the fork. 'Get the other one.'

'I can't, Mama,' I say. 'I'll do anything, but don't make me do that.'

She went to the corner of the fence and broke the biggest switch over there she could find. I knelt 'side the trap, crying.

'Get him out of there,' she say.

'I can't, Mama.'

She started hitting me 'cross the back. I went down on the ground, crying.

'Get him,' she say.

'Octavia?' Auntie say.

'Cause she had come out of the house and she was standing by the tree looking at us.

'Get him out of there,' Mama say.

'Octavia,' Auntie say, 'explain to him. Explain to him. Just don't beat him. Explain to him.'

But she hit me and hit me and hit me.

I'm still young – I ain't no more than eight; but I know now; I know why I had to do it. (They was so little, though. They was so little. I 'member how I picked the feathers off them and cleaned them and helt them over the fire. Then we all ate them. Ain't had but a little bitty piece each, but we all had a little bitty piece, and everybody just looked at me 'cause they was so proud.) Suppose she had to go away? That's why I had to do it. Suppose she had to go away like Daddy went away? Then who was go'n look after us? They had to be somebody left to carry on. I didn't know it then, but I know it now. Auntie and Monsieur Bayonne talked to me and made me see.

V

Time I see it I get out my handkerchief and start waving. It's still 'way down there, but I keep waving anyhow. Then it come up and stop and me and Mama get on. Mama tell me go sit in the back while she pay. I do like she say, and the people look at me. When I pass the little sign that say 'White' and 'Colored,' I start looking for a seat. I just see one of them back there, but I don't take it, 'cause I want my mama to sit down herself. She comes in the back and sit down, and I lean on the seat. They got seats in the front, but I know I can't sit there, 'cause I have to sit back of the sign. Anyhow, I don't want sit there if my mama go'n sit back here.

They got a lady sitting 'side my mama and she looks at me and smiles little bit. I smile back, but I don't open my mouth, 'cause the wind'll get in and make that tooth ache. The lady take out a pack of gum and reach me a slice, but I shake my head. The lady just can't understand why a little boy'll turn down gum, and she reach me a slice again. This time I point to my jaw. The lady understands and smiles little bit, and I smile little bit, but I don't open my mouth, though.

They got a girl sitting 'cross from me. She got on a red overcoat and her hair's plaited in one big plait. First, I make 'tend I don't see her over there, but then I start looking at her little

147

bit. She make 'tend she don't see me, either, but I catch her looking that way. She got a cold, and every now and then she h'ist that little handkerchief to her nose. She ought to blow it, but she don't. Must think she's too much a lady or something.

Every time she h'ist that little handkerchief, the lady 'side her say something in her ear. She shakes her head and lays her hands in her lap again. Then I catch her kind of looking where I'm at. I smile at her little bit. But think she'll smile back? Uh-uh. She just turn up her little old nose and turn her head. Well, I show her both of us can turn us head. I turn mine too and look out at the river.

The river is gray. The sky is gray. They have pool-doos on the water. The water is wavy, and the pool-doos go up and down. The bus go round a turn, and you got plenty trees hiding the river. Then the bus go round another turn, and I can see the river again.

I look toward the front where all the white people sitting. Then I look at that little old gal again. I don't look right at her, 'cause I don't want all them people to know I love her. I just look at her little bit, like I'm looking out that window over there. But she knows I'm looking that way, and she kind of look at me, too. The lady sitting 'side her catch her this time, and she leans over and says something in her ear.

'I don't love him nothing,' that little old gal says out loud.

Everybody back there hear her mouth, and all of them look at us and laugh.

'I don't love you, either,' I say. 'So you don't have to turn up your nose, Miss.'

'You the one looking,' she say.

'I wasn't looking at you,' I say. 'I was looking out that window, there.'

'Out that window, my foot,' she say. 'I seen you. Every-time I turned round you was looking at me.'

'You must of been looking yourself if you seen me all them times,' I say.

'Shucks,' she say, 'I got me all kind of boyfriends.'

'I got girlfriends, too,' I say.

'Well, I just don't want you getting your hopes up,' she say.

I don't say no more to that little old gal 'cause I don't want have to bust her in the mouth. I lean on the seat where Mama sitting, and I don't even look that way no more. When we get to Bayonne, she jugg her little old tongue out at me. I make 'tend I'm go'n hit her, and she duck down 'side her mama. And all the people laugh at us again.

VI

Me and Mama get off and start walking in town. Bayonne is a little bitty town. Baton Rouge is a hundred times bigger than Bayonne. I went to Baton Rouge once – me, Ty, Mama, and Daddy. But that was 'way back yonder, 'fore Daddy went in the Army. I wonder when we go'n see him again. I wonder when. Look like he ain't ever coming back home. . . . Even the pavement all cracked in Bayonne. Got grass shooting right out the sidewalk. Got weeds in the ditch, too; just like they got at home.

It's some cold in Bayonne. Look like it's colder than it is home. The wind blows in my face, and I feel that stuff running down my nose. I sniff. Mama says use that hand-kerchief. I blow my nose and put it back.

We pass a school and I see them white children playing in the yard. Big old red school, and them children just running and playing. Then we pass a café, and I see a bunch of people in there eating. I wish I was in there 'cause I'm cold. Mama tells me keep my eyes in front where they belong.

149

We pass stores that's got dummies, and we pass another café, and then we pass a shoe shop, and that bald-head man in there fixing on a shoe. I look at him and I butt into that white lady, and Mama jerks me in front and tells me stay there.

We come up to the courthouse, and I see the flag waving there. This flag ain't like the one we got at school. This one here ain't got but a handful of stars. One at school got a big pile of stars – one for every state. We pass it and we turn and there it is – the dentist office. Me and Mama go in, and they got people sitting everywhere you look. They even got a little boy in there younger than me.

Me and Mama sit on that bench, and a white lady come in there and ask me what my name is. Mama tells her and the white lady goes on back. Then I hear somebody hollering in there. Soon 's that little boy hear him hollering, he starts hollering, too. His mama pats him and pats him, trying to make him hush up, but he ain't thinking 'bout his mama.

The man that was hollering in there comes out holding his jaw. He is a big old man and he's wearing overalls and a jumper.

'Got it, hanh?' another man asks him.

The man shakes his head – don't want open his mouth.

'Man, I thought they was killing you in there,' the other man says. 'Hollering like a pig under a gate.'

The man don't say nothing. He just heads for the door, and the other man follows him.

'John Lee,' the white lady says. 'John Lee Williams.'

The little boy juggs his head down in his mama's lap and holler more now. His mama tells him go with the nurse, but he ain't thinking 'bout his mama. His mama tells him again, but he don't even hear her. His mama picks him up and takes him in there, and even when the white lady shuts the door I can still hear little old John Lee.

'I often wonder why the Lord let a child like that suffer,' a lady says to my mama. The lady's sitting right in front of us on another bench. She's got on a white dress and a black sweater. She must be a nurse or something herself, I reckon.

'Not us to question,' a man says.

'Sometimes I don't know if we shouldn't,' the lady says.

'I know definitely we shouldn't,' the man says. The man looks like a preacher. He's big and fat and he's got on a black suit. He's got a gold chain, too.

'Why?' the lady says.

'Why anything?' the preacher says.

'Yes,' the lady says. 'Why anything?'

'Not us to question,' the preacher says.

The lady looks at the preacher a little while and looks at Mama again.

'And look like it's the poor who suffers the most,' she says. 'I don't understand it.'

'Best not to even try,' the preacher says. 'He works in mysterious ways – wonders to perform.'

Right then little John Lee bust out hollering, and everybody turn they head to listen.

'He's not a good dentist,' the lady says. 'Dr Robillard is much better. But more expensive. That's why most of the colored people come here. The white people go to Dr Robillard. Y'all from Bayonne?'

'Down the river,' my mama says. And that's all she go'n say, 'cause she don't talk much. But the lady keeps on looking at her, and so she says, 'Near Morgan.'

'I see,' the lady says.

VII

'That's the trouble with the black people in this country today,' somebody else says. This one here's sitting on the same side me and Mama's sitting, and he is kind of sitting in front of that preacher. He looks like a teacher or somebody that goes to college. He's got on a suit, and he's got a book that he's been reading. 'We don't question is exactly our problem,' he says. 'We should question and question and question – question everything.'

The preacher just looks at him a long time. He done put a toothpick or something in his mouth, and he just keeps on turning it and turning it. You can see he don't like that boy with that book.

'Maybe you can explain what you mean,' he says.

'I said what I meant,' the boy says. 'Question everything. Every stripe, every star, every word spoken. Everything.'

'It 'pears to me that this young lady and I was talking 'bout God, young man,' the preacher says.

'Question Him, too,' the boy says.

'Wait,' the preacher says. 'Wait now.'

'You heard me right,' the boy says. 'His existence as well as everything else. Everything.'

The preacher just looks across the room at the boy. You can see he's getting madder and madder. But mad or no mad, the boy ain't thinking 'bout him. He looks at that preacher just 's hard 's the preacher looks at him.

'Is this what they coming to?' the preacher says. 'Is this what we educating them for?'

'You're not educating me,' the boy says. 'I wash dishes at night so that I can go to school in the day. So even the words you spoke need questioning.'

The preacher just looks at him and shakes his head.

'When I come in this room and seen you there with your book, I said to myself, "There's an intelligent man." How wrong a person can be.'

'Show me one reason to believe in the existence of a God,' the boy says.

'My heart tells me,' the preacher says.

' "My heart tells me," ' the boy says. ' "My heart tells me." Sure, "My heart tells me." And as long as you listen to what your heart tells you, you will have only what the white man gives you and nothing more. Me, I don't listen to my heart. The purpose of the heart is to pump blood throughout the body, and nothing else.'

'Who's your paw, boy?' the preacher says.

'Why?'

'Who is he?'

'He's dead.'

'And your mom?'

'She's in Charity Hospital with pneumonia. Half killed herself, working for nothing.'

'And 'cause he's dead and she's sick, you mad at the world?'

'I'm not mad at the world. I'm questioning the world. I'm questioning it with cold logic, sir. What do words like Freedom, Liberty, God, White, Colored mean? I want to know. That's why *you* are sending us to school, to read and to ask questions. And because we ask these questions, you call us mad. No sir, it is not us who are mad.'

'You keep saying "us"?'

' "Us." Yes – us. I'm not alone.'

The preacher just shakes his head. Then he looks at everybody in the room – everybody. Some of the people look down at the floor, keep from looking at him. I kind of look 'way myself, but soon 's I know he done turn his head, I look that way again.

'I'm sorry for you,' he says to the boy.

'Why?' the boy says. 'Why not be sorry for yourself? Why are you so much better off than I am? Why aren't you sorry for these other people in here? Why not be sorry for the lady who had to drag her child into the dentist office? Why not be sorry for the lady sitting on that bench over there? Be sorry for them. Not for me. Some way or the other I'm going to make it.'

'No, I'm sorry for you,' the preacher says.

'Of course, of course,' the boy says, nodding his head. 'You're sorry for me because I rock that pillar you're leaning on.'

'You can't ever rock the pillar I'm leaning on, young man. It's stronger than anything man can ever do.'

'You believe in God because a man told you to believe in God,' the boy says. 'A white man told you to believe in God. And why? To keep you ignorant so he can keep his feet on your neck.'

'So now we the ignorant?' the preacher says.

'Yes,' the boy says. 'Yes.' And he opens his book again.

The preacher just looks at him sitting there. The boy done forgot all about him. Everybody else make 'tend they done forgot the squabble, too.

Then I see that preacher getting up real slow. Preacher's a great big old man and he got to brace himself to get up. He comes over where the boy is sitting. He just stands there a little while looking down at him, but the boy don't raise his head.

'Get up, boy,' preacher says.

The boy looks up at him, then he shuts his book real slow and stands up. Preacher just hauls back and hit him in the face. The boy falls back 'gainst the wall, but he straightens himself up and looks right back at that preacher.

'You forgot the other cheek,' he says.

The preacher hauls back and hit him again on the other side. But this time the boy braces himself and don't fall.

'That hasn't changed a thing,' he says.

The preacher just looks at the boy. The preacher's breathing real hard like he just run up a big hill. The boy sits down and opens his book again.

'I feel sorry for you,' the preacher says. 'I never felt so sorry for a man before.'

The boy makes 'tend he don't even hear that preacher. He keeps on reading his book. The preacher goes back and gets his hat off the chair.

'Excuse me,' he says to us. 'I'll come back some other time. Y'all, please excuse me.'

And he looks at the boy and goes out the room. The boy h'ist his hand up to his mouth one time to wipe 'way some blood. All the rest of the time he keeps on reading. And nobody else in there say a word.

VIII

Little John Lee and his mama come out the dentist office, and the nurse calls somebody else in. Then little bit later they come out, and the nurse calls another name. But fast 's she calls somebody in there, somebody else comes in the place where we sitting, and the room stays full.

The people coming in now, all of them wearing big coats. One of them says something 'bout sleeting, another one says he hope not. Another one says he think it ain't nothing but rain. 'Cause, he says, rain can get awful cold this time of year.

All round the room they talking. Some of them talking to people right by them, some of them talking to people clear 'cross the room, some of them talking to anybody'll listen. It's a little bitty room, no bigger than us kitchen, and I can see everybody in there. The little old room's full of smoke, 'cause you got two old men smoking pipes over by that side door. I think I feel my tooth thumping me some, and I hold my breath and wait. I wait and wait, but it don't thump me no more. Thank God for that.

I feel like going to sleep, and I lean back 'gainst the wall. But I'm scared to go to sleep. Scared 'cause the nurse might call my name and I won't hear her. And Mama might go to sleep, too, and she'll be mad if neither one of us heard the nurse.

I look up at Mama. I love my mama. I love my mama. And when cotton come I'm go'n get her a new coat. And I ain't go'n get a black one, either. I think I'm go'n get her a red one.

'They got some books over there,' I say. 'Want read one of them?'

Mama looks at the books, but she don't answer me.

'You got yourself a little man there,' the lady says.

Mama don't say nothing to the lady, but she must've smiled, 'cause I seen the lady smiling back. The lady looks at me a little while, like she's feeling sorry for me.

'You sure got that preacher out here in a hurry,' she says to that boy.

The boy looks up at her and looks in his book again. When I grow up I want be just like him. I want clothes like that and I want keep a book with me, too.

'You really don't believe in God?' the lady says.

'No,' he says.

'But why?' the lady says.

'Because the wind is pink,' he says.

'What?' the lady says.

The boy don't answer her no more. He just reads in his book.

'Talking 'bout the wind is pink,' that old lady says. She's sitting on the same bench with the boy and she's trying to look in his face. The boy makes 'tend the old lady ain't even there. He just keeps on reading. 'Wind is pink,' she says again. 'Eh, Lord, what children go'n be saying next?'

The lady 'cross from us bust out laughing.

'That's a good one,' she says. 'The wind is pink. Yes sir, that's a good one.'

'Don't you believe the wind is pink?' the boy says. He keeps his head down in the book.

'Course I believe it, honey,' the lady says. 'Course I do.' She looks at us and winks her eye. 'And what color is grass, honey?'

'Grass? Grass is black.'

She bust out laughing again. The boy looks at her.

'Don't you believe grass is black?' he says.

The lady quits her laughing and looks at him. Everybody else looking at him, too. The place quiet, quiet.

'Grass is green, honey,' the lady says. 'It was green yesterday, it's green today, and it's go'n be green tomorrow.'

'How do you know it's green?'

'I know because I know.'

'You don't know it's green,' the boy says. 'You believe it's green because someone told you it was green. If someone had told you it was black you'd believe it was black.'

'It's green,' the lady says. 'I know green when I see green.'

'Prove it's green,' the boy says.

'Sure, now,' the lady says. 'Don't tell me it's coming to that.'

'It's coming to just that,' the boy says. 'Words mean nothing. One means no more than the other.'

157

'That's what it all coming to?' that old lady says. That old lady got on a turban and she got on two sweaters. She got a green sweater under a black sweater. I can see the green sweater 'cause some of the buttons on the other sweater's missing.

'Yes ma'am,' the boy says. 'Words mean nothing. Action is the only thing. Doing. That's the only thing.'

'Other words, you want the Lord to come down here and show Hisself to you?' she says.

'Exactly, ma'am,' he says.

'You don't mean that, I'm sure?' she says.

'I do, ma'am,' he says.

'Done, Jesus,' the old lady says, shaking her head.

'I didn't go 'long with that preacher at first,' the other lady says; 'but now – I don't know. When a person say the grass is black, he's either a lunatic or something's wrong.'

'Prove to me that it's green,' the boy says.

'It's green because the people say it's green.'

'Those same people say we're citizens of these United States,' the boy says.

'I think I'm a citizen,' the lady says.

'Citizens have certain rights,' the boy says. 'Name me one right that you have. One right, granted by the Constitution, that you can exercise in Bayonne.'

The lady don't answer him. She just looks at him like she don't know what he's talking 'bout. I know I don't.

'Things changing,' she says.

'Things are changing because some black men have begun to think with their brains and not their hearts,' the boy says.

'You trying to say these people don't believe in God?'

'I'm sure some of them do. Maybe most of them do. But they don't believe that God is going to touch these white people's hearts and change things tomorrow. Things change through action. By no other way.'

Everybody sit quiet and look at the boy. Nobody says a thing. Then the lady 'cross the room from me and Mama just shakes her head.

'Let's hope that not all your generation feel the same way you do,' she says.

'Think what you please, it doesn't matter,' the boy says. 'But it will be men who listen to their heads and not their hearts who will see that your children have a better chance than you had.'

'Let's hope they ain't all like you, though,' the old lady says. 'Done forgot the heart absolutely.'

'Yes ma'am, I hope they aren't all like me,' the boy says. 'Unfortunately, I was born too late to believe in your God. Let's hope that the ones who come after will have your faith – if not in your God, then in something else, something definitely that they can lean on. I haven't anything. For me, the wind is pink, the grass is black.'

IX

The nurse comes in the room where we all sitting and waiting and says the doctor won't take no more patients till one o'clock this evening. My mama jumps up off the bench and goes up to the white lady.

'Nurse, I have to go back in the field this evening,' she says.

'The doctor is treating his last patient now,' the nurse says. 'One o'clock this evening.'

'Can I at least speak to the doctor?' my mama asks.

'I'm his nurse,' the lady says.

'My little boy's sick,' my mama says. 'Right now his tooth almost killing him.'

The nurse looks at me. She's trying to make up her mind

159

if to let me come in. I look at her real pitiful. The tooth ain't hurting me at all, but Mama say it is, so I make 'tend for her sake.

'This evening,' the nurse says, and goes on back in the office.

'Don't feel 'jected, honey,' the lady says to Mama. 'I been round them a long time – they take you when they want to. If you was white, that's something else; but we the wrong color.'

Mama don't say nothing to the lady, and me and her go outside and stand 'gainst the wall. It's cold out there. I can feel that wind going through my coat. Some of the other people come out of the room and go up the street. Me and Mama stand there a little while and we start walking. I don't know where we going. When we come to the other street we just stand there.

'You don't have to make water, do you?' Mama says.

'No, ma'am,' I say.

We go on up the street. Walking real slow. I can tell Mama don't know where she's going. When we come to a store we stand there and look at the dummies. I look at a little boy wearing a brown overcoat. He's got on brown shoes, too. I look at my old shoes and look at his'n again. You wait till summer, I say.

Me and Mama walk away. We come up to another store and we stop and look at them dummies, too. Then we go on again. We pass a café where the white people in there eating. Mama tells me keep my eyes in front where they belong, but I can't help from seeing them people eat. My stomach starts to growling 'cause I'm hungry. When I see people eating, I get hungry; when I see a coat, I get cold.

A man whistles at my mama when we go by a filling station. She makes 'tend she don't even see him. I look back and I feel like hitting him in the mouth. If I was bigger, I say; if I was bigger, you'd see.

We keep on going. I'm getting colder and colder, but I don't say nothing. I feel that stuff running down my nose and I sniff.

'That rag,' Mama says.

I get it out and wipe my nose. I'm getting cold all over now – my face, my hands, my feet, everything. We pass another little café, but this'n for white people, too, and we can't go in there, either. So we just walk. I'm so cold now I'm 'bout ready to say it. If I knowed where we was going I wouldn't be so cold, but I don't know where we going. We go, we go, we go. We walk clean out of Bayonne. Then we cross the street and we come back. Same thing I seen when I got off the bus this morning. Same old trees, same old walk, same old weeds, same old cracked pave – same old everything.

I sniff again.

'That rag,' Mama says.

I wipe my nose real fast and jugg that handkerchief back in my pocket 'fore my hand gets too cold. I raise my head and I can see David's hardware store. When we come up to it, we go in. I don't know why, but I'm glad.

It's warm in there. It's so warm in there you don't ever want to leave. I look for the heater, and I see it over by them barrels. Three white men standing round the heater talking in Creole. One of them comes over to see what my mama want.

'Got any axe handles?' she says.

Me, Mama and the white man start to the back, but Mama stops me when we come up to the heater. She and the white man go on. I hold my hands over the heater and look at them. They go all the way to the back, and I see the white man pointing to the axe handles 'gainst the wall. Mama takes one of them and shakes it like she's trying to figure how much it weighs. Then she rubs her hand over it from one end to the other end. She turns it over and looks at the other side, then she shakes it again, and shakes her head and puts it back. She gets another one and she does it just like she did the first one, then she shakes her head. Then she gets a brown one and do it that, too. But she don't like this one, either. Then she gets another one, but 'fore she shakes it or anything, she looks at me. Look like she's trying to say something to me, but I don't know what it is. All I know is I done got warm now and I'm feeling right smart better. Mama shakes this axe handle just like she did the others, and shakes her head and says something to the white man. The white man just looks at his pile of axe handles, and when Mama pass him to come to the front, the white man just scratch his head and follows her. She tells me come on and we go on out and start walking again.

We walk and walk, and no time at all I'm cold again. Look like I'm colder now 'cause I can still remember how good it was back there. My stomach growls and I suck it in to keep Mama from hearing it. She's walking right 'side me, and it growls so loud you can hear it a mile. But Mama don't say a word.

X

When we come up to the courthouse, I look at the clock. It's got quarter to twelve. Mean we got another hour and a quarter to be out here in the cold. We go and stand 'side a building. Something hits my cap and I look up at the sky. Sleet's falling.

I look at Mama standing there. I want stand close 'side her, but she don't like that. She say that's crybaby stuff. She say you got to stand for yourself, by yourself.

'Let's go back to that office,' she says.

We cross the street. When we get to the dentist office I try to open the door, but I can't. I twist and twist, but I can't. Mama pushes me to the side and she twist the knob, but she can't open the door, either. She turns 'way from the door. I look at her, but I don't move and I don't say nothing. I done seen her like this before and I'm scared of her.

'You hungry?' she says. She says it like she's mad at me, like I'm the cause of everything.

'No, ma'am,' I say.

'You want eat and walk back, or you rather don't eat and ride?'

'I ain't hungry,' I say.

I ain't just hungry, but I'm cold, too. I'm so hungry and cold I want to cry. And look like I'm getting colder and colder. My feet done got numb. I try to work my toes, but I don't even feel them. Look like I'm go'n die. Look like I'm go'n stand right here and freeze to death. I think 'bout home. I think 'bout Val and Auntie and Ty and Louis and Walker. It's 'bout twelve o'clock and I know they eating dinner now. I can hear Ty making jokes. He done forgot 'bout getting up early this morning and right now he's probably making jokes. Always trying to make somebody laugh. I wish I was right there listening to him. Give anything in the world if I was home round the fire.

'Come on,' Mama says.

We start walking again. My feet so numb I can't hardly feel them. We turn the corner and go on back up the street. The clock on the courthouse starts hitting for twelve.

The sleet's coming down plenty now. They hit the pave

and bounce like rice. Oh, Lord; oh, Lord, I pray. Don't let me die, don't let me die, don't let me die, Lord.

XI

Now I know where we going. We going back of town where the colored people eat. I don't care if I don't eat. I been hungry before. I can stand it. But I can't stand the cold.

I can see we go'n have a long walk. It's 'bout a mile down there. But I don't mind. I know when I get there I'm go'n warm myself. I think I can hold out. My hands numb in my pockets and my feet numb, too, but if I keep moving I can hold out. Just don't stop no more, that's all.

The sky's gray. The sleet keeps on falling. Falling like rain now – plenty, plenty. You can hear it hitting the pave. You can see it bouncing. Sometimes it bounces two times 'fore it settles.

We keep on going. We don't say nothing. We just keep on going, keep on going.

I wonder what Mama's thinking. I hope she ain't mad at me. When summer come I'm go'n pick plenty cotton and get her a coat. I'm go'n get her a red one.

I hope they'd make it summer all the time. I'd be glad if it was summer all the time – but it ain't. We got to have winter, too. Lord, I hate the winter. I guess everybody hate the winter.

I don't sniff this time. I get out my handkerchief and wipe my nose. My hands's so cold I can hardly hold the handkerchief.

I think we getting close, but we ain't there yet. I wonder where everybody is. Can't see a soul but us. Look like we the only two people moving round today. Must be too cold for the rest of the people to move round in.

I can hear my teeth. I hope they don't knock together too hard and make that bad one hurt. Lord, that's all I need, for that bad one to start off.

I hear a church bell somewhere. But today ain't Sunday. They must be ringing for a funeral or something.

I wonder what they doing at home. They must be eating. Monsieur Bayonne might be there with his guitar. One day Ty played with Monsieur Bayonne's guitar and broke one of the strings. Monsieur Bayonne was some mad with Ty. He say Ty wasn't go'n ever 'mount to nothing. Ty can go just like Monsieur Bayonne when he ain't there. Ty can make everybody laugh when he starts to mocking Monsieur Bayonne.

I used to like to be with Mama and Daddy. We used to be happy. But they took him in the Army. Now, nobody happy no more. . . . I be glad when Daddy comes home.

Monsieur Bayonne say it wasn't fair for them to take Daddy and give Mama nothing and give us nothing. Auntie say, 'Shhh, Etienne. Don't let them hear you talk like that.' Monsieur Bayonne say, 'It's God truth. What they giving his children? They have to walk three and a half miles to school hot or cold. That's anything to give for a paw? She's got to work in the field rain or shine just to make ends meet. That's anything to give for a husband?' Auntie say, 'Shhh, Etienne, shhh.' 'Yes, you right,' Monsieur Bayonne say. 'Best don't say it in front of them now. But one day they go'n find out. One day.' 'Yes, I suppose so,' Auntie say. 'Then what, Rose Mary?' Monsieur Bayonne say. 'I don't know, Etienne,' Auntie say. 'All we can do is us job, and leave everything else in His hand . . .'

We getting closer, now. We getting closer. I can even see the railroad tracks.

We cross the tracks, and now I see the café. Just to get in there, I say. Just to get in there. Already I'm starting to feel little better.

XII

We go in. Ahh, it's good. I look for the heater; there 'gainst the wall. One of them little brown ones. I just stand there and hold my hands over it. I can't open my hands too wide 'cause they almost froze.

Mama's standing right 'side me. She done unbuttoned her coat. Smoke rises out of the coat, and the coat smells like a wet dog.

I move to the side so Mama can have more room. She opens out her hands and rubs them together. I rub mine together, too, 'cause this keep them from hurting. If you let them warm too fast, they hurt you sure. But if you let them warm just little bit at a time, and you keep rubbing them, they be all right every time.

They got just two more people in the café. A lady back of the counter, and a man on this side the counter. They been watching us ever since we come in.

Mama gets out the handkerchief and count up the money. Both of us know how much money she's got there. Three dollars. No, she ain't got three dollars, 'cause she had to pay us way up here. She ain't got but two dollars and a half left. Dollar and a half to get my tooth pulled, and fifty cents for us to go back on, and fifty cents worth of salt meat.

She stirs the money round with her finger. Most of the money is change 'cause I can hear it rubbing together. She stirs it and stirs it. Then she looks at the door. It's still sleeting. I can hear it hitting 'gainst the wall like rice.

'I ain't hungry, Mama,' I say.

'Got to pay them something for they heat,' she says.

She takes a quarter out the handkerchief and ties the handkerchief up again. She looks over her shoulder at the people, but she still don't move. I hope she don't spend the money. I don't want her spending it on me. I'm hungry, I'm almost starving I'm so hungry, but I don't want her spending the money on me.

She flips the quarter over like she's thinking. She's must be thinking 'bout us walking back home. Lord, I sure don't want walk home. If I thought it'd do any good to say something, I'd say it. But Mama makes up her own mind 'bout things.

She turns 'way from the heater right fast, like she better hurry up and spend the quarter 'fore she change her mind. I watch her go toward the counter. The man and the lady look at her, too. She tells the lady something and the lady walks away. The man keeps on looking at her. Her back's turned to the man, and she don't even know he's standing there.

The lady puts some cakes and a glass of milk on the counter. Then she pours up a cup of coffee and sets it 'side the other stuff. Mama pays her for the things and comes on back where I'm standing. She tells me sit down at the table 'gainst the wall.

The milk and the cakes's for me; the coffee's for Mama. I eat slow and I look at her. She's looking outside at the sleet. She's looking real sad. I say to myself, I'm go'n make all this up one day. You see, one day, I'm go'n make all this up. I want say it now; I want tell her how I feel right now; but Mama don't like for us to talk like that.

'I can't eat all this,' I say.

They ain't got but just three little old cakes there. I'm so hungry right now, the Lord knows I can eat a hundred times three, but I want my mama to have one.

Mama don't even look my way. She knows I'm hungry, she knows I want it. I let it stay there a little while, then I get it and eat it. I eat just on my front teeth, though, 'cause if cake touch that back tooth I know what'll happen. Thank God it ain't hurt me at all today.

After I finish eating I see the man go to the juke box. He drops a nickel in it, then he just stand there a little while looking at the record. Mama tells me keep my eyes in front where they belong. I turn my head like she say, but then I hear the man coming toward us.

'Dance, pretty?' he says.

Mama gets up to dance with him. But 'fore you know it, she done grabbed the little man in the collar and done heaved him 'side the wall. He hit the wall so hard he stop the juke box from playing.

'Some pimp,' the lady back of the counter says. 'Some pimp.'

The little man jumps up off the floor and starts toward my mama. 'Fore you know it, Mama done sprung open her knife and she's waiting for him.

'Come on,' she says. 'Come on. I'll gut you from your neighbo to your throat. Come on.'

I go up to the little man to hit him, but Mama makes me come and stand 'side her. The little man looks at me and Mama and goes on back to the counter.

'Some pimp,' the lady back of the counter says. 'Some pimp.' She starts laughing and pointing at the little man. 'Yes sir, you a pimp, all right. Yes sir-ree.'

XIII

'Fasten that coat, let's go,' Mama says.

'You don't have to leave,' the lady says.

Mama don't answer the lady, and we right out in the cold
again. I'm warm right now — my hands, my ears, my feet —
but I know this ain't go'n last too long. It done sleet so much
now you got ice everywhere you look.

We cross the railroad tracks, and soon's we do, I get cold.
That wind goes through this little old coat like it ain't even
there. I got on a shirt and a sweater under the coat, but that
wind don't pay them no mind. I look up and I can see we
got a long way to go. I wonder if we go'n make it 'fore I get
too cold.

We cross over to walk on the sidewalk. They got just one
sidewalk back here, and it's over there.

After we go just a little piece, I smell bread cooking. I look,
then I see a baker shop. When we get closer, I can smell it
more better. I shut my eyes and make 'tend I'm eating. But
I keep them shut too long and I butt up 'gainst a telephone
post. Mama grabs me and see if I'm hurt. I ain't bleeding or
nothing and she turns me loose.

I can feel I'm getting colder and colder, and I look up to
see how far we still got to go. Uptown is 'way up yonder.
A half mile more, I reckon. I try to think of something. They
say think and you won't get cold. I think of that poem, 'Annabel Lee.' I ain't been to school in so long — this bad weather —
I reckon they done passed 'Annabel Lee' by now. But passed
it or not, I'm sure Miss Walker go'n make me recite it when
I get there. That woman don't never forget nothing. I ain't
never seen nobody like that in my life.

I'm still getting cold. 'Annabel Lee' or no 'Annabel Lee,'

I'm still getting cold. But I can see we getting closer. We getting there gradually.

Soon 's we turn the corner, I see a little old white lady up in front of us. She's the only lady on the street. She's all in black and she's got a long black rag over her head.

'Stop,' she says.

Me and Mama stop and look at her. She must be crazy to be out in all this bad weather. Ain't got but a few other people out there, and all of them's men.

'Y'all done ate?' she says.

'Just finish,' Mama says.

'Y'all must be cold then?' she says.

'We headed for the dentist,' Mama says. 'We'll warm up when we get there.'

'What dentist?' the old lady says. 'Mr Bassett?'

'Yes, ma'am,' Mama says.

'Come on in,' the old lady says. 'I'll telephone him and tell him y'all coming.'

Me and Mama follow the old lady in the store. It's a little bitty store, and it don't have much in there. The old lady takes off her head rag and folds it up.

'Helena?' somebody calls from the back.

'Yes, Alnest?' the old lady says.

'Did you see them?'

'They're here. Standing beside me.'

'Good. Now you can stay inside.'

The old lady looks at Mama. Mama's waiting to hear what she brought us in here for. I'm waiting for that, too.

'I saw y'all each time you went by,' she says. 'I came out to catch you, but you were gone.'

'We went back of town,' Mama says.

'Did you eat?'

'Yes, ma'am.'

The old lady looks at Mama a long time, like she's thinking Mama might be just saying that. Mama looks right back at her. The old lady looks at me to see what I have to say. I don't say nothing. I sure ain't going 'gainst my mama.

'There's food in the kitchen,' she says to Mama. 'I've been keeping it warm.'

Mama turns right around and starts for the door.

'Just a minute,' the old lady says. Mama stops. 'The boy'll have to work for it. It isn't free.'

'We don't take no handout,' Mama says.

'I'm not handing out anything,' the old lady says. 'I need my garbage moved to the front. Ernest has a bad cold and can't go out there.'

'James'll move it for you,' Mama says.

'Not unless you eat,' the old lady says. 'I'm old, but I have my pride, too, you know.'

Mama can see she ain't go'n beat this old lady down, so she just shakes her head.

'All right,' the old lady says. 'Come into the kitchen.'

She leads the way with that rag in her hand. The kitchen is a little bitty little old thing, too. The table and the stove just 'bout fill it up. They got a little room to the side. Somebody in there laying 'cross the bed – 'cause I can see one of his feet. Must be the person she was talking to: Ernest or Alnest – something like that.

'Sit down,' the old lady says to Mama. 'Not you,' she says to me. 'You have to move the cans.'

'Helena?' the man says in the other room.

'Yes, Alnest?' the old lady says.

'Are you going out there again?'

'I must show the boy where the garbage is, Alnest,' the old lady says.

'Keep that shawl over your head,' the old man says.

'You don't have to remind me, Alnest. Come, boy,' the old lady says.

We go out in the yard. Little old back yard ain't no bigger than the store or the kitchen. But it can sleet here just like it can sleet in any big back yard. And 'fore you know it, I'm trembling.

'There,' the old lady says, pointing to the cans. I pick up one of the cans and set it right back down. The can's so light, I'm go'n see what's inside of it.

'Here,' the old lady says. 'Leave that can alone.'

I look back at her standing there in the door. She's got that black rag wrapped round her shoulders, and she's pointing one of her little old fingers at me.

'Pick it up and carry it to the front,' she says. I go by her with the can, and she's looking at me all the time. I'm sure the can's empty. I'm sure she could've carried it herself – maybe both of them at the same time. 'Set it on the sidewalk by the door and come back for the other one,' she says.

I go and come back, and Mama looks at me when I pass her. I get the other can and take it to the front. It don't feel a bit heavier than that first one. I tell myself I ain't go'n be nobody's fool, and I'm go'n look inside this can to see just what I been hauling. First, I look up the street, then down the street. Nobody coming. Then I look over my shoulder toward the door. That little old lady done slipped up there quiet 's mouse, watching me again. Look like she knowed what I was go'n do.

'Ehh, Lord,' she says. 'Children, children. Come in here, boy, and go wash your hands.'

I follow her in the kitchen. She points toward the bathroom, and I go in there and wash up. Little bitty old bathroom, but it's clean, clean. I don't use any of her towels; I wipe my hands on my pants legs.

When I come back in the kitchen, the old lady done dished up the food. Rice, gravy, meat – and she even got some lettuce and tomato in a saucer. She even got a glass of milk and a piece of cake there, too. It looks so good, I almost start eating 'fore I say my blessing.

'Helena?' the old man says.

'Yes, Alnest?'

'Are they eating?'

'Yes,' she says.

'Good,' he says. 'Now you'll stay inside.'

The old lady goes in there where he is and I can hear them talking. I look at Mama. She's eating slow like she's thinking. I wonder what's the matter now. I reckon she's thinking 'bout home.

The old lady comes back in the kitchen.

'I talked to Dr Bassett's nurse,' she says. 'Dr Bassett will take you as soon as you get there.'

'Thank you, ma'am,' Mama says.

'Perfectly all right,' the old lady says. 'Which one is it?'

Mama nods toward me. The old lady looks at me real sad. I look sad, too.

'You're not afraid, are you?' she says.

'No, ma'am,' I say.

'That's a good boy,' the old lady says. 'Nothing to be afraid of. Dr Bassett will not hurt you.'

When me and Mama get through eating, we thank the old lady again.

'Helena, are they leaving?' the old man says.

'Yes, Alnest.'

'Tell them I say good-bye.'

'They can hear you, Alnest.'

'Good-bye both mother and son,' the old man says. 'And may God be with you.'

Me and Mama tell the old man good-bye, and we follow the old lady in the front room. Mama opens the door to go out, but she stops and comes back in the store.

'You sell salt meat?' she says.

'Yes.'

'Give me two bits worth.'

'That isn't very much salt meat,' the old lady says.

'That's all I have,' Mama says.

The old lady goes back of the counter and cuts a big piece off the chunk. Then she wraps it up and puts it in a paper bag.

'Two bits,' she says.

'That looks like awful lot of meat for a quarter,' Mama says.

'Two bits,' the old lady says. 'I've been selling salt meat behind this counter twenty-five years. I think I know what I'm doing.'

'You got a scale there,' Mama says.

'What?' the old lady says.

'Weigh it,' Mama says.

'What?' the old lady says. 'Are you telling me how to run my business?'

'Thanks very much for the food,' Mama says.

'Just a minute,' the old lady says.

'James,' Mama says to me. I move toward the door.

'Just one minute, I said,' the old lady says.

Me and Mama stop again and look at her. The old lady takes the meat out of the bag and unwraps it and cuts 'bout half of it off. Then she wraps it up again and juggs it back in the bag and gives the bag to Mama. Mama lays the quarter on the counter.

'Your kindness will never be forgotten,' she says. 'James,' she says to me.

We go out, and the old lady comes to the door to look

at us. After we go a little piece I look back, and she's still there watching us.

The sleet's coming down heavy, heavy now, and I turn up my coat collar to keep my neck warm. My mama tells me turn it right back down.

'You not a bum,' she says. 'You a man.'

WILLA CATHER

THE BURGLAR'S CHRISTMAS

TWO VERY SHABBY-LOOKING young men stood at the corner of Prairie Avenue and Eighteenth Street, looking despondently at the carriages that whirled by. It was Christmas Eve, and the streets were full of vehicles; florists' wagons, grocers' carts and carriages. The streets were in that half-liquid, half-congealed condition peculiar to the streets of Chicago at that season of the year. The swift wheels that spun by sometimes threw the slush of mud and snow over the two young men who were talking on the corner.

'Well,' remarked the elder of the two, 'I guess we are at our rope's end, sure enough. How do you feel?'

'Pretty shaky. The wind's sharp tonight. If I had had anything to eat I mightn't mind it so much. There is simply no show. I'm sick of the whole business. Looks like there's nothing for it but the lake.'

'O, nonsense, I thought you had more grit. Got anything left you can hock?'

'Nothing but my beard, and I am afraid they wouldn't find it worth a pawn ticket,' said the younger man ruefully, rubbing the week's growth of stubble on his face.

'Got any folks anywhere? Now's your time to strike 'em if you have.'

'Never mind if I have, they're out of the question.'

'Well, you'll be out of it before many hours if you don't make a move of some sort. A man's got to eat. See here, I am going down to Longtin's saloon. I used to play the banjo in there with a couple of coons, and I'll bone him for some of his free-lunch stuff. You'd better come along, perhaps they'll fill an order for two.'

'How far down is it?'

'Well, it's clear downtown, of course, way down on Michigan Avenue.'

'Thanks, I guess I'll loaf around here. I don't feel equal to the walk, and the cars – well, the cars are crowded.' His features drew themselves into what might have been a smile under happier circumstances.

'No, you never did like street cars, you're too aristocratic. See here, Crawford, I don't like leaving you here. You ain't good company for yourself tonight.'

'Crawford? O, yes, that's the last one. There have been so many I forget them.'

'Have you got a real name, anyway?'

'O, yes, but it's one of the ones I've forgotten. Don't you worry about me. You go along and get your free lunch. I think I had a row in Longtin's place once. I'd better not show myself there again.' As he spoke the young man nodded and turned slowly up the avenue.

He was miserable enough to want to be quite alone. Even the crowd that jostled by him annoyed him. He wanted to think about himself. He had avoided this final reckoning with himself for a year now. He had laughed it off and drunk it off. But now, when all those artificial devices which are employed to turn our thoughts into other channels and shield us from ourselves had failed him, it must come. Hunger is a powerful incentive to introspection.

It is a tragic hour, that hour when we are finally driven to reckon with ourselves, when every avenue of mental distraction has been cut off and our own life and all its ineffaceable failures closes about us like the walls of that old torture chamber of the Inquisition. Tonight, as this man stood stranded in the streets of the city, his hour came. It was not the first time he had been hungry and desperate and alone. But always before there had been some outlook, some chance ahead, some pleasure yet untasted that seemed worth the effort, some face that he fancied was, or would be, dear. But it was not so tonight. The unyielding conviction was upon him that he had failed in everything, had outlived everything. It had been near him for a long time, that Pale Spectre. He had caught its shadow at the bottom of his glass many a time, at the head of his bed when he was sleepless at night, in the twilight shadows when some great sunset broke upon him. It had made life hateful to him when he awoke in the morning before now. But now it settled slowly over him, like night, the endless Northern nights that bid the sun a long farewell. It rose up before him like granite. From this brilliant city with its glad bustle of Yuletide he was shut off as completely as though he were a creature of another species. His days seemed numbered and done, sealed over like the little coral cells at the bottom of the sea. Involuntarily he drew that cold air through his lungs slowly, as though he were tasting it for the last time.

Yet he was but four and twenty, this man – he looked even younger – and he had a father some place down East who had been very proud of him once. Well, he had taken his life into his own hands, and this was what he had made of it. That was all there was to be said. He could remember the hopeful things they used to say about him at college in the old days, before he had cut away and begun to live by his wits, and he found courage to smile at them now. They had read him wrongly. He knew now that he never had the essentials of success, only the superficial agility that is often mistaken for it. He was tow without the tinder, and he had burnt himself out at other people's fires. He had helped other people to make it win, but he himself – he had never touched an enterprise that had not failed eventually. Or, if it survived his connection with it, it left him behind.

His last venture had been with some ten-cent specialty company, a little lower than all the others, that had gone to pieces in Buffalo, and he had worked his way to Chicago by boat. When the boat made up its crew for the outward voyage, he was dispensed with as usual. He was used to that. The reason for it? O, there are so many reasons for failure! His was a very common one.

As he stood there in the wet under the street light he drew up his reckoning with the world and decided that it had treated him as well as he deserved. He had overdrawn his account once too often. There had been a day when he thought otherwise; when he had said he was unjustly handled, that his failure was merely the lack of proper adjustment between himself and other men, that some day he would be recognized and it would all come right. But he knew better than that now, and he was still man enough to bear no grudge against any one – man or woman.

Tonight was his birthday, too. There seemed something particularly amusing in that. He turned up a limp little coat collar to try to keep a little of the wet chill from his throat, and instinctively began to remember all the birthday parties he used to have. He was so cold and empty that his mind seemed unable to grapple with any serious question. He kept thinking about gingerbread and frosted cakes like a child. He could remember the splendid birthday parties his mother used to give him, when all the other little boys in the block came in their Sunday clothes and creaking shoes, with their ears still red from their mother's towel, and the pink and white birthday cake, and the stuffed olives and all the dishes of which he had been particularly fond, and how he would eat and eat and then go to bed and dream of Santa Claus. And in the morning he would awaken and eat again, until by night the family doctor arrived with his castor oil, and poor William used to dolefully say that it was altogether too much to have your birthday and Christmas all at once. He could remember, too, the royal birthday suppers he had given at college, and the stag dinners, and the toasts, and the music, and the good fellows who had wished him happiness and really meant what they said.

And since then there were other birthday suppers that he could not remember so clearly; the memory of them was heavy and flat, like cigarette smoke that has been shut in a room all night, like champagne that has been a day opened, a song that has been too often sung, an acute sensation that has been overstrained. They seemed tawdry and garish, discordant to him now. He rather wished he could forget them altogether.

Whichever way his mind now turned there was one thought that it could not escape, and that was the idea of food. He caught the scent of a cigar suddenly, and felt a sharp pain in the pit of his abdomen and a sudden moisture in his mouth. His cold hands clenched angrily, and for a moment he felt that bitter hatred of wealth, of ease, of everything that is well fed and well housed that is common to starving men. At any rate he had a right to eat! He had demanded great things from the world once: fame and wealth and admiration. Now it was simply bread – and he would have it! He looked about him quickly and felt the blood begin to stir in his veins. In all his straits he had never stolen anything, his tastes were above it. But tonight there would be no tomorrow. He was amused at the way in which the idea excited him. Was it possible there was yet one more experience that would distract him, one thing that had power to excite his jaded interest? Good! he had failed at everything else, now he would see what his chances would be as a common thief. It would be amusing to watch the beautiful consistency of his destiny work itself out even in that role. It would be interesting to add another study to his gallery of futile attempts, and then label them all: 'the failure as a journalist', 'the failure as a lecturer', 'the failure as a business man', 'the failure as a thief', and so on, like the titles under the pictures of the Dance of Death. It was time that Childe Roland came to the dark tower.

A girl hastened by him with her arms full of packages. She walked quickly and nervously, keeping well within the shadow, as if she were not accustomed to carrying bundles and did not care to meet any of her friends. As she crossed the muddy street, she made an effort to lift her skirt a little, and as she did so one of the packages slipped unnoticed from beneath her arm. He caught it up and overtook her. 'Excuse me, but I think you dropped something.'

She started, 'O, yes, thank you, I would rather have lost anything than that.'

The young man turned angrily upon himself. The package must have contained something of value. Why had he not kept it? Was this the sort of thief he would make? He ground his teeth together. There is nothing more maddening than to have morally consented to crime and then lack the nerve force to carry it out.

A carriage drove up to the house before which he stood. Several richly dressed women alighted and went in. It was a new house, and must have been built since he was in Chicago last. The front door was open and he could see down the hallway and up the staircase. The servant had left the door and gone with the guests. The first floor was brilliantly lighted, but the windows upstairs were dark. It looked very easy, just to slip upstairs to the darkened chambers where the jewels and trinkets of the fashionable occupants were kept.

Still burning with impatience against himself he entered quickly. Instinctively he removed his mud-stained hat as he passed quickly and quietly up the staircase. It struck him as being a rather superfluous courtesy in a burglar, but he had done it before he had thought. His way was clear enough, he met no one on the stairway or in the upper hall. The gas was lit in the upper hall. He passed the first chamber door through sheer cowardice. The second he entered quickly, thinking of something else lest his courage should fail him, and closed the door behind him. The light from the hall shone into the room through the transom. The apartment was furnished richly enough to justify his expectations. He went at once to the dressing case. A number of rings and small trinkets lay in a silver tray. These he put hastily in his pocket. He opened the upper drawer and found, as he expected, several leather cases. In the first he opened was a lady's watch, in the second a pair of old-fashioned bracelets; he seemed to dimly remember having seen bracelets like them before, somewhere. The third case was heavier, the spring was much worn, and it opened easily. It held a cup of some kind. He held it up to the light and then his strained nerves gave way and he uttered a sharp exclamation. It was the silver mug he used to drink from when he was a little boy.

The door opened, and a woman stood in the doorway facing him. She was a tall woman, with white hair, in evening dress. The light from the hall streamed in upon him, but she was not afraid. She stood looking at him a moment, then she threw out her hand and went quickly toward him.

'Willie, Willie! Is it you?'

He struggled to loose her arms from him, to keep her lips

from his cheek. 'Mother – you must not! You do not understand! O, my God, this is worst of all!' Hunger, weakness, cold, shame, all came back to him, and shook his self-control completely. Physically he was too weak to stand a shock like this. Why could it not have been an ordinary discovery, arrest, the station house and all the rest of it. Anything but this! A hard dry sob broke from him. Again he strove to disengage himself.

'Who is it says I shall not kiss my son? O, my boy, we have waited so long for this! You have been so long in coming, even I almost gave you up.'

Her lips upon his cheek burnt him like fire. He put his hand to his throat, and spoke thickly and incoherently: 'You do not understand. I did not know you were here. I came here to rob – it is the first time – I swear it – but I am a common thief. My pockets are full of your jewels now. Can't you hear me? I am a common thief!'

'Hush, my boy, those are ugly words. How could you rob your own house? How could you take what is your own? They are all yours, my son, as wholly yours as my great love – and you can't doubt that, Will, do you?'

That soft voice, the warmth and fragrance of her person stole through his chill, empty veins like a gentle stimulant. He felt as though all his strength were leaving him and even consciousness. He held fast to her and bowed his head on her strong shoulder, and groaned aloud.

'O, mother, life is hard, hard!'

She said nothing, but held him closer. And O, the strength of those white arms that held him! O, the assurance of safety in that warm bosom that rose and fell under his cheek! For a moment they stood so, silently. Then they heard a heavy step upon the stair. She led him to a chair and went out and closed the door. At the top of the staircase she met a tall, broad-shouldered man, with iron-gray hair, and a face alert and stern. Her eyes were shining and her cheeks on fire, her whole face was one expression of intense determination.

'James, it is William in there, come home. You must keep him at any cost. If he goes this time, I go with him. O, James, be easy with him, he has suffered so.' She broke from a command to an entreaty, and laid her hand on his shoulder. He looked questioningly at her a moment, then went in the room and quietly shut the door.

She stood leaning against the wall, clasping her temples with her hands and listening to the low indistinct sound of the voices within. Her own lips moved silently. She waited a long time, scarcely breathing. At last the door opened, and her husband came out. He stopped to say in a shaken voice, 'You go to him now, he will stay. I will go to my room. I will see him again in the morning.'

She put her arm about his neck. 'O, James, I thank you, I thank you! This is the night he came so long ago, you remember? I gave him to you then, and now you give him back to me!'

'Don't, Helen,' he muttered. 'He is my son, I have never forgotten that. I failed with him. I don't like to fail, it cuts my pride. Take him and make a man of him.' He passed on down the hall.

She flew into the room where the young man sat with his head bowed upon his knee. She dropped upon her knees beside him. Ah, it was so good to him to feel those arms again!

'He is so glad, Willie, so glad! He may not show it, but he is as happy as I. He never was demonstrative with either of us, you know.'

'O, my God, he was good enough,' groaned the man. 'I told him everything, and he was good enough. I don't see how either of you can look at me, speak to me, touch me.'

187

He shivered under her clasp again as when she had first touched him, and tried weakly to throw her off. But she whispered softly, 'This is my right, my son.'

Presently, when he was calmer, she rose. 'Now, come with me into the library, and I will have your dinner brought there.'

As they went downstairs she remarked apologetically, 'I will not call Ellen tonight; she has a number of guests to attend to. She is a big girl now, you know, and came out last winter. Besides, I want you all to myself tonight.'

When the dinner came, and it came very soon, he fell upon it savagely. As he ate she told him all that had transpired during the years of his absence, and how his father's business had brought them there. 'I was glad when we came. I thought you would drift West. I seemed a good deal nearer to you here.'

There was a gentle unobtrusive sadness in her tone that was too soft for a reproach.

'Have you everything you want? It is a comfort to see you eat.'

He smiled grimly. 'It is certainly a comfort to me. I have not indulged in this frivolous habit for some thirty-five hours.'

She caught his hand and pressed it sharply, uttering a quick remonstrance.

'Don't say that! I know, but I can't hear you say it – it's too terrible! My boy, food has choked me many a time when I have thought of the possibility of that. Now take the old lounging chair by the fire, and if you are too tired to talk, we will just sit and rest together.'

He sank into the depths of the big leather chair with the lions' heads on the arms, where he had sat so often in the days when his feet did not touch the floor and he was half afraid of the grim monsters cut in the polished wood. That chair seemed to speak to him of things long forgotten. It was like the touch of an old familiar friend. He felt a sudden yearning tenderness for the happy little boy who had sat there and dreamed of the big world so long ago. Alas, he had been dead many a summer, that little boy!

He sat looking up at the magnificent woman beside him. He had almost forgotten how handsome she was; how lustrous and sad were the eyes that were set under that serene brow, how impetuous and wayward the mouth even now, how superb the white throat and shoulders! Ah, the wit and grace and fineness of this woman! He remembered how proud he had been of her as a boy when she came to see him at school. Then in the deep red coals of the grate he saw the faces of other women who had come since then into his vexed, disordered life. Laughing faces, with eyes artificially bright, eyes without depth or meaning, features without the stamp of high sensibilities. And he had left this face for such as those!

He sighed restlessly and laid his hand on hers. There seemed refuge and protection in the touch of her, as in the old days when he was afraid of the dark. He had been in the dark so long now, his confidence was so thoroughly shaken, and he was bitterly afraid of the night and of himself.

'Ah, mother, you make other things seem so false. You must feel that I owe you an explanation, but I can't make any, even to myself. Ah, but we make poor exchanges in life. I can't make out the riddle of it all. Yet there are things I ought to tell you before I accept your confidence like this.'

'I'd rather you wouldn't, Will. Listen: Between you and me there can be no secrets. We are more alike than other people. Dear boy, I know all about it. I am a woman, and circumstances were different with me, but we are of one blood.

I have lived all your life before you. You have never had an impulse that I have not known, you have never touched a brink that my feet have not trod. This is your birthday night. Twenty-four years ago I foresaw all this. I was a young woman then and I had hot battles of my own, and I felt your likeness to me. You were not like other babies. From the hour you were born you were restless and discontented, as I had been before you. You used to brace your strong little limbs against mine and try to throw me off as you did tonight. Tonight you have come back to me, just as you always did after you ran away to swim in the river that was forbidden you, the river you loved because it was forbidden. You are tired and sleepy, just as you used to be then, only a little older and a little paler and a little more foolish. I never asked you where you had been then, nor will I now. You have come back to me, that's all in all to me. I know your every possibility and limitation, as a composer knows his instrument.'

He found no answer that was worthy to give to talk like this. He had not found life easy since he had lived by his wits. He had come to know poverty at close quarters. He had known what it was to be gay with an empty pocket, to wear violets in his buttonhole when he had not breakfasted, and all the hateful shams of the poverty of idleness. He had been a reporter on a big metropolitan daily, where men grind out their brains on paper until they have not one idea left – and still grind on. He had worked in a real estate office, where ignorant men were swindled. He had sung in a comic opera chorus and played Harris in an Uncle Tom's Cabin company, and edited a socialist weekly. He had been dogged by debt and hunger and grinding poverty, until to sit here by a warm fire without concern as to how it would be paid for seemed unnatural.

He looked up at her questioningly. 'I wonder if you know how much you pardon?'

'O, my poor boy, much or little, what does it matter? Have you wandered so far and paid such a bitter price for knowledge and not yet learned that love has nothing to do with pardon or forgiveness, that it only loves, and loves – and loves? They have not taught you well, the women of your world.' She leaned over and kissed him, as no woman had kissed him since he left her.

He drew a long sigh of rich content. The old life, with all its bitterness and useless antagonism and flimsy sophistries, its brief delights that were always tinged with fear and distrust and unfaith, that whole miserable, futile, swindled world of Bohemia seemed immeasurably distant and far away, like a dream that is over and done. And as the chimes rang joyfully outside and sleep pressed heavily upon his eyelids, he wondered dimly if the Author of this sad little riddle of ours were not able to solve it after all, and if the Potter would not finally mete out his all comprehensive justice, such as none but he could have, to his Things of Clay, which are made in his own patterns, weak or strong, for his own ends; and if some day we will not awaken and find that all evil is a dream, a mental distortion that will pass when the dawn shall break.

SHERWOOD ANDERSON

MOTHER

ELIZABETH WILLARD, the mother of George Willard, was tall and gaunt and her face was marked with smallpox scars. Although she was but forty-five, some obscure disease had taken the fire out of her figure. Listlessly she went about the disorderly old hotel looking at the faded wall-paper and the ragged carpets and, when she was able to be about, doing the work of a chambermaid among beds soiled by the slumbers of fat traveling men. Her husband, Tom Willard, a slender, graceful man with square shoulders, a quick military step, and a black mustache trained to turn sharply up at the ends, tried to put the wife out of his mind. The presence of the tall ghostly figure, moving slowly through the halls, he took as a reproach to himself. When he thought of her he grew angry and swore. The hotel was unprofitable and forever on the edge of failure and he wished himself out of it. He thought of the old house and the woman who lived there with him as things defeated and done for. The hotel in which he had begun life so hopefully was now a mere ghost of what a hotel should be. As he went spruce and business-like through the streets of Winesburg, he sometimes stopped and turned quickly about as though fearing that the spirit of the hotel and of the woman would follow him even into the streets. 'Damn such a life, damn it!' he sputtered aimlessly.

Tom Willard had a passion for village politics and for years had been the leading Democrat in a strongly Republican community. Some day, he told himself, the tide of things political will turn in my favor and the years of ineffectual service count big in the bestowal of rewards. He dreamed of going to Congress and even of becoming governor. Once when a younger member of the party arose at a political conference and began to boast of his faithful service, Tom Willard grew white with fury. 'Shut up, you,' he roared, glaring about. 'What do you know of service? What are you but a boy? Look at what I've done here! I was a Democrat here in Winesburg when it was a crime to be a Democrat. In the old days they fairly hunted us with guns.'

Between Elizabeth and her one son George there was a deep unexpressed bond of sympathy, based on a girlhood dream that had long ago died. In the son's presence she was timid and reserved, but sometimes while he hurried about town intent upon his duties as a reporter, she went into his room and closing the door knelt by a little desk, made of a kitchen table, that sat near a window. In the room by the desk she went through a ceremony that was half a prayer, half a demand, addressed to the skies. In the boyish figure she yearned to see something half forgotten that had once been a part of herself re-created. The prayer concerned that. 'Even though I die, I will in some way keep defeat from you,' she cried, and so deep was her determination that her whole body shook. Her eyes glowed and she clenched her fists. 'If I am dead and see him becoming a meaningless drab figure like myself, I will come back,' she declared. 'I ask God now to give me that privilege. I demand it. I will pay for it. God may beat me with his fists. I will take any blow that may befall if but this my boy be allowed to express something for us both.' Pausing uncertainly, the woman stared about the boy's room. 'And do not let him become smart and successful either,' she added vaguely.

The communion between George Willard and his mother

was outwardly a formal thing without meaning. When she was ill and sat by the window in her room he sometimes went in the evening to make her a visit. They sat by a window that looked over the roof of a small frame building into Main Street. By turning their heads they could see through another window, along an alleyway that ran behind the Main Street stores and into the back door of Abner Groff's bakery. Sometimes as they sat thus a picture of village life presented itself to them. At the back door of his shop appeared Abner Groff with a stick or an empty milk bottle in his hand. For a long time there was a feud between the baker and a grey cat that belonged to Sylvester West, the druggist. The boy and his mother saw the cat creep into the door of the bakery and presently emerge followed by the baker, who swore and waved his arms about. The baker's eyes were small and red and his black hair and beard were filled with flour dust. Sometimes he was so angry that, although the cat had disappeared, he hurled sticks, bits of broken glass, and even some of the tools of his trade about. Once he broke a window at the back of Sinning's Hardware Store. In the alley the grey cat crouched behind barrels filled with torn paper and broken bottles above which flew a black swarm of flies. Once when she was alone, and after watching a prolonged and ineffectual outburst on the part of the baker, Elizabeth Willard put her head down on her long white hands and wept. After that she did not look along the alleyway any more, but tried to forget the contest between the bearded man and the cat. It seemed like a rehearsal of her own life, terrible in its vividness.

In the evening when the son sat in the room with his mother, the silence made them both feel awkward. Darkness came on and the evening train came in at the station. In the street below feet tramped up and down upon a board sidewalk. In the station yard, after the evening train had gone, there was a heavy silence. Perhaps Skinner Leason, the express agent, moved a truck the length of the station platform. Over on Main Street sounded a man's voice, laughing. The door of the express office banged. George Willard arose and crossing the room fumbled for the doorknob. Sometimes he knocked against a chair, making it scrape along the floor. By the window sat the sick woman, perfectly still, listless. Her long hands, white and bloodless, could be seen drooping over the ends of the arms of the chair. 'I think you had better be out among the boys. You are too much indoors,' she said, striving to relieve the embarrassment of the departure. 'I thought I would take a walk,' replied George Willard, who felt awkward and confused.

One evening in July, when the transient guests who made the New Willard House their temporary home had become scarce, and the hallways, lighted only by kerosene lamps turned low, were plunged in gloom, Elizabeth Willard had an adventure. She had been ill in bed for several days and her son had not come to visit her. She was alarmed. The feeble blaze of life that remained in her body was blown into a flame by her anxiety and she crept out of bed, dressed and hurried along the hallway toward her son's room, shaking with exaggerated fears. As she went along she steadied herself with her hand, slipped along the papered walls of the hall and breathed with difficulty. The air whistled through her teeth. As she hurried forward she thought how foolish she was. 'He is concerned with boyish affairs,' she told herself. 'Perhaps he has now begun to walk about in the evening with girls.'

Elizabeth Willard had a dread of being seen by guests in the hotel that had once belonged to her father and the ownership of which still stood recorded in her name in the county courthouse. The hotel was continually losing patronage because of its shabbiness and she thought of herself as also shabby. Her own room was in an obscure corner and when she felt able to work she voluntarily worked among the beds, preferring the labor that could be done when the guests were abroad seeking trade among the merchants of Winesburg.

By the door of her son's room the mother knelt upon the floor and listened for some sound from within. When she heard the boy moving about and talking in low tones a smile came to her lips. George Willard had a habit of talking aloud to himself and to hear him doing so had always given his mother a peculiar pleasure. The habit in him, she felt, strengthened the secret bond that existed between them. A thousand times she had whispered to herself of the matter. 'He is groping about, trying to find himself,' she thought. 'He is not a dull clod, all words and smartness. Within him there is a secret something that is striving to grow. It is the thing I let be killed in myself.'

In the darkness in the hallway by the door the sick woman arose and started again toward her own room. She was afraid that the door would open and the boy come upon her. When she had reached a safe distance and was about to turn a corner into a second hallway she stopped and bracing herself with her hands waited, thinking to shake off a trembling fit of weakness that had come upon her. The presence of the boy in the room had made her happy. In her bed, during the long hours alone, the little fears that had visited her had become giants. Now they were all gone. 'When I get back to my room I shall sleep,' she murmured gratefully.

But Elizabeth Willard was not to return to her bed and to sleep. As she stood trembling in the darkness the door of her son's room opened and the boy's father, Tom Willard, stepped out. In the light that steamed out at the door he stood with the knob in his hand and talked. What he said infuriated the woman.

Tom Willard was ambitious for his son. He had always thought of himself as a successful man, although nothing he had ever done had turned out successfully. However, when he was out of sight of the New Willard House and had no fear of coming upon his wife, he swaggered and began to dramatize himself as one of the chief men of the town. He wanted his son to succeed. He it was who had secured for the boy the position on the *Winesburg Eagle*. Now, with a ring of earnestness in his voice, he was advising concerning some course of conduct. 'I tell you what, George, you've got to wake up,' he said sharply. 'Will Henderson has spoken to me three times concerning the matter. He says you go along for hours not hearing when you are spoken to and acting like a gawky girl. What ails you?' Tom Willard laughed good-naturedly. 'Well, I guess you'll get over it,' he said. 'I told Will that. You're not a fool and you're not a woman. You're Tom Willard's son and you'll wake up. I'm not afraid. What you say clears things up. If being a newspaper man had put the notion of becoming a writer into your mind that's all right. Only I guess you'll have to wake up to do that too, eh?'

Tom Willard went briskly along the hallway and down a flight of stairs to the office. The woman in the darkness could hear him laughing and talking with a guest who was striving to wear away a dull evening by dozing in a chair by the office door. She returned to the door of her son's room. The weakness had passed from her body as by a miracle and she stepped boldly along. A thousand ideas raced through her head. When she heard the scraping of a chair and the sound of a pen scratching upon paper, she again turned and went back along the hallway to her own room.

A definite determination had come into the mind of the defeated wife of the Winesburg hotel keeper. The determination was the result of long years of quiet and rather ineffectual thinking. 'Now,' she told herself, 'I will act. There is something threatening my boy and I will ward it off.' The fact that the conversation between Tom Willard and his son had been rather quiet and natural, as though an understanding existed between them, maddened her. Although for years she had hated her husband, her hatred had always before been a quite impersonal thing. He had been merely a part of something else that she hated. Now, and by the few words at the door, he had become the thing personified. In the darkness of her own room she clenched her fists and glared about. Going to a cloth bag that hung on a nail by the wall she took out a long pair of sewing scissors and held them in her hand like a dagger. 'I will stab him,' she said aloud. 'He has chosen to be the voice of evil and I will kill him. When I have killed him something will snap within myself and I will die also. It will be a release for all of us.'

In her girlhood and before her marriage with Tom Willard, Elizabeth had borne a somewhat shaky reputation in Winesburg. For years she had been what is called 'stage-struck' and had paraded through the streets with traveling men guests at her father's hotel, wearing loud clothes and urging them to tell her of life in the cities out of which they had come. Once she startled the town by putting on men's clothes and riding a bicycle down Main Street.

In her own mind the tall dark girl had been in those days much confused. A great restlessness was in her and it expressed itself in two ways. First there was an uneasy desire for change, for some big definite movement to her life. It was this feeling that had turned her mind to the stage. She dreamed of joining some company and wandering over the world, seeing always new faces and giving something out of herself to all people. Sometimes at night she was quite beside herself with the thought, but when she tried to talk of the matter to the members of the theatrical companies that came to Winesburg and stopped at her father's hotel, she got nowhere. They did not seem to know what she meant, or if she did get something of her passion expressed, they only laughed. 'It's not like that,' they said. 'It's as dull and un-interesting as this here. Nothing comes of it.'

With the traveling men when she walked about with them, and later with Tom Willard, it was quite different. Always they seemed to understand and sympathize with her. On the side streets of the village, in the darkness under the trees, they took hold of her hand and she thought that some-thing unexpressed in herself came forth and became a part of an unexpressed something in them.

And then there was the second expression of her rest-lessness. When that came she felt for a time released and happy. She did not blame the men who walked with her and later she did not blame Tom Willard. It was always the same, beginning with kisses and ending, after strange wild emo-tions, with peace and then sobbing repentance. When she sobbed she put her hand upon the face of the man and had always the same thought. Even though he were large and bearded she thought he had become suddenly a little boy. She wondered why he did not sob also.

In her room, tucked away in a corner of the old Willard House, Elizabeth Willard lighted a lamp and put it on a dressing table that stood by the door. A thought had come into her mind and she went to a closet and brought out a small square box and set it on the table. The box contained material for make-up and had been left with other things by a theatrical company that had once been stranded in Winesburg. Elizabeth Willard had decided that she would be beautiful. Her hair was still black and there was a great mass of it braided and coiled about her head. The scene that was to take place in the office below began to grow in her mind. No ghostly worn-out figure should confront Tom Willard, but something quite unexpected and startling. Tall and with dusky cheeks and hair that fell in a mass from her shoulders, a figure should come striding down the stairway before the startled loungers in the hotel office. The figure would be silent – it would be swift and terrible. As a tigress whose cub had been threatened would she appear, coming out of the shadows, stealing noiselessly along and holding the long wicked scissors in her hand.

With a little broken sob in her throat, Elizabeth Willard blew out the light that stood upon the table and stood weak and trembling in the darkness. The strength that had been as a miracle in her body left and she half reeled across the floor, clutching at the back of the chair in which she had spent so many long days staring out over the tin roofs into the main street of Winesburg. In the hallway there was the sound of footsteps and George Willard came in at the door. Sitting in a chair beside his mother he began to talk. 'I'm going to get out of here,' he said. 'I don't know where I shall go or what I shall do but I am going away.'

The woman in the chair waited and trembled. An impulse came to her. 'I suppose you had better wake up,' she said. 'You think that? You will go to the city and make money, eh? It will be better for you, you think, to be a business man, to be brisk and smart and alive?' She waited and trembled.

The son shook his head. 'I suppose I can't make you understand, but oh, I wish I could,' he said earnestly. 'I can't even talk to father about it. I don't try. There isn't any use. I don't know what I shall do. I just want to go away and look at people and think.'

Silence fell upon the room where the boy and woman sat together. Again, as on the other evenings, they were embarrassed. After a time the boy tried again to talk. 'I suppose it won't be for a year or two but I've been thinking about it,' he said, rising and going toward the door. 'Something father said makes it sure that I shall have to go away.' He fumbled with the doorknob. In the room the silence became unbearable to the woman. She wanted to cry out with joy because of the words that had come from the lips of her son, but the expression of joy had become impossible to her. 'I think you had better go out among the boys. You are too much indoors,' she said. 'I thought I would go for a little walk,' replied the son stepping awkwardly out of the room and closing the door.

TILLIE OLSEN

I STAND HERE
IRONING

I STAND HERE IRONING, and what you asked me moves tormented back and forth with the iron.

'I wish you would manage the time to come in and talk with me about your daughter. I'm sure you can help me understand her. She's a youngster who needs help and whom I'm deeply interested in helping.'

'Who needs help.' Even if I came, what good would it do? You think because I am her mother I have a key, or that in some way you could use me as a key? She has lived for nineteen years. There is all that life that has happened outside of me, beyond me.

And when is there time to remember, to sift, to weigh, to estimate, to total? I will start and there will be an interruption and I will have to gather it all together again. Or I will become engulfed with all I did or did not do, with what should have been and what cannot be helped.

She was a beautiful baby. The first and only one of our five that was beautiful at birth. You do not guess how new and uneasy her tenancy in her now-loveliness. You did not know her all those years she was thought homely, or see her poring over her baby pictures, making me tell her over and over how beautiful she had been – and would be, I would tell her – and was now, to the seeing eye. But the seeing eyes were few or nonexistent. Including mine.

I nursed her. They feel that's important nowadays.

I nursed all the children, but with her, with all the fierce rigidity of first motherhood, I did like the books then said. Though her cries battered me to trembling and my breasts ached with swollenness, I waited till the clock decreed.

Why do I put that first? I do not even know if it matters, or if it explains anything.

She was a beautiful baby. She blew shining bubbles of sound. She loved motion, loved light, loved color and music and textures. She would lie on the floor in her blue overalls patting the surface so hard in ecstasy her hands and feet would blur. She was a miracle to me, but when she was eight months old I had to leave her daytimes with the woman downstairs to whom she was no miracle at all, for I worked or looked for work and for Emily's father, who 'could no longer endure' (he wrote in his good-bye note) 'sharing want with us.'

I was nineteen. It was the pre-relief, pre-WPA world of the depression. I would start running as soon as I got off the streetcar, running up the stairs, the place smelling sour, and awake or asleep to startle awake, when she saw me she would break into a clogged weeping that could not be comforted, a weeping I can hear yet.

After a while I found a job hashing at night so I could be with her days, and it was better. But it came to where I had to bring her to his family and leave her.

It took a long time to raise the money for her fare back. Then she got chicken pox and I had to wait longer. When she finally came, I hardly knew her, walking quick and nervous like her father, looking like her father, thin, and dressed in a shoddy red that yellowed her skin and glared at the pockmarks. All the baby loveliness gone.

She was two. Old enough for nursery school they said, and I did not know then what I know now – the fatigue of the long day, and the lacerations of group life in nurseries that are only parking places for children.

Except that it would have made no difference if I had known. It was the only place there was. It was the only way we could be together, the only way I could hold a job.

And even without knowing, I knew. I knew the teacher that was evil because all these years it has curdled into my memory, the little boy hunched in the corner, her rasp, 'why aren't you outside, because Alvin hits you? that's no reason, go out, scaredy.' I knew Emily hated it even if she did not clutch and implore 'don't go Mommy' like the other children, mornings.

She always had a reason why we should stay home. Momma, you look sick, Momma. I feel sick. Momma, the teachers aren't there today, they're sick. Momma, we can't go, there was a fire there last night. Momma, it's a holiday today, no school, they told me.

But never a direct protest, never rebellion. I think of our others in their three-, four-year-oldness – the explosions, the tempers, the denunciations, the demands – and I feel suddenly ill. I put the iron down. What in me demanded that goodness in her? And what was the cost, the cost to her of such goodness?

The old man living in the back once said in his gentle way: 'You should smile at Emily more when you look at her.' What *was* in my face when I looked at her? I loved her. There were all the acts of love.

It was only with the others I remembered what he said, and it was the face of joy, and not of care or tightness or worry I turned to them – too late for Emily. She does not smile easily, let alone almost always as her brothers and sisters do. Her face is closed and sombre, but when she wants, how fluid. You must have seen it in her pantomimes, you spoke of her rare gift for comedy on the stage that rouses a laughter out of the audience so dear they applaud and applaud and do not want to let her go.

Where does it come from, that comedy? There was none of it in her when she came back to me that second time, after I had had to send her away again. She had a new daddy now to learn to love, and I think perhaps it was a better time.

Except when we left her alone nights, telling ourselves she was old enough.

'Can't you go some other time, Mommy, like tomorrow?' she would ask. 'Will it be just a little while you'll be gone? Do you promise?'

The time we came back, the front door open, the clock on the floor in the hall. She rigid awake. 'It wasn't just a little while. I didn't cry. Three times I called you, just three times, and then I ran downstairs to open the door so you could come faster. The clock talked loud. I threw it away, it scared me what it talked.'

She said the clock talked loud again that night I went to the hospital to have Susan. She was delirious with the fever that comes before red measles, but she was fully conscious all the week I was gone and the week after we were home when she could not come near the new baby or me.

She did not get well. She stayed skeleton thin, not wanting to eat, and night after night she had nightmares. She would call for me, and I would rouse from exhaustion to sleepily call back: 'You're all right, darling, go to sleep, it's just a dream,' and if she still called, in a sterner voice, 'now go to sleep, Emily, there's nothing to hurt you.' Twice, only twice, when I had to get up for Susan anyhow, I went in to sit with her.

Now when it is too late (as if she would let me hold and comfort her like I do the others) I get up and go to her at once at her moan or restless stirring. 'Are you awake, Emily? Can I get you something?' And the answer is always the same: 'No, I'm all right, go back to sleep, Mother.'

They persuaded me at the clinic to send her away to a convalescent home in the country where 'she can have the kind of food and care you can't manage for her, and you'll be free to concentrate on the new baby.' They still send children to that place. I see pictures on the society page of sleek young women planning affairs to raise money for it, or dancing at the affairs, or decorating Easter eggs or filling Christmas stockings for the children.

They never have a picture of the children so I do not know if the girls still wear those gigantic red bows and the ravaged looks on the every other Sunday when parents can come to visit 'unless otherwise notified' – as we were notified the first six weeks.

Oh it is a handsome place, green lawns and tall trees and fluted flower beds. High up on the balconies of each cottage the children stand, the girls in their red bows and white dresses, the boys in white suits and giant red ties. The parents stand below shrieking up to be heard and the children shriek down to be heard, and between them the invisible wall 'Not To Be Contaminated by Parental Germs or Physical Affection.'

There was a tiny girl who always stood hand in hand with Emily. Her parents never came. One visit she was gone. 'They moved her to Rose College,' Emily shouted in explanation. 'They don't like you to love anybody here.'

She wrote once a week, the labored writing of a seven-year-old. 'I am fine. How is the baby. If I write my leter nicly I will have a star. Love.' There never was a star. We wrote every other day, letters she could never hold or keep but only hear read – once. 'We simply do not have room for children

211

to keep any personal possessions,' they patiently explained when we pieced one Sunday's shrieking together to plead how much it would mean to Emily, who loved so to keep things, to be allowed to keep her letters and cards.

Each visit she looked frailer. 'She isn't eating,' they told us.

(They had runny eggs for breakfast or mush with lumps, Emily said later, I'd hold it in in my mouth and not swallow. Nothing ever tasted good, just when they had chicken.)

It took us eight months to get her released home, and only the fact that she gained back so little of her seven lost pounds convinced the social worker.

I used to try to hold and love her after she came back, but her body would stay stiff, and after a while she'd push away. She ate little. Food sickened her, and I think much of life too. Oh she had physical lightness and brightness, twinkling by on skates, bouncing like a ball up and down up and down over the jump rope, skimming over the hill; but these were momentary.

She fretted about her appearance, thin and dark and foreign-looking at a time when every little girl was supposed to look or thought she should look a chubby blonde replica of Shirley Temple. The doorbell sometimes rang for her, but no one seemed to come and play in the house or be a best friend. Maybe because we moved so much.

There was a boy she loved painfully through two school semesters. Months later she told me how she had taken pennies from my purse to buy him candy. 'Licorice was his favorite and I brought him some every day, but he still liked Jennifer better'n me. Why, Mommy?' The kind of question for which there is no answer.

School was a worry to her. She was not glib or quick in a world where glibness and quickness were easily confused with ability to learn. To her overworked and exasperated teachers she was an overconscientious 'slow learner' who kept trying to catch up and was absent entirely too often.

I let her be absent, though sometimes the illness was imaginary. How different from my now-strictness about attendance with the others. I wasn't working. We had a new baby, I was home anyhow. Sometimes, after Susan grew old enough, I would keep her home from school, too, to have them all together.

Mostly Emily had asthma, and her breathing, harsh and labored, would fill the house with a curiously tranquil sound. I would bring the two old dresser mirrors and her boxes of collections to her bed. She would select beads and single earrings, bottle tops and shells, dried flowers and pebbles, old postcards and scraps, all sorts of oddments; then she and Susan would play Kingdom, setting up landscapes and furniture, peopling them with action.

Those were the only times of peaceful companionship between her and Susan. I have edged away from it, that poisonous feeling between them, that terrible balancing of hurts and needs I had to do between the two, and did so badly, those earlier years.

Oh there are conflicts between the others too, each one human, needing, demanding, hurting, taking – but only between Emily and Susan, no, Emily toward Susan that corroding resentment. It seems so obvious on the surface, yet it is not obvious. Susan, the second child, Susan, golden- and curly-haired and chubby, quick and articulate and assured, everything in appearance and manner Emily was not; Susan, not able to resist Emily's precious things, losing or sometimes clumsily breaking them; Susan telling jokes and riddles to company for applause while Emily sat silent (to say to me later: that was *my* riddle, Mother, I told it to Susan); Susan, who for all the five years' difference in age was just a year behind Emily in developing physically.

I am glad for that slow physical development that widened the difference between her and her contemporaries, though she suffered over it. She was too vulnerable for that terrible world of youthful competition, of preening and parading, of constant measuring of yourself against every other, of envy, 'If I had that copper hair,' 'If I had that skin....' She tormented herself enough about not looking like the others, there was enough of the unsureness, the having to be conscious of words before you speak, the constant caring – what are they thinking of me? without having it all magnified by the merciless physical drives.

Ronnie is calling. He is wet and I change him. It is rare there is such a cry now. That time of motherhood is almost behind me when the ear is not one's own but must always be racked and listening for the child cry, the child call. We sit for a while and I hold him, looking out over the city spread in charcoal with its soft aisles of light. '*Shoogily,*' he breathes and curls closer. I carry him back to bed, asleep. *Shoogily.* A funny word, a family word, inherited from Emily, invented by her to say: *comfort.*

In this and other ways she leaves her seal, I say aloud. And startle at my saying it. What do I mean? What did I start to gather together, to try and make coherent? I was at the terrible, growing years. War years. I do not remember them well. I was working, there were four smaller ones now, there was not time for her. She had to help be a mother, and housekeeper, and shopper. She had to set her seal. Mornings of crisis and near hysteria trying to get lunches packed, hair combed, coats and shoes found, everyone to school or Child Care on time, the baby ready for transportation. And always the paper scribbled on by a smaller one, the book looked at by Susan then mislaid, the homework not done. Running out to that huge school where she was one, she was lost, she was a drop; suffering over the unpreparedness, stammering and unsure in her classes.

There was so little time left at night after the kids were bedded down. She would struggle over books, always eating (it was in those years she developed her enormous appetite that is legendary in our family) and I would be ironing, or preparing food for the next day, or writing V-mail to Bill, or tending the baby. Sometimes, to make me laugh, or out of her despair, she would imitate happenings or types at school.

I think I said once: 'Why don't you do something like this in the school amateur show?' One morning she phoned me at work, hardly understandable through the weeping: 'Mother, I did it. I won, I won; they gave me first prize; they clapped and clapped and wouldn't let me go.'

Now suddenly she was Somebody, and as imprisoned in her difference as she had been in anonymity.

She began to be asked to perform at other high schools, even in colleges, then at city and statewide affairs. The first one we went to, I only recognized her that first moment when thin, shy, she almost drowned herself into the curtains. Then: Was this Emily? The control, the command, the convulsing and deadly clowning, the spell, then the roaring, stamping audience, unwilling to let this rare and precious laughter out of their lives.

Afterwards: You ought to do something about her with a gift like that – but without money or knowing how, what does one do? We have left it all to her, and the gift has as often eddied inside, clogged and clotted, as been used and growing.

She is coming. She runs up the stairs two at a time with

her light graceful step, and I know she is happy tonight. Whatever it was that occasioned your call did not happen today.

'Aren't you ever going to finish the ironing, Mother? Whistler painted his mother in a rocker. I'd have to paint mine standing over an ironing board.' This is one of her communicative nights and she tells me everything and nothing as she fixes herself a plate of food out of the icebox.

She is so lovely. Why did you want me to come in at all? Why were you concerned? She will find her way.

She starts up the stairs to bed. 'Don't get me up with the rest in the morning.' 'But I thought you were having midterms.' 'Oh, those,' she comes back in, kisses me, and says quite lightly, 'in a couple of years when we'll all be atom-dead they won't matter a bit.'

She has said it before. She *believes* it. But because I have been dredging the past, and all that compounds a human being is so heavy and meaningful in me, I cannot endure it tonight.

I will never total it all. I will never come in to say: She was a child seldom smiled at. Her father left me before she was a year old. I had to work her first six years when there was work, or I sent her home and to his relatives. There were years she had care she hated. She was dark and thin and foreign-looking in a world where the prestige went to blondeness and curly hair and dimples, she was slow where glibness was prized. She was a child of anxious, not proud, love. We were poor and could not afford for her the soil of easy growth. I was a young mother, I was a distracted mother. There were the other children pushing up, demanding. Her younger sister seemed all that she was not. There were years she did not want me to touch her. She kept too much in herself, her life was such she had to keep too much in herself.

My wisdom came too late. She has much to her and probably nothing will come of it. She is a child of her age, of depression, of war, of fear.

Let her be. So all that is in her will not bloom – but in how many does it? There is still enough left to live by. Only help her to know – help make it so there is cause for her to know – that she is more than this dress on the ironing board, helpless before the iron.

– 1961

AMY TAN

TWO KINDS

MY MOTHER BELIEVED you could be anything you wanted to be in America. You could open a restaurant. You could work for the government and get good retirement. You could buy a house with almost no money down. You could become rich. You could become instantly famous.

'Of course you can be prodigy, too,' my mother told me when I was nine. 'You can be best anything. What does Auntie Lindo know? Her daughter, she is only best tricky.'

America was where all my mother's hopes lay. She had come here in 1949 after losing everything in China: her mother and father, her family home, her first husband, and two daughters, twin baby girls. But she never looked back with regret. There were so many ways for things to get better.

We didn't immediately pick the right kind of prodigy. At first my mother thought I could be a Chinese Shirley Temple. We'd watch Shirley's old movies on TV as though they were training films. My mother would poke my arm and say, '*Ni kan*' – You watch. And I would see Shirley tapping her feet, or singing a sailor song, or pursing her lips into a very round O while saying, 'Oh my goodness.'

'*Ni kan*,' said my mother as Shirley's eyes flooded with tears. 'You already know how. Don't need talent for crying!'

Soon after my mother got this idea about Shirley Temple, she took me to a beauty training school in the Mission district and put me in the hands of a student who could barely hold the scissors without shaking. Instead of getting big fat curls, I emerged with an uneven mass of crinkly black fuzz. My mother dragged me off to the bathroom and tried to wet down my hair.

'You look like Negro Chinese,' she lamented, as if I had done this on purpose.

The instructor of the beauty training school had to lop off these soggy clumps to make my hair even again. 'Peter Pan is very popular these days,' the instructor assured my mother. I now had hair the length of a boy's, with straight-across bangs that hung at a slant two inches above my eyebrows. I liked the haircut and it made me actually look forward to my future fame.

In fact, in the beginning, I was just as excited as my mother, maybe even more so. I pictured this prodigy part of me as many different images, trying each one on for size. I was a dainty ballerina girl standing by the curtains, waiting to hear the right music that would send me floating on my tiptoes. I was like the Christ child lifted out of the straw manger, crying with holy indignity. I was Cinderella stepping from her pumpkin carriage with sparkly cartoon music filling the air.

In all of my imaginings, I was filled with a sense that I would soon become *perfect*. My mother and father would adore me. I would be beyond reproach. I would never feel the need to sulk for anything.

But sometimes the prodigy in me became impatient. 'If you don't hurry up and get me out of here, I'm disappearing for good,' it warned. 'And then you'll always be nothing.'

Every night after dinner, my mother and I would sit at the Formica kitchen table. She would present new tests, taking her examples from stories of amazing children she had read in *Ripley's Believe It or Not*, or *Good Housekeeping*, *Reader's Digest*, and a dozen other magazines she kept in a pile in our bathroom. My mother got these magazines from people whose houses she cleaned. And since she cleaned many houses each week, we had a great assortment. She would look through them all, searching for stories about remarkable children.

The first night she brought out a story about a three-year-old boy who knew the capitals of all the states and even most of the European countries. A teacher was quoted as saying the little boy could also pronounce the names of the foreign cities correctly.

'What's the capital of Finland?' my mother asked me, looking at the magazine story.

All I knew was the capital of California, because Sacramento was the name of the street we lived on in Chinatown. 'Nairobi!' I guessed, saying the most foreign word I could think of. She checked to see if that was possibly one way to pronounce 'Helsinki' before showing me the answer.

The tests got harder – multiplying numbers in my head, finding the queen of hearts in a deck of cards, trying to stand on my head without using my hands, predicting the daily temperatures in Los Angeles, New York, and London.

One night I had to look at a page from the Bible for three minutes and then report everything I could remember. 'Now Jehoshaphat had riches and honor in abundance and ... that's all I remember, Ma,' I said.

And after seeing my mother's disappointed face once again, something inside of me began to die. I hated the tests, the raised hopes and failed expectations. Before going to bed that night, I looked in the mirror above the bathroom sink and when I saw only my face staring back – and that it would always be this ordinary face – I began to cry. Such a sad, ugly girl! I made high-pitched noises like a crazed animal, trying to scratch out the face in the mirror.

And then I saw what seemed to be the prodigy side of me – because I had never seen that face before. I looked at my reflection, blinking so I could see more clearly. The girl staring back at me was angry, powerful. This girl and I were the same. I had new thoughts, willful thoughts, or rather thoughts filled with lots of won'ts. I won't let her change me, I promised myself. I won't be what I'm not.

So now on nights when my mother presented her tests, I performed listlessly, my head propped on one arm. I pretended to be bored. And I was. I got so bored I started counting the bellows of the foghorns out on the bay while my mother drilled me in other areas. The sound was comforting and reminded me of the cow jumping over the moon. And the next day, I played a game with myself, seeing if my mother would give up on me before eight bellows. After a while I usually counted only one, maybe two bellows at most. At last she was beginning to give up hope.

Two or three months had gone by without any mention of my being a prodigy again. And then one day my mother was watching *The Ed Sullivan Show* on TV. The TV was old and the sound kept shorting out. Every time my mother got halfway up from the sofa to adjust the set, the sound would go back on and Ed would be talking. As soon as she sat down, Ed would go silent again. She got up, the TV broke into loud piano music. She sat down. Silence. Up and down, back and forth, quiet and loud. It was like a stiff embraceless dance between her and the TV set. Finally she stood by the set with her hand on the sound dial.

She seemed entranced by the music, a little frenzied piano piece with this mesmerizing quality, sort of quick passages and then teasing lilting ones before it returned to the quick playful parts.

'*Ni kan*,' my mother said, calling me over with hurried hand gestures. 'Look here.'

I could see why my mother was fascinated by the music. It was being pounded out by a little Chinese girl, about nine years old, with a Peter Pan haircut. The girl had the sauciness of a Shirley Temple. She was proudly modest like a proper Chinese child. And she also did this fancy sweep of a curtsy, so that the fluffy skirt of her white dress cascaded slowly to the floor like the petals of a large carnation.

In spite of these warning signs, I wasn't worried. Our family had no piano and we couldn't afford to buy one, let alone reams of sheet music and piano lessons. So I could be generous in my comments when my mother bad-mouthed the little girl on TV.

'Play note right, but doesn't sound good! No singing sound,' complained my mother.

'What are you picking on her for?' I said carelessly. 'She's pretty good. Maybe she's not the best, but she's trying hard.' I knew almost immediately I would be sorry I said that.

'Just like you,' she said. 'Not the best. Because you not trying.' She gave a little huff as she let go of the sound dial and sat down on the sofa.

The little Chinese girl sat down also to play an encore of 'Anitra's Dance' by Grieg. I remember the song, because later on I had to learn how to play it.

Three days after watching *The Ed Sullivan Show*, my mother told me what my schedule would be for piano lessons and piano practice. She had talked to Mr Chong, who lived on the first floor of our apartment building. Mr Chong was a retired piano teacher and my mother had traded housecleaning

225

services for weekly lessons and a piano for me to practice on every day, two hours a day, from four until six.

When my mother told me this, I felt as though I had been sent to hell. I whined and then kicked my foot a little when I couldn't stand it anymore.

'Why don't you like me the way I am? I'm *not* a genius! I can't play the piano. And even if I could, I wouldn't go on TV if you paid me a million dollars!' I cried.

My mother slapped me. 'Who ask you be genius?' she shouted. 'Only ask you be your best. For you sake. You think I want you be genius? Hnnh! What for! Who ask you!'

'So ungrateful,' I heard her mutter in Chinese. 'If she had as much talent as she has temper, she would be famous now.'

Mr Chong, whom I secretly nicknamed Old Chong, was very strange, always tapping his fingers to the silent music of an invisible orchestra. He looked ancient in my eyes. He had lost most of the hair on top of his head and he wore thick glasses and had eyes that always looked tired and sleepy. But he must have been younger than I thought, since he lived with his mother and was not yet married.

I met Old Lady Chong once and that was enough. She had this peculiar smell like a baby that had done something in its pants. And her fingers felt like a dead person's, like an old peach I once found in the back of the refrigerator; the skin just slid off the meat when I picked it up.

I soon found out why Old Chong had retired from teaching piano. He was deaf. 'Like Beethoven!' he shouted to me. 'We're both listening only in our head!' And he would start to conduct his frantic silent sonatas.

Our lessons went like this. He would open the book and point to different things, explaining their purpose: 'Key! Treble! Bass! No sharps or flats! So this is C major! Listen now and play after me!'

And then he would play the C scale a few times, a simple chord, and then, as if inspired by an old, unreachable itch, he gradually added more notes and running trills and a pounding bass until the music was really something quite grand.

I would play after him, the simple scale, the simple chord, and then I just played some nonsense that sounded like a cat running up and down on top of garbage cans. Old Chong smiled and applauded and then said, 'Very good! But now you must learn to keep time!'

So that's how I discovered that Old Chong's eyes were too slow to keep up with the wrong notes I was playing. He went through the motions in half-time. To help me keep rhythm, he stood behind me, pushing down on my right shoulder for every beat. He balanced pennies on top of my wrists so I would keep them still as I slowly played scales and arpeggios. He had me curve my hand around an apple and keep that shape when playing chords. He marched stiffly to show me how to make each finger dance up and down, staccato like an obedient little soldier.

He taught me all these things, and that was how I also learned I could be lazy and get away with mistakes, lots of mistakes. If I hit the wrong notes because I hadn't practiced enough, I never corrected myself. I just kept playing in rhythm. And Old Chong kept conducting his own private reverie.

So maybe I never really gave myself a fair chance. I did pick up the basics pretty quickly, and I might have become a good pianist at that young age. But I was so determined not to try, not to be anybody different that I learned to play only the most ear-splitting preludes, the most discordant hymns.

Over the next year, I practiced like this, dutifully in my

own way. And then one day I heard my mother and her friend Lindo Jong both talking in a loud bragging tone of voice so others could hear. It was after church, and I was leaning against the brick wall wearing a dress with stiff white petticoats. Auntie Lindo's daughter, Waverly, who was about my age, was standing farther down the wall about five feet away. We had grown up together and shared all the closeness of two sisters squabbling over crayons and dolls. In other words, for the most part, we hated each other. I thought she was snotty. Waverly Jong had gained a certain amount of fame as 'Chinatown's Littlest Chinese Chess Champion.'

'She bring home too many trophy,' lamented Auntie Lindo that Sunday. 'All day she play chess. All day I have no time do nothing but dust off her winnings.' She threw a scolding look at Waverly, who pretended not to see her.

'You lucky you don't have this problem,' said Auntie Lindo with a sigh to my mother.

And my mother squared her shoulders and bragged: 'Our problem worser than yours. If we ask Jing-mei wash dish, she hear nothing but music. It's like you can't stop this natural talent.'

And right then, I was determined to put a stop to her foolish pride.

A few weeks later, Old Chong and my mother conspired to have me play in a talent show which would be held in the church hall. By then, my parents had saved up enough to buy me a second-hand piano, a black Wurlitzer spinet with a scarred bench. It was the showpiece of our living-room.

For the talent show, I was to play a piece called 'Pleading Child' from Schumann's *Scenes from Childhood*. It was a simple, moody piece that sounded more difficult than it was. I was supposed to memorize the whole thing, playing the repeat parts twice to make the piece sound longer. But I dawdled over it, playing a few bars and then cheating, looking up to see what notes followed. I never really listened to what I was playing. I daydreamed about being somewhere else, about being someone else.

The part I liked to practice best was the fancy curtsy: right foot out, touch the rose on the carpet with a pointed foot, sweep to the side, left leg bends, look up and smile.

My parents invited all the couples from the Joy Luck Club to witness my debut. Auntie Lindo and Uncle Tin were there. Waverly and her two older brothers had also come. The first two rows were filled with children both younger and older than I was. The littlest ones got to go first. They recited simple nursery rhymes, squawked out tunes on miniature violins, twirled Hula Hoops, pranced in pink ballet tutus, and when they bowed or curtsied, the audience would sigh in unison, 'Awww,' and then clap enthusiastically.

When my turn came, I was very confident. I remember my childish excitement. It was as if I knew, without a doubt, that the prodigy side of me really did exist. I had no fear whatsoever, no nervousness. I remember thinking to myself, This is it! This is it! I looked out over the audience, at my mother's blank face, my father's yawn, Auntie Lindo's stiff-lipped smile, Waverly's sulky expression. I had on a white dress layered with sheets of lace, and a pink bow in my Peter Pan haircut. As I sat down I envisioned people jumping to their feet and Ed Sullivan rushing up to introduce me to everyone on TV.

And I started to play. It was so beautiful. I was so caught up in how lovely I looked that at first I didn't worry how I would sound. So it was a surprise to me when I hit the first wrong note and I realized something didn't sound quite right. And then I hit another and another followed that.

A chill started at the top of my head and began to trickle down. Yet I couldn't stop playing, as though my hands were bewitched. I kept thinking my fingers would adjust themselves back, like a train switching to the right track. I played this strange jumble through two repeats, the sour notes staying with me all the way to the end.

When I stood up, I discovered my legs were shaking. Maybe I had just been nervous and the audience, like Old Chong, had seen me go through the right motions and had not heard anything wrong at all. I swept my right foot out, went down on my knee, looked up and smiled. The room was quiet, except for Old Chong, who was beaming and shouting, 'Bravo! Bravo! Well done!' But then I saw my mother's face, her stricken face. The audience clapped weakly, and as I walked back to my chair, with my whole face quivering as I tried not to cry, I heard a little boy whisper loudly to his mother, 'That was awful,' and the mother whispered back, 'Well, she certainly tried.'

And now I realized how many people were in the audience, the whole world it seemed. I was aware of eyes burning into my back. I felt the shame of my mother and father as they sat stiffly throughout the rest of the show.

We could have escaped during intermission. Pride and some strange sense of honor must have anchored my parents to their chairs. And so we watched it all: the eighteen-year-old boy with a fake mustache who did a magic show and juggled flaming hoops while riding a unicycle. The breasted girl with white makeup who sang from *Madama Butterfly* and got honorable mention. And the eleven-year-old boy who won first prize playing a tricky violin song that sounded like a busy bee.

After the show, the Hsus, the Jongs, and the St Clairs from the Joy Luck Club came up to my mother and father.

'Lots of talented kids,' Auntie Lindo said vaguely, smiling broadly.

'That was somethin' else,' said my father, and I wondered if he was referring to me in a humorous way, or whether he even remembered what I had done.

Waverly looked at me and shrugged her shoulders. 'You aren't a genius like me,' she said matter-of-factly. And if I hadn't felt so bad, I would have pulled her braids and punched her stomach.

But my mother's expression was what devastated me: a quiet, blank look that said she had lost everything. I felt the same way, and it seemed as if everybody were now coming up, like gawkers at the scene of an accident, to see what parts were actually missing. When we got on the bus to go home, my father was humming the busy-bee tune and my mother was silent. I kept thinking she wanted to wait until we got home before shouting at me. But when my father unlocked the door to our apartment, my mother walked in and then went to the back, into the bedroom. No accusations. No blame. And in a way, I felt disappointed. I had been waiting for her to start shouting, so I could shout back and cry and blame her for all my misery.

I assumed my talent-show fiasco meant I never had to play the piano again. But two days later, after school, my mother came out of the kitchen and saw me watching TV.

'Four clock,' she reminded me as if it were any other day. I was stunned, as though she were asking me to go through the talent-show torture again. I wedged myself more tightly in front of the TV.

'Turn off TV,' she called from the kitchen five minutes later.

I didn't budge. And then I decided. I didn't have to do

231

what my mother said anymore. I wasn't her slave. This wasn't China. I had listened to her before and look what happened. She was the stupid one.

She came out from the kitchen and stood in the arched entryway of the living-room. 'Four clock,' she said once again, louder.

'I'm not going to play anymore,' I said nonchalantly. 'Why should I? I'm not a genius.'

She walked over and stood in front of the TV. I saw her chest was heaving up and down in an angry way.

'No!' I said, and I now felt stronger, as if my true self had finally emerged. So this was what had been inside me all along.

'No! I won't!' I screamed.

She yanked me by the arm, pulled me off the floor, snapped off the TV. She was frighteningly strong, half pulling, half carrying me toward the piano as I kicked the throw rugs under my feet. She lifted me up and onto the hard bench. I was sobbing by now, looking at her bitterly. Her chest was heaving even more and her mouth was open, smiling crazily as if she were pleased I was crying.

'You want me to be someone that I'm not!' I sobbed. 'I'll never be the kind of daughter you want me to be!'

'Only two kinds of daughters,' she shouted in Chinese. 'Those who are obedient and those who follow their own mind! Only one kind of daughter can live in this house. Obedient daughter!'

'Then I wish I wasn't your daughter. I wish you weren't my mother,' I shouted. As I said these things I got scared. It felt like worms and toads and slimy things crawling out of my chest, but it also felt good, as if this awful side of me had surfaced, at last.

'Too late change this,' said my mother shrilly.

And I could sense her anger rising to its breaking point.

232

I wanted to see it spill over. And that's when I remembered the babies she had lost in China, the ones we never talked about. 'Then I wish I'd never been born!' I shouted. 'I wish I were dead! Like them.'

It was as if I had said the magic words. Alakazam! – and her face went blank, her mouth closed, her arms went slack, and she backed out of the room, stunned, as if she were blowing away like a small brown leaf, thin, brittle, lifeless.

It was not the only disappointment my mother felt in me. In the years that followed, I failed her so many times, each time asserting my own will, my right to fall short of expectations. I didn't get straight As. I didn't become class president. I didn't get into Stanford. I dropped out of college.

For unlike my mother, I did not believe I could be anything I wanted to be. I could only be me.

And for all those years, we never talked about the disaster at the recital or my terrible accusations afterward at the piano bench. All that remained unchecked, like a betrayal that was now unspeakable. So I never found a way to ask her why she had hoped for something so large that failure was inevitable.

And even worse, I never asked her what frightened me the most: Why had she given up hope?

For after our struggle at the piano, she never mentioned my playing again. The lessons stopped. The lid to the piano was closed, shutting out the dust, my misery, and her dreams.

So she surprised me. A few years ago, she offered to give me the piano, for my thirtieth birthday. I had not played in all those years. I saw the offer as a sign of forgiveness, a tremendous burden removed.

'Are you sure?' I asked shyly. 'I mean, won't you and Dad miss it?'

'No, this your piano,' she said firmly. 'Always your piano. You only one can play.'

'Well, I probably can't play anymore,' I said. 'It's been years.'

'You pick up fast,' said my mother, as if she knew this was certain. 'You have natural talent. You could been genius if you want to.'

'No I couldn't.'

'You just not trying,' said my mother. And she was neither angry nor sad. She said it as if to announce a fact that could never be disproved. 'Take it,' she said.

But I didn't at first. It was enough that she had offered it to me. And after that, every time I saw it in my parents' living-room, standing in front of the bay windows, it made me feel proud, as if it were a shiny trophy I had won back.

Last week I sent a tuner over to my parents' apartment and had the piano reconditioned, for purely sentimental reasons. My mother had died a few months before and I had been getting things in order for my father, a little bit at a time. I put the jewelry in special silk pouches. The sweaters she had knitted in yellow, pink, bright orange – all the colors I hated – I put those in moth-proof boxes. I found some old Chinese silk dresses, the kind with little slits up the sides. I rubbed the old silk against my skin, then wrapped them in tissue and decided to take them home with me.

After I had the piano tuned, I opened the lid and touched the keys. It sounded even richer than I remembered. Really, it was a very good piano. Inside the bench were the same exercise notes with handwritten scales, the same second-hand music books with their covers held together with yellow tape.

I opened up the Schumann book to the dark little piece

I had played at the recital. It was on the left-hand side of the page, 'Pleading Child.' It looked more difficult than I remembered. I played a few bars, surprised at how easily the notes came back to me.

And for the first time, or so it seemed, I noticed the piece on the right-hand side. It was called 'Perfectly Contented.' I tried to play this one as well. It had a lighter melody but the same flowing rhythm and turned out to be quite easy. 'Pleading Child' was shorter but slower; 'Perfectly Contented' was longer, but faster. And after I played them both a few times, I realized they were two halves of the same song.

ANITA DESAI

WINTERSCAPE

SHE STANDS WITH the baby in her arms in front of the refrigerator, and points at the pictures she has taped on its white enamel surface, each in turn, calling out the names of the people in the photographs. It is a game they play often to pass the time, the great stretches of time they spend alone together. The baby jabs his short pink finger at a photograph, and the mother cries, 'That's Daddy, in his new car!' or 'Susan and cousin Ted, on his first birthday!' and 'Grandma by the Christmas tree!' All these pictures are as bright and festive as bits of tinsel or confetti. Everyone is smiling in them, and there are birthday cakes and Christmas trees, the shining chrome of new cars, bright green lawns and white houses. 'Da-dee!' the baby shouts. 'Soo-sun!' The bright colours make the baby smile. The mother is happy to play the game, and laughs: her baby is learning the names of all the members of the family; he is becoming a part of the family.

Then the baby reaches out and waves an ineffectual hand at a photograph that is almost entirely white, only a few shades of grey to bring out the shapes and figures in it. There are two, and both are draped in snow-white clothes which cover their shoulders, exposing only the backs of their heads which are white too, and they are standing beside the very same white refrigerator in the same white-painted kitchen, in front of a white-framed window. They are looking out of it, not at the camera but at the snow that is falling past the windowpanes, covering the leafless tree and the wooden fence and the ground outside, providing them with a white snow-scape into which they seem nearly to have merged. Nearly.

The baby's pink finger jabs at the white photograph. The mother says nothing immediately: she seems silenced, as if she too has joined the two figures at the window and with them is looking out of the white kitchen into a white world. The photograph somehow calls for silence, creates silence, like snow.

The baby too drops his hand, lowers his head on his mother's shoulder, and yawns. Snow, silence, and sleep: the white picture has filled him with sleep, he is overcome by it. His mother holds him and rocks him, swaying on her feet. She loves the feel of the baby's head on her shoulder; she tucks it under her chin protectively. She swivels around to the window as if she sees the two white figures there now, vanishing into the green dusk of a summer evening. She sings softly into the baby's dark hair: 'Ma and Masi – Ma and Masi together.'

'*Two?*' Beth turned her head on the pillow and stared at him over the top of her glasses, lowering the book she was reading to the rounded dome of her belly under the blue coverlet. '*Two* tickets? For *whom?*' because she knew Rakesh did not have a father, that his mother was a widow.

'For my mother and my aunt,' he said, in a low, almost sullen voice, sitting on the edge of the bed in his pyjamas and twisting his fingers together. His back was turned to her, his shoulders stooped. Because of the time difference, he had had to place the call to the village in India in the middle of the night.

'Your *aunt?*' Beth heard her own voice escalate. 'Why do we have to pay for your aunt to visit us? Why does *she* have to visit us when the baby is born? I can't have so many guests in the house, Rakesh!'

He turned around towards her slowly, and she saw dark circles under his eyes. Another time they might have caused her to put her finger out to touch those big, bluish pouches, like bruises, but now she felt herself tense at the thought of not just one, but two strangers, foreigners, part of Rakesh's past, invading their house. She had already wished she had not allowed Rakesh to send for his mother to attend to the birth of their child. It had seemed an outlandish, archaic idea even when it was first suggested; now it was positively bizarre. 'Why both of them? We only asked your mother,' she insisted.

Rakesh was normally quick with his smile, his reassuring words, soft and comforting murmurs. He had seemed nervous ever since she became pregnant, more inclined to worry about what she took as a natural process. But she could see it was not that, it was something else that made him brood, silently, on the edge of the bed, the blue pouches hanging under his eyes, and his hands twisted.

'What's the matter?' she said sharply, and took off her glasses and turned over her book. 'What's wrong?'

He roused himself to shake his head, attempted to smile, and failed. Then he lifted up his legs and lay down on the bed, beside her, turning to her with that same brooding expression, not really seeing her. He put out his hand and tried to stroke the hair at her temple. It annoyed her: he was so clearly about to make a request, a difficult request. She tensed, ready to refuse. He ought not to be asking anything of her in her condition. Two guests, two foreigners – at such a time. 'Tell me,' she demanded.

So he began to tell her. 'They are both my mothers, Beth,' he said. 'I have two mothers.'

* * *

241

There were three years between them and those seemed to have made all the difference. Asha was the first child in the family. So delighted was her father that it never crossed his mind she should have been a son. He tossed her up and caught her in his arms and put his face into her neck to make growling sounds that sent her into squeals of laughter. That she was fair-skinned, plump and had curly hair and bright black eyes all pleased him. He liked his wife to dress the child in frilly, flounced, flowered dresses and put ribbons in her hair. She was glad and relieved he was so pleased with his daughter: it could have been otherwise, but he said, 'A pretty daughter is an ornament to the home.'

So Asha grew up knowing she was an ornament, and a joy. She had no hesitation ever in asking for a toy or a sweet, in climbing onto her parents' laps or standing in the centre of a circle to sing or skip.

When Anu was born, three years later, it was different. Although her father bent over her and fondled her head and said nothing to express disappointment, disappointment was in the air. It swaddled baby Anu (no one even remembered her full name, the more majestic Annapurna), and among the first things she heard were the mutterings of the older people in the family who had no compunction about pronouncing their disappointment. And while her mother held her close and defended her against them, baby Anu knew she was in a weak position. So one might have thought, watching her grow. Although she stayed close to her elder sister, clinging to the hem of her dress, shadowing her, and Asha was pleased to have someone so entirely under her control, there remained something hesitant, nervous and tentative about Anu's steps, her movements and speech. Everything about her expressed diffidence.

While Asha proved a natural housekeeper and joined,

with gusto, in the cooking, the washing, the sweeping, all those household tasks shared between the women, pinning her chunni back behind her ears, rolling up the sleeves of her kameez, and settling down to kneading the dough, or pounding spices, or rolling out chapatis with a fine vigour, Anu proved sadly incompetent. She managed to get her hand burnt when frying pakoras, took so long to grind chillies that her mother grew impatient and pushed her out of the way, and was too weak to haul up a full bucket of water from the well, needing to do it half a bucket at a time. When visitors filled the house and everything was in an uproar, Anu would try to slip away and make herself invisible and only return when summoned – to be scolded soundly for shirking work. 'Look at your sister,' she was always counselled, and she did, raising her eyes with timid admiration. Asha, used to her sister's ways, gave her a wink and slipped her one of the snacks or sweets she had missed. An understanding grew between them, strengthened by strand upon strand upon strand of complicity.

Later, sons were born to their parents, and the pressure, the tension in their relationships with their daughters was relieved. Good-naturedly, the father allowed both of them to go to school. 'What is the harm?' he asked the elderly critics of this unusual move. 'These days it is good for girls to be educated. One day, who knows, they may work in an office – or a bank!'

That certainly did not happen. Another generation would be born and raised before any girl in that Punjab village became an office clerk or a bank teller. Asha and Anu had a few years in the local government school where they wore blue cotton kameezes with white chunnis, and white gym shoes, and sat on benches learning the Punjabi alphabet and their numbers. Here the scales may well have tipped the other way, because Asha found the work ferociously difficult and grew hot and bothered as she tried to work out problems in addition and subtraction or to read her lessons from the tattered, illustrated text books, while Anu discovered an unexpected nimbleness of mind that skipped about the numbers with the agility of a young goat, and scampered through the letters quite friskily. Asha threw her sister exasperated looks but did not mind so much when Anu took over her homework and did it for her in her beautiful hand. Anu drew praise when she wrote essays on 'The Cow' and 'My Favourite Festival' – but, alas, the latter proved to be her swan song because at this point Asha turned fifteen and the family found her a bridegroom and married her off and Anu had to stay home from then on to help her mother.

Asha's bridegroom was a large man, not so young, but it did not matter because he owned so much land and cattle. He had a great handlebar moustache and a turban and Anu was terrified for Asha when she first saw him, but was later to find no cause for terror: he was a kindly, good-natured man who clearly adored his bright-eyed, quick-tongued, lively young wife and was generous to her and to her entire family. His voice was unexpectedly soft and melodious, and he often regaled his visitors, or a gathering in the village, with his songs. Asha – who had plenty of talents but not artistic ones – looked at him with admiration then, sitting back on her haunches and cupping her chin in her hands which were bedecked with the rings and bracelets he had given her.

They often asked Anu to come and stay with them. Asha found she was so accustomed to having her younger sister at her heels, she really could not do without her. She might have done, had she had children, but, though many were born to her, they were either stillborn or died soon after birth, none living for more than a few days. This created an emptiness in the big house so full of goods and comforts, and Asha grew querulous and plaintive, a kind of bitterness informing her every gesture and expression, while her husband became prone to depression which no one would have predicted earlier. Anu often came upon him seated in an armchair at the end of the veranda, or up on the flat roof of the house in the cool evenings, looking out with an expression of deep melancholy across his fields to the horizon where the white spire and the golden dome of the Sikh temple stood against the sky. He left the work on the farm to a trusted headman to supervise and became idle himself, exasperating Asha who tended to throw herself into every possible activity with determined vigour and thought a man should too.

After yet another miscarriage, Asha roused herself with a grim wilfulness to join in the preparation for Anu's wedding, arranged by the parents to a clerk in a neighbouring town, a sullen, silent young man with large teeth and large hands that he rubbed together all the time. Anu kept her face and her tears hidden throughout the wedding, as brides did, and Asha was both consoling and encouraging, as women were.

Unexpectedly, that unpromising young man who blinked through his spectacles and could scarcely croak one sentence at a time, showed no hesitation whatsoever when it came to fathering a child. Nor did Anu, who was so slight of frame and mousy in manner, seem to be in any way handicapped as a woman or mother – her child was born easily, and it was a son. A round, black-haired, red-cheeked boy who roared lustily for his milk and thrashed out with his legs and grabbed with his hands, clearly meant for survival and success.

If Anu and her husband were astonished by him, it could scarcely have matched Asha and her husband's wonder. They were enthralled by the boy: he was the child of their dreams, their thwarted hopes and desires. Anu lay back and watched how Asha scooped Rakesh up into her large, soft arms, how she cradled and kissed him, then how her husband took him from her, wrapped in the candy pink wool shawl knitted by Asha, and crooned over him. She was touched and grateful for Asha's competence, as adept at handling the baby as in churning butter or making sweets. Anu stayed in bed, letting her sister fuss over both her and the baby – making Anu special milk and almond and jaggery drinks in tall metal tumblers, keeping the baby happy and content, massaging him with mustard oil, feeding him sips of sweetened milk from a silver shell, tickling him till he smiled.

Anu's husband looked on, awkwardly, too nervous to hold his own child: small creatures made him afraid; he never failed to kick a puppy or a kitten out of his way, fiercely. Anu rose from her bed occasionally to make a few tentative gestures of motherhood but soon relinquished them, one by one, first letting Asha feed the baby and dress him, then giving up attempts to nurse the boy and letting Asha take over the feeding.

At the first hint of illness – actually, the baby was teething which caused a tummy upset – Asha bundled him up in his blanket and took him home, promising, 'I'll bring him back as soon as he is well. Now you go and rest, Anu, you haven't slept and you look sick yourself.'

When Anu went to fetch him after a week, she came upon Asha's husband, sitting on that upright chair of his on the veranda, but now transformed. He had the baby on his knee and was hopping him up and down while singing a rhyme, and his eyes sparkled as vivaciously as the child's. Instead of taking her son from him, Anu held back, enjoying the scene. Noticing her at last, the large man in the turban beamed at her. 'A prince!' he said, 'and one day he will have all my fields, my cattle, the dairy, the cane-crushing factory, everything. He will grow up to be a prince!'

Rakesh's first birthday was to be celebrated at Asha's house – 'We will do it in style,' she said, revealing how little she thought Anu and her husband were capable of achieving it. Preparations went on for weeks beforehand. There was to be a feast for the whole village. A goat was to be slaughtered and roasted, and the women in the family were busy making sweets and delicacies with no expense spared: Asha's husband was seeing to that. He himself went out to shoot partridges for the festive dinner, setting out before dawn into the rippling grainfields and calling back to the women to have the fire ready for his return.

Those were his last words – to have the fire ready. 'As if he knew', wept Asha's mother, 'that it was the funeral pyre we would light.' Apparently there had been an accident with the gun. It had gone off unexpectedly and the bullet had pierced his shoulder and a lung; he had bled to death. There were no birthday festivities for one-year-old Rakesh.

Knowing that the one thing that could comfort Asha was the presence of the baby in her arms, Anu refrained from suggesting she take him home. At first she had planned to leave the boy with her widowed sister for the first month of mourning, then drew it out to two and even three months. When her husband, taunted by his own family for his failure to establish himself as head of his household, ordered her to bring their son home, Anu surprised herself by answering, 'Let him be. Asha needs him. We can have more sons for ourselves.' Their house was empty and melancholy – it had always been a mean place, a narrow set of rooms in the bazaar, with no sunlight or air – but she sat in its gloom, stitching clothes for her rapidly growing son, a chunni drawn over her head, a picture of acceptance that her

247

husband was not able to disturb, except briefly, with fits of violence.

After one of these, they would go and visit the boy, with gifts, and Rakesh came to look upon his parents as a visiting aunt and uncle, who offered him sweets and toys with a dumbly appeasing, appealing air. No one remembered when he started calling them Masi and Masa. Asha he already addressed as Ma: it was so clearly her role.

Anu had been confident other children would follow. She hoped for a daughter next time, somehow feeling a daughter might be more like her, and more likely to stay with her. But Rakesh had his second and third birthday in Asha's house, and there was no other child. Anu's husband looked discouraged now, and resentful, his own family turning into a chorus of mocking voices. He stayed away at work for long hours; there were rumours – quickly brought to Anu's attention – that he had taken to gambling, and drugs, and some even hinted at having seen him in quarters of the town where respectable people did not go. She was not too perturbed: their relationship was a furtive, nocturnal thing that never survived daylight. She was concerned, of course, when he began to look ill, to break out in boils and rashes, and come down with frequent fevers, and she nursed him in her usual bungling, tentative way. His family came to take over, criticizing her sharply for her failings as a nurse, but he only seemed to grow worse, and died shortly before Rakesh's fifth birthday. His family set up a loud lament and clearly blamed her for the way he had dwindled away in spite of their care. She packed her belongings – in the same tin trunk in which she had brought them as a bride, having added nothing more to them – and went to live with Asha – and the child.

* * *

In the dark, Beth found it was she who was stroking the hair at Rakesh's temple now, and he who lay stretched out with his hands folded on his chest and his eyes staring at the ceiling.

'Then the woman you call Ma – she is really your aunt?' Beth queried.

Rakesh gave a long sigh. 'I always knew her as my mother.'

'And your aunt is your real mother? When did they tell you?'

'I don't know,' he admitted. 'I grew up knowing it – perhaps people spoke of it in the village, but when you are small you don't question. You just accept.'

'But didn't your *real* mother ever tell you, or try to take you away?'

'No!' he exclaimed. 'That's just it, Beth. She never did – she had given me to her sister, out of love, out of sympathy when her husband died. She never tried to break up the relationship I had with her. It was out of love.' He tried to explain again, 'The love sisters feel.'

Beth, unlike Rakesh, had a sister. Susan. She thought of her now, living with her jobless, worthless husband in a trailer somewhere in Manitoba with a string of children. The thought of handing over her child to her was so bizarre that it made her snort. 'I know I couldn't give my baby to Susan for anything,' she declared, removing her hand from his temple and placing it on her belly.

'You don't know, you can't say – what may happen, what things one may do –'

'*Of course* I know,' she said, more loudly. 'Nothing, no one, could make me do that. Give my baby away?' Her voice became shrill and he turned on his side, closing his eyes to show her he did not wish to continue the conversation.

She understood that gesture but she persisted. 'But didn't they ever fight? Or disagree about the way you were brought

249

up? Didn't they have different ideas of how to do that? You know, I've told Susan –'

He sighed again. 'It was not like that. They understood each other. Ma looked after me – she cooked for me and fed me, made me sit down on a mat and sat in front of me and fed me with her own hands. And what a cook she is! Beth, you'll love –' he broke off, knowing he was going too far, growing foolish now. 'And Masi,' he recovered himself, 'she took me by the hand to school. In the evening, she lit the lamp and made me show her my books. She helped me with my lessons – and I think learned with me. She is a reader, Beth, like you,' he was able to say with greater confidence.

'But weren't they jealous of each other – of one for cooking for you and feeding you, and the other for sharing your lessons? Each was doing what the other didn't, after all.'

He caught her hand, on the coverlet, to stop her talking. 'It wasn't like that,' he said again, and wished she would be silent so he could remember for himself that brick-walled courtyard in the village, the pump gushing out the sweet water from the tube well, the sounds of cattle stirring in the sheaves of fodder in the sheds, the can of frothing milk the dairyman brought to the door, the low earthen stove over which his mother – his aunt – stirred a pan in the smoky dimness of dawn, making him tea. The pigeons in the rafters, cooing, a feather drifting down –

'Well, I suppose I'll be seeing them both, then – and I'll find out for myself,' Beth said, a bit grimly, and snapped off the light.

'Never heard of anything so daft,' pronounced her mother, pouring out a cup of coffee for Beth who sat at her kitchen table with her elbows on its plastic cover and her chin cupped in her hands. Doris was still in her housecoat and slippers, going about her morning in the sunlit kitchen. Beth had come early.

When Beth did not reply, Doris planted her hands on the table and stared into her brooding face. 'Well, isn't it?' she demanded. 'Whoever heard of such a thing? Rakesh having two mothers! Why ever didn't he tell us before?'

'He told me about them both of course,' Beth flared up, and began to stir her coffee. 'He talked of them as his mother and aunt. I knew they were both widows, lived together, that's all.'

Doris looked as if she had plenty more to say on the subject than that. She tightened the belt around her red-striped housecoat and sat down squarely across from Beth. 'Looks as if he never told you who his mother was though, or his father. The real ones, I mean. I call that peculiar, Beth, pec-u-liar!'

Beth stirred resentfully. 'I s'pose he hardly thinks of it that way – he was a baby when it happened. He says he grew up just accepting it. They *love* each other, he said.'

Doris scratched at her head with one hand, rattled the coffee cup in its saucer with the other. 'Two sisters loving each other – that much? That's what's so daft – who in her right mind would give away her baby to her sister just like that? I mean, would you hand yours over to Susan? And would Susan take it? I mean, as if it were a birthday present!'

'Oh, Mum!'

'Now you've spilt your coffee! Wait, I'll get a sponge. Don't get up. You're getting big, girl. You OK? You mustn't mind me.'

'I'm OK, Mum, but now I'm going to have *two* women visiting. Rakesh's mum would be one thing, but two of 'em together – I don't know.'

'That's what I say,' Doris added quickly. 'And all that

expense – why's he sending them tickets? I thought they had money: he keeps talking about that farm as if they were landlords –'

'Oh, that's where he grew up, Mum. They sold it long ago – that's what paid for his education at McGill, you know. That *costs*.'

'What – it cost them the whole farm? He's always talking about how big it was –'

'They sold it a bit at a time. They helped pay for our house, too, and then set up his practice.'

'Hmm,' said Doris, as she shook a cigarette out of a packet and put it in her mouth.

'Oh, Mum, I can't stand smoke now! It makes me nauseous – you know that –' Beth protested.

'Sorry, love,' Doris said, and laid down the matchbox she had picked up but with the cigarette still between her lips. 'I'm just worried about you – dealing with two Indian women – in your condition –'

'I guess they know about babies,' Beth said hopefully.

'But do they know about Canada?' Doris came back smartly, as one who had learned. 'And about the Canadian *winter*?'

They thought they did – from Rakesh's dutiful, although not very informative, letters over the years. After Rakesh had graduated from the local college, it was Asha who insisted he go abroad 'for further studies'. Anu would not have had the courage to suggest it, and had no money of her own to spend, but here was another instance of her sister's courage and boldness. Asha had seen all the bright young people of the village leave and told Anu, 'He' – meaning her late husband – 'wanted Rakesh to study abroad. "We will give him the best education," he had said, so I am only doing what he told me to.' She tucked her widow's white chunni behind her ears and lifted her chin, looking proud. When Anu raised the matter of expense, she waved her hand – so competent at raising the boy, at running the farm, and now at handling the accounts. 'We will sell some of the land. Where is the need for so much? Rakesh will never be a farmer,' she said. So Rakesh began to apply to foreign universities, and although his two mothers felt tightness in their chests at the prospect of his leaving them, they also swelled with pride to think he might do so, the first in the family to leave the country 'for further studies'. When he had completed his studies – the two women selling off bits and pieces of the land to pay for them till there was nothing left but the old farmhouse – he wrote to tell them he had been offered jobs by several firms. They wiped their eyes with the corners of their chunnis, weeping for joy at his success and the sorrowful knowledge that he would not come back. Instead, they received letters about his achievements: his salary, his promotion, and with it the apartment in the city, then his own office and practice, photographs accompanying each as proof.

Then, one day, the photograph that left them speechless: it showed him standing with his arm around a girl, a blonde girl, at an office party. She was smiling. She had fair hair cut short and wore a green hairband and a green dress. Rakesh was beaming. He had grown rather fat, his stomach bulging out of a striped shirt, above a leather belt with a big buckle. He was also rather bald. The girl looked small and slim and young beside him. Rakesh did not tell them how old she was, what family she came from, what schooling she had had, when was the wedding, should they come, and other such particulars of importance to them. Rakesh, when he wrote, managed to avoid almost all such particulars, mentioning only that the wedding would be small, merely an official matter of registration at the town hall, they need not trouble to come – as they had ventured to suggest.

They were hurt. They tried to hide it from their neighbours as they went around with boxes of tinsel-spread sweets as gifts to celebrate the far-off occasion. So when the letter arrived announcing Beth's punctual pregnancy and the impending birth, they did not again make the mistake of tactful enquiries: Anu's letter stated with unaccustomed boldness their intention to travel to Canada and see their grandchild for themselves. That was her term – 'our grandchild'.

Yet it was with the greatest trepidation that they set out on this adventure. Everyone in the village was encouraging and supportive. Many of them had flown to the US, to Canada, to England, to visit their children abroad. It had become almost commonplace for the families to travel to New Delhi, catch a plane and fly off to some distant continent, bearing bundles and boxes full of the favourite pickles, chutneys and sweets of their far-flung progeny. Stories abounded of these goodies being confiscated on arrival at the airports, taken away by indignant customs officers to be burnt: 'He asked me, "What is *this*? What is *this*?" He had never seen mango pickle before, can you believe?' 'He didn't know what is betel nut! "Beetle? You are bringing in an insect?" he asked!' – and of being stranded at airports by great blizzards or lightning strikes by airline staff – 'We were lucky we had taken our bedroll and could spread out on the floor and sleep' – and of course they vied with each other with reports of their sons' and daughters' palatial mansions, immense cars, stocked refrigerators, prodigies of shopping in the most extensive of department stores. They brought back with them electrical appliances, cosmetics, watches, these symbols of what was 'foreign'.

The two mothers had taken no part in this, saying, 'We

can get those here too,' and contenting themselves by passing around the latest photographs of Rakesh and his wife and their home in Toronto. Now that they too were to join this great adventure, they became nervous – even Asha did. Young, travelled daughters and granddaughters of old friends came around to reassure them: 'Auntie, it is not difficult at all! Just buy a ticket at the booth, put it in the slot, and step into the subway. It will take you where you like,' or 'Over there you won't need kerosene or coal for the stove, Auntie. You have only to switch on the stove, it will light by itself,' or 'You won't need to wash your clothes, Auntie. They have machines, you put everything in, with soap, it washes by itself.' The two women wondered if these self-confident youngsters were pulling their legs: they were not reassured. Every piece of information, meant to help, threw them into greater agitation. They were convinced they would be swallowed up by the subway if they went out, or electrocuted at home if they stayed in. By the time the day of their departure came around, they were feverish with anxiety and sleeplessness. Anu would gladly have abandoned the plan – but Asha reminded her that Rakesh had sent them tickets, his first present to them after leaving home, how could they refuse?

It was ten years since Rakesh had seen his mothers, and he had forgotten how thinly they tended to dress, how unequipped they might be. Beth's first impression of them as they came out of the immigration control area, wheeling a trolley between them with their luggage precariously balanced on it, was of their wisps of widows' white clothing – muslin, clearly – and slippers flapping at their feet. Rakesh was embarrassed by their skimpy apparel, Beth unexpectedly moved. She had always thought of them as having so much; now her reaction was: they have so little!

She took them to the stores at once to fit them out with overcoats, gloves, mufflers – and woollen socks. They drew the line at shoes: they had never worn shoes, could not fit their feet into them, insisting on wearing their sandals with thick socks instead. She brought them back barely able to totter out of the car and up the drive, weighed down as they were by great duffle coats that kept their arms lifted from their sides, with their hands fitted into huge gloves, and with their heads almost invisible under the wrappings of woollen mufflers. Under it all, their white cotton kameezes hung out like rags of their past, sadly.

When Doris came around to visit them, she brought along all the spare blankets she had in her apartment, presciently. 'Thought you'd be cold,' she told them. 'I went through the war in England, and I know what that's like, I can tell you. And it isn't half cold yet. Wait till it starts to snow.' They smiled eagerly, in polite anticipation.

While Beth and Doris bustled about, 'settling them in', Rakesh stood around, unexpectedly awkward and ill at ease. After the first ecstatic embrace and the deep breath of their lingering odour of the barnyard and woodsmoke and the old soft muslin of their clothing, their sparse hair, he felt himself in their way and didn't know quite what to do with himself or with them. It was Beth who made them tea and tested their English while Rakesh sat with his feet apart, cracking his knuckles and smiling somewhat vacantly.

At the table, it was different: his mothers unpacked all the foods they had brought along, tied up in small bundles or packed in small boxes, and coaxed him to eat, laughing as they remembered how he had pestered them for these as a child. To them, he was still that: a child, and now he ate, and a glistening look of remembrance covered his face like a film of oil on his fingers, but he also glanced sideways at

Beth, guiltily, afraid of betraying any disloyalty to her. She wrinkled her nose slightly, put her hand on her belly and excused herself from eating on account of her pregnancy. They nodded sympathetically and promised to make special preparations for her.

On weekends, Beth insisted he take them out and show them the sights, and they dutifully allowed themselves to be led into his car, and then around museums, up radio towers and into department stores – but they tended to become car-sick on these excursions, foot-weary in museums and confused in stores. They clearly preferred to stay in. That was painful, and the only way out of the boredom was to bring home videos and put them on. Then everyone could put their heads back and sleep, or pretend to sleep.

On weekdays, in desperation, Beth too took to switching on the television set, tuned to programmes she surmised were blandly innocent, and imagined they would sit together on the sofa and find amusement in the nature, travel and cooking programmes. Unfortunately these had a way of changing when her back was turned and she would return to find them in a state of shock from watching a torrid sex scene or violent battle taking place before their affronted and disbelieving eyes. They sat side by side with their feet dangling and their eyes screwed up, munching on their dentures with fear at the popping of guns, the exploding of bombs and grunting of naked bodies. Their relief when she suggested a break for tea was palpable. Once in the kitchen, the kettle whistling shrilly, cups standing ready with the threads of tea bags dangling out of them, they seemed reluctant to leave the sanctuary. The kitchen was their great joy, once they had got used to the shiny enamel and chrome and up-to-date gadgetry. They became expert at punching the buttons of the microwave although they never learned what items could and what could not be placed in it. To Rakesh's surprise it was Anu who seemed to comprehend the rules better, she who peered at any scrap of writing, trying to decipher some meaning. Together the two would open the refrigerator twenty times in one morning, never able to resist looking in at its crowded, illuminated shelves; that reassurance of food seemed to satisfy them on some deep level – their eyes gleamed and they closed the door on it gently, with a dreamy expression.

Still, the resources of the kitchen were not limitless. Beth found they had soon run through them, and the hours dragged for her, in the company of the two mothers. There were just so many times she could ask Doris to come over and relieve her, and just so many times she could invent errands that would allow them all to escape from the house so crowded with their hopes, expectations, confusion and disappointments. She knew Rakesh disappointed them. She watched them trying to re-create what he had always described to her as his most warmly close and intimate relationship, and invariably failing. The only way they knew to do this was to cook him the foods of his childhood – as best they could reproduce these in this strange land or retail the gossip of the village, not realizing he had forgotten the people they spoke of, had not the slightest interest in who had married whom, or sold land or bought cattle. He would give embarrassed laughs, glance at Beth in appeal, and find reasons to stay late at work. She was exasperated by his failure but also secretly relieved to see how completely he had transformed himself into a husband, a Canadian, and, guiltily, she too dragged out her increasingly frequent escapes – spending the afternoon at her mother's house, describing to a fascinated Doris the village ways of these foreign mothers, or meeting girlfriends for coffee, going to the library to read child-rearing manuals – then returning in a rush of concern for the two imprisoned women at home.

She had spent one afternoon at the library, deep in an old stuffed chair in an undisturbed corner she knew, reading – something she found she could not do at home where the two mothers would watch her as she read, intently, as if waiting to see where it would take her and when she would be done – when she became aware of the light fading, darkness filling the tall window under which she sat. When she looked up, she was startled to see flakes of snow drifting through the dark, minute as tiny bees flying in excited hordes. They flew faster and faster as she watched, and in no time they would grow larger, she knew. She closed the magazine hastily, replaced it on the rack, put on her beret and gloves, picked up her bag and went out to the car outside. She opened the door and got in clumsily; she was so large now it was difficult to fit behind the steering wheel.

The streets were very full, everyone hurrying home before the snowfall became heavier. Her windscreen wiper going furiously, Beth drove home carefully. The first snowfall generally had its element of surprise; something childish in her responded with excitement. But this time she could only think of how surprised the two mothers would be, how much more intense their confinement.

When she let herself into the house with her key, she could look straight down the hall to the kitchen, and there she saw them standing, at the window, looking out to see the snow collect on the twigs and branches of the bare cherry tree and the tiles of the garden shed and the top of the wooden fence outside. Their white cotton saris were wrapped about them like shawls, their two heads leaned against each other as they peered out, speechlessly.

They did not hear her, they were so absorbed in the falling of the snow and the whitening of the stark scene on the other side of the glass pane. She shut the door silently, slipped into her bedroom and fetched the camera from where it lay on the closet shelf. Then she came out into the hall again and, standing there, took a photograph.

Later, when it was developed – together with the first pictures of the baby – she showed the mothers the print, and they put their hands to their mouths in astonishment. 'Why didn't you tell us?' they said. 'We didn't know – our backs were turned.' Beth wanted to tell them it didn't matter, it was their postures that expressed everything, but then they would have wanted to know what 'everything' was, and she found she did not want to explain, she did not want words to break the silent completeness of that small, still scene. It was as complete, and as fragile, after all, as a snow crystal.

The birth of the baby broke through it, of course. The sisters revived as if he were a reincarnation of Rakesh. They wanted to hold him, flat on the palms of their hands, or sit cross-legged on the sofa and rock him by pumping one knee up and down, and could not at all understand why Beth insisted they place him in his cot in a darkened bedroom instead. 'He has to learn to go to sleep by himself,' she told them when he cried and cried in protest and she refused to give them permission to snatch him up to their flat bosoms and console him.

They could not understand the rituals of baby care that Beth imposed – the regular feeding and sleeping times, the boiling and sterilizing of bottles and teats, the cans of formula and the use of disposable diapers. The first euphoria and excitement soon led to little nervous dissensions and explosions, then to dejection. Beth was too absorbed in her child to care.

The winter proved too hard, too long for the visitors. They began to fall ill, to grow listless, to show signs of depression and restlessness. Rakesh either did not notice or pretended not to, so that when Beth spoke of it one night in their bedroom, he asked if she were not 'over-reacting', one of his favourite terms. 'Ask them, just ask them,' she retorted. 'How can I?' he replied. 'Can I say to them "D'you want to go home?" They'll think I want them to.' She flung her arms over her head in exasperation. 'Why can't you just talk to each other?' she asked.

She was restless too, eager to bring to an end a visit that had gone on too long. The two little old women were in her way, underfoot, as she hurried between cot and kitchen. She tried to throw them sympathetic smiles but knew they were more like grimaces. She often thought about the inexplicable relationship of these two women, how Masi, small, mousy Masi, had borne Rakesh and then given him over to Ma, her sister. What could have made her do that? How could she have? Thinking of her own baby, the way he filled her arms and fitted against her breast, Beth could not help but direct a piercing, perplexed stare at them. She knew she would not give up her baby for anything, anyone, certainly not to her sister Susan who was hardly capable of bringing up her own, and yet these two had lived their lives ruled by that one impulse, totally unnatural to her. They looked back at her, questioningly, sensing her hostility.

And eventually they asked Rakesh — very hesitantly, delicately, but clearly after having discussed the matter between themselves and having come to a joint decision. They wanted to go home. The baby had arrived safely, and Beth was on her feet again, very much so. And it was too much for her, they said, a strain. No, no, she had not said a thing, of course not, nothing like that, and nor had he, even inadvertently. They were happy – they had been happy – but now – and they coughed and coughed, in embarrassment as much as on account of the cold. And out of pity he cut short their fumbling explanations, and agreed to book their seats on a flight home. Yes, he and Beth would come and visit them, with the baby, as soon as he was old enough to travel.

This was the right thing to say. Their creased faces lifted up to him in gratitude. He might have spilt some water on wilting plants: they revived; they smiled; they began to shop for presents for everyone at home. They began to think of those at home, laugh in anticipation of seeing home again.

At the farewell in the airport – he took them there while Beth stayed at home with the baby, who had a cold – they cast their tender, grateful looks upon him again, then turned to wheel their trolley with its boxes and trunks away, full of gifts for family and neighbours. He watched as their shoulders, swathed in their white chunnis, and their bent white heads, turned away from him and disappeared. He lifted a fist to his eyes in an automatic gesture, then sighed with relief and headed for his car waiting in the grey snow.

At home Beth had put the baby to sleep in his cot. She had cooked dinner, and on hearing Rakesh enter, she lit candles on the table, as though it were a celebration. He looked at her questioningly but she only smiled. She had cooked his favourite pasta. He sat at the table and lifted his fork, trying to eat. Why, what was she celebrating? He found a small, annoying knot of resentment fastened onto the fork at her evident pleasure at being alone with him and her baby again. He kept the fork suspended to look at her, to demand if this were so, and then saw, over her shoulder, the refrigerator with its array of the photographs and memos she liked to tape to its white enamel surface. What caught his eye was the photograph she had newly taped to it – with the view of the white window, and the two widows in white, and the whirling snow.

He put down his forkful of pasta. 'Rakesh? Rakesh?' Beth asked a few times, then turned to look herself. Together they stared at the winterscape.

'Why?' he asked.

Beth shrugged. 'Let it be,' she said.

LOUISE ERDRICH

THE LEAP

MY MOTHER IS the surviving half of a blindfold trapeze act, not a fact I think about much even now that she is sightless, the result of encroaching and stubborn cataracts. She walks slowly through our house here in New Hampshire, lightly touching her way along walls and running her hands over shelves, books, the drift of a grown child's belongings and castoffs. She has never upset an object or so much as brushed a magazine onto the floor. She has never lost her balance or bumped into a closet door left carelessly open.

The catlike precision of her movements in old age might be the result of her early training, but she shows so little of the drama or flair one might expect from a performer that I tend to forget the Flying Avalons. She has kept no sequined costume, no photographs, no fliers or posters from that part of her youth. I would, in fact, tend to think that all memory of double somersaults and heart-stopping catches has left her arms and legs, were it not for the fact that sometimes, as I sit sewing in the room of the rebuilt house that I slept in as a child, I hear the crackle, catch a whiff of smoke from the stove downstairs. Suddenly the room goes dark, the stitches burn beneath my fingers, and I am sewing with a needle of hot silver, a thread of fire.

I owe her my existence three times. The first was when she saved herself. In the town square a replica tent pole, cracked and splintered, now stands, cast in concrete. It commemorates the disaster that put the town on the front page of the

Boston and New York tabloids. It is from those old newspapers, now historical records, that I get my information, not from Anna of the Flying Avalons, nor from any of her relatives, now dead, or certainly from the other half of her particular act, Harold Avalon, her first husband. In one news account, it says, 'The day was mildly overcast but nothing in the air or temperature gave any hint of the sudden force with which the deadly gale would strike.'

I have lived in the West, where you can see the weather coming for miles, and it is true that in town we are at something of a disadvantage. When extremes of temperatures collide, a hot and cold front, winds generate instantaneously behind a hill and crash upon you without warning. That, I think, was the likely situation on that day in June. People probably commented on the pleasant air, grateful that no hot sun beat upon the striped tent that stretched over the entire center green. They bought their tickets and surrendered them in anticipation. They sat. They ate caramelized popcorn and roasted peanuts. There was time, before the storm, for three acts. The White Arabians of Ali-Khazar rose on their hind legs and waltzed. The Mysterious Bernie folded himself into a painted cracker tin, and the Lady of the Mists made herself appear and disappear in surprising places. As the clouds gathered outside, unnoticed, the ringmaster cracked his whip, shouted his introduction, and pointed to the ceiling of the tent, where the Flying Avalons were perched.

They loved to drop gracefully from nowhere, like two sparkling birds, and blow kisses as they doffed their glittering, plumed helmets and high-collared capes. They laughed and flirted openly as they beat their way up again on the trapeze bars. In the final vignette of their act, they actually would kiss in midair, pausing, almost hovering as they swooped past each other. On the ground, between bows,

Harry Avalon would skip lightly to the front rows and point out the smear of Anna's lipstick, just off the edge of his mouth. They made a romantic pair all right, especially in the blindfold sequence.

That afternoon, as the anticipation increased, as Mr and Mrs Avalon tied sparkling strips of cloth onto each other's faces and as they puckered their lips in mock kisses, lips destined 'never again to meet' as one long breathless article put it, the wind rose, only miles off, wrapped itself into a cone, and howled. There came a rumble of electrical energy, drowned out by the sudden roll of drums. One detail, not mentioned by the press, perhaps unknown – Anna was pregnant at the time, seven months and hardly showing, her stomach muscles were that strong. It seems incredible that she would work high above the ground, when any fall could be so dangerous, but the explanation – I know from watching her go blind – is that my mother lives comfortably in extreme elements. She is one with the constant dark now, just as the air was her home, familiar to her, safe, before the storm that afternoon.

From opposite ends of the tent they waved, blind and smiling, to the crowd below. The ringmaster removed his hat and called for silence, so that the two above could concentrate. They rubbed their hands in chalky powder, then Harry launched himself and swung, once, twice, in huge calibrated beats across space. He hung from his knees and on the third swing stretched wide his arms, held his hands out to receive his pregnant wife as she dove from her shining bar.

It was while the two were in midair, their hands about to meet, that lightning struck the main pole and sizzled down the guy wires, filling the air with a blue radiance that Harry Avalon must certainly have seen even through the cloth of his blindfold as the tent buckled and the edifice toppled

269

him forward. The swing continued and did not return in its sweep, and Harry went down, down into the crowd with his last thought, perhaps, just a prickle of surprise at his empty hands.

My mother once told me that I'd be amazed at how many things a person can do in the act of falling. Perhaps at the time she was teaching me to dive off a board at the town pool, for I associate the idea with midair somersaults. But I also think she meant that even in that awful doomed second one could think. She certainly did. When her hands did not meet her husband's, my mother tore her blindfold away. As he swept past her on the wrong side she could have grasped his ankle, or the toe-end of his tights, and gone down clutching him. Instead, she changed direction. Her body twisted toward a heavy wire and she managed to hang on to the braided metal, still hot from the lightning strike. Her palms were burned so terribly that once healed they bore no lines, only the blank scar tissue of a quieter future. She was lowered, gently, to the sawdust ring just underneath the dome of the canvas roof, which did not entirely settle but was held up on one end and jabbed through, torn, and even on fire in places from the giant spark, though rain and men's jackets soon put that out.

Three people died, but except for her hands my mother was not seriously harmed until an overeager rescuer broke her arm in extricating her and also, in the process, collapsed a portion of the tent bearing a huge buckle that knocked her unconscious. She was taken to the local hospital, and there she must have hemorrhaged, for they kept her confined to her bed a month and a half before her baby was born without life.

Harry Avalon had always wanted to be buried in the circus cemetery next to the original Avalon, his uncle, and so she sent him back with his brothers. The child, however, is buried around the corner, beyond this house and just down the highway. Sometimes I used to walk there, just to sit. She was a girl, but I never thought of her as a sister, or even as a separate person, really. I suppose you could call it the egocentrism of a child, of all young children, but I always considered her a less finished version of myself.

When the snow falls, throwing shadows among the stones, I could pick hers out easily from the road, for hers is bigger than the others and is the shape of an actual lamb at rest, its legs curled beneath. The carved lamb looms larger in my thoughts as the years pass, though it is probably just my eyes, the vision dimming the way it has for my mother, as what is close to me blurs and distances sharpen. In odd moments, I think it is the edge drawing near, the edge of everything, the horizon we do not really speak of in the eastern woods. And it also seems to me, although this is probably an idle fantasy, that somewhere the statue is growing more sharply etched as if, instead of weathering itself into a porous mass, it is hardening on the hillside with each snowfall, perfecting itself.

It was during her confinement in the hospital that my mother met my father. He was called in to look at the set of her arm, which was complicated. He stayed, sitting at her bedside, for he was something of an armchair traveler, and had spent his war quietly, at an Air Force training grounds, where he became a specialist in arms and legs broken during parachute training exercises. Anna Avalon had been to many of the places he longed to visit – Venice, Rome, Mexico, all through France and Spain. She had no family of her own, and had been taken in by the Avalons, trained to perform from a very young age. They toured Europe before the war, then based themselves in New York. She was illiterate.

It was in the hospital that she learned to read and write,

as a way of overcoming the boredom and depression of those months, and it was my father who insisted on teaching her. In return for stories of her adventures, he graded her first exercises. He brought her first book to her, and over her bold letters, which the pale guides of the penmanship pads could not contain, they fell in love.

I wonder whether my father calculated the exchange he offered: one form of flight for another. For after that, and for as long as I can remember, my mother was never without a book. Until now, that is, and it remains the greatest difficulty of her blindness. Since my father's recent death, there is no one to read to her, which is why I returned, in fact, from my failed life where the land is flat. I came home to read to my mother, to read out loud, to read long into the dark if I must, to read all night.

Once my father and mother married, they moved onto the old farm he had inherited but didn't care much for. Though he'd been thinking of moving to a larger city, he settled down and broadened his practice in this valley. It still seems odd to me that they chose to stay in the town where the disaster occurred, and which my father in the first place had found so constricting. It was my mother who insisted upon it, after her child did not survive. And then, too, she loved the sagging farmhouse with its scrap of what was left of the vast acreage of woods and hidden hay fields that stretched to the game park.

I owe my existence, the second time then, to the two of them and the hospital that brought them together. That is the debt we take for granted since none of us asks for life. It is only once we have it that we hang on so dearly.

I was seven the year that the house caught fire, probably from standing ash. It can rekindle, and my father, forgetful around the house and perpetually exhausted from night hours on call, often emptied what he thought were ashes from cold stoves into wooden or cardboard containers. The fire could have started from a flaming box. Or perhaps a buildup of creosote inside the chimney was the culprit. It started right around the stove, and the heart of the house was gutted. The babysitter, fallen asleep in my father's den on the first floor, woke to find the stairway to my upstairs room cut off by flames. She used the phone, then ran outside to stand beneath my window.

When my parents arrived, the town volunteers had drawn water from the fire pond and were spraying the outside of the house, preparing to go inside after me, not knowing at the time that there was only one staircase and that it was lost. On the other side of the house, the superannuated extension ladder broke in half. Perhaps the clatter of it falling against the walls woke me, for I'd been asleep up to that point.

As soon as I awakened, I smelled the smoke. I did things by the letter then, was good at memorizing instructions, and so I did exactly what was taught in the second-grade home fire drill. I got up. I touched the back of my door without opening it. Finding it hot, I left it closed and stuffed my rolled-up rug against the crack. I did not hide beneath my bed or crawl into my closet. I put on my flannel robe, and then I sat down to wait.

Outside, my mother stood below my dark window and saw clearly that there was no rescue. Flames had pierced one side wall and the glare of the fire lighted the mammoth limbs and trunk of the vigorous old maple that had probably been planted the year the house was built. No leaf touched the wall, and just one thin limb scraped the roof. From below, it looked as though even a squirrel would have had trouble jumping from the tree onto the house, for the breadth of that small branch was no bigger than my mother's wrist.

Standing there, my mother asked my father to unzip her dress.

When he treated her too gently, as if she'd lost her mind, she made him understand. He couldn't make his hands work, so she finally tore it off and stood there in her pearls and stockings. She directed one of the men to lean the broken half of the extension ladder up against the trunk of the tree. In surprise, he complied. She ascended. She vanished. Then she could be seen easily among the leafless branches of late November as she made her way up and up and, along her stomach, inched the length of a bough that curved above the branch that brushed the roof.

Once there, swaying, she stood and balanced. There were plenty of people in the crowd and many who still remember, or think they do, my mother's leap through the ice-dark air toward that thinnest extension, and how she broke the branch falling so that it cracked in her hands, cracked louder than the flames as she vaulted with it toward the edge of the roof, and how it hurtled down end over end without her, and their eyes went up, again, to see where she had flown.

I didn't see her leap through air, only heard the sudden thump and looked out my window. She was hanging by her heels from the new gutter we had put in that year, and she was smiling. I was not surprised to see her, she was so matter-of-fact. She tapped on the window. I remember how she did it, too; it was the friendliest tap, a bit tentative, as if she were afraid she had arrived too early at a friend's house. Then she gestured at the latch, and when I opened the window she told me to raise it wider, and prop it up with the stick, so it wouldn't crush her fingers. She swung down, caught the ledge, and crawled through the opening. Once she was in my room, I realized she had on only underclothing, a tight bra of the heavy circular-stitched cotton women used to wear and step-in, lace-trimmed drawers. I remember feeling light-headed, of course, terribly relieved and then embarrassed for her, to be seen by the crowd undressed.

I was still embarrassed as we flew out the window, toward earth, me in her lap, her toes pointed as we skimmed toward the painted target of the firefighter's tarp held below.

I know that she's right. I knew it even then. As you fall there is time to think. Curled as I was, against her stomach, I was not startled by the cries of the crowd or the looming faces. The wind roared and beat its hot breath at our back, the flames whistled. I slowly wondered what would happen if we missed the circle or bounced out of it. Then I forgot fear. I wrapped my hands around my mother's hands. I felt the brush of her lips, and I heard the beat of her heart in my ears, loud as thunder, long as the roll of drums.

HORTENSE CALISHER

THE MIDDLE
DRAWER

THE DRAWER WAS always kept locked. In a household where the tangled rubbish of existence had collected on surfaces like a scurf, which was forever being cleared away by her mother and the maid, then by her mother, and, finally, hardly at all, it had been a permanent cell – rather like, Hester thought wryly, the gene that is carried over from one generation to the other. Now, holding the small, square, indelibly known key in her hand, she shrank before it, reluctant to perform the blasphemy that the living must inevitably perpetrate on the possessions of the dead. There were no revelations to be expected when she opened the drawer, only the painful reiteration of her mother's personality and the power it had held over her own, which would rise – an emanation, a mist, that she herself had long since shredded away, parted, and escaped.

She repeated to herself, like an incantation, 'I am married. I have a child of my own, a home of my own five hundred miles away. I have not even lived in this house – my parents' house – for over seven years.' Stepping back, she sat on the bed where her mother had died the week before, slowly, from cancer, where Hester had held the large, long-fingered, competent hand for a whole night, watching the asphyxiating action of the fluid mounting in the lungs until it had extinguished the breath. She sat facing the drawer.

It had taken her all her own lifetime to get to know its full contents, starting from the first glimpses, when she was just able to lean her chin on the side and have her hand pushed away from the packets and japanned boxes, to the last weeks, when she had made a careful show of not noticing while she got out the necessary bankbooks and safe-deposit keys. Many times during her childhood, when she had lain blandly ill herself, elevated to the honor of the parental bed while she suffered from the 'autointoxication' that must have been 1918's euphemism for plain piggishness, the drawer had been opened. Then she had been allowed to play with the two pairs of pearled opera glasses or the long string of graduated white china beads, each with its oval sides flushed like cheeks. Over these she had sometimes spent the whole afternoon, pencilling two eyes and a pursed mouth on each bead, until she had achieved an incredible string of minute, doll-like heads that made even her mother laugh.

Once while Hester was in college, the drawer had been opened for the replacement of her grandmother's great sunburst pin, which she had never before seen and which had been in pawn, and doggedly reclaimed over a long period by her mother. And for Hester's wedding her mother had taken out the delicate diamond chain – the 'lavaliere' of the Gibson-girl era – that had been her father's wedding gift to her mother, and the ugly, expensive bar pin that had been his gift to his wife on the birth of her son. Hester had never before seen either of them, for the fashion of wearing diamonds indiscriminately had never been her mother's, who was contemptuous of other women's display, although she might spend minutes in front of the mirror debating a choice between two relatively gimcrack pieces of costume jewelry. Hester had never known why this was until recently, when the separation of the last few years had relaxed the tension between her mother and herself – not enough to prevent explosions when they met but enough for her to see obscurely the long motivations of her mother's life. In the European sense, family jewelry was Property, and with all her faultless English and New World poise, her mother had never exorcised her European core.

In the back of the middle drawer, there was a small square of brown-toned photograph that had never escaped into the large, ramshackle portfolio of family pictures kept in the drawer of the old break-front bookcase, open to any hand. Seated on a bench, Hedwig Licht, aged two, brows knitted under ragged hair, stared mournfully into the camera with the huge, heavy-lidded eyes that had continued to brood in her face as a woman, the eyes that she had transmitted to Hester, along with the high cheekbones that she had deplored. Fat, wrinkled stockings were bowed into arcs that almost met at the high-stretched boots, which did not touch the floor; to hold up the stockings, strips of calico matching the dumpy little dress were bound around the knees.

Long ago, Hester, in her teens, staring tenaciously into the drawer under her mother's impatient glance, had found the little square and exclaimed over it, and her mother, snatching it away from her, had muttered, 'If that isn't Dutchy!' But she had looked at it long and ruefully before she had pushed it back into a corner. Hester had added the picture to the legend of her mother's childhood built up from the bitter little anecdotes that her mother had let drop casually over the years.

She saw the small Hedwig, as clearly as if it had been herself, haunting the stiff rooms of the house in the townlet of Oberelsbach, motherless since birth and almost immediately stepmothered by a woman who had been unloving, if not unkind, and had soon borne the stern, *Haustyrann* father a son. The small figure she saw had no connection with the all-powerful figure of her mother but, rather, seemed akin to the legion of lonely children who were a constant motif in the literature that had been her own drug – the Sara Crewes and Little Dorrits, all those children who inhabited the familiar terror-struck dark that crouched under the lash of the adult. She saw Hedwig receiving from her dead mother's mother – the Grandmother Rosenberg, warm and loving but, alas, too far away to be of help – the beautiful, satin-incrusted bisque doll, and she saw the bad stepmother taking it away from Hedwig and putting it in the drawing-room, because 'it is too beautiful for a child to play with.' She saw all this as if it had happened to her and she had never forgotten.

Years later, when this woman, Hester's step-grandmother, had come to the United States in the long train of refugees from Hitler, her mother had urged the grown Hester to visit her, and she had refused, knowing her own childishness but feeling the resentment rise in her as if she were six, saying, 'I won't go. She wouldn't let you have your doll.' Her mother had smiled at her sadly and had shrugged her shoulders resignedly. 'You wouldn't say that if you could see her. She's an old woman. She has no teeth.' Looking at her mother, Hester had wondered what her feelings were after forty years, but her mother, private as always in her emotions, had given no sign.

There had been no sign for Hester – never an open demonstration of love or an appeal – until the telephone call of a few months before, when she had heard her mother say quietly, over the distance, 'I think you'd better come,' and she had turned away from the phone saying bitterly, almost in awe, 'If she *asks me* to come, she must be dying!'

Turning the key over in her hand, Hester looked back at the composite figure of her mother – that far-off figure of the legendary child, the nearer object of her own depend-ence, love, and hate – looked at it from behind the safe, dry wall of her own 'American' education. We are told, she thought, that people who do not experience love in their earliest years cannot open up; they cannot give it to others; but by the time we have learned this from books or dredged it out of reminiscence, they have long since left upon us their chill, irremediable stain.

If Hester searched in her memory for moments of animal maternal warmth, like those she self-consciously gave her own child (as if her own childhood prodded her from behind), she thought always of the blue-shot twilight of one New York evening, the winter she was eight, when she and her mother were returning from a shopping expedition, gay and united in the shared guilt of being late for supper. In her mind, now, their arrested figures stood like two silhouettes caught in the spotlight of time. They had paused under the brightly agitated bulbs of a movie-theatre marquee, behind them the broad, rose-red sign of a Happiness candy store. Her mother, suddenly leaning down to her, had encircled her with her arm and nuzzled her, saying almost anxiously, 'We do have fun together, don't we?' Hester had stared back stolidly, almost suspiciously, into the looming, pleading eyes, but she had rested against the encircling arm, and warmth had trickled through her as from a closed wound reopening.

After this, her mother's part in the years that followed seemed blurred with the recriminations from which Hester had retreated ever farther, always seeking the remote corners of the household – the sofa-fortressed alcoves, the store closet, the servants' bathroom – always bearing her amulet, a book. It seemed to her now, wincing, that the barrier of her mother's dissatisfaction with her had risen imperceptibly, like a coral cliff built inexorably from the slow accretion of carelessly ejaculated criticisms that had grown into solid being in the heavy fullness of time. Meanwhile, her father's uncritical affection, his open caresses, had been steadiness under her feet after the shifting waters of her mother's personality, but he had been away from home on business for long periods, and when at home he, too, was increasingly a target for her mother's deep-burning rage against life. Adored member of a large family that was almost tribal in its affections and unity, he could not cope with this smoldering force and never tried to understand it, but the shield of his adulthood gave him a protection that Hester did not have. He stood on equal ground.

Hester's parents had met at Saratoga, at the races. So dissimilar were their backgrounds that it was improbable that they would ever have met elsewhere than in the somewhat easy social flux of a spa, although their brownstone homes in New York were not many blocks apart, his in the gentility of upper Madison Avenue, hers in the solid, Germanic comfort of Yorkville. By this time, Hedwig had been in America ten years.

All Hester knew of her mother's coming to America was that she had arrived when she was sixteen. Now that she knew how old her mother had been at death, knew the birth date so zealously guarded during a lifetime of evasion and so quickly exposed by the noncommittal nakedness of funeral routine, she realized that her mother must have arrived in 1900. She had come to the home of an aunt, a sister of her own dead mother. What family drama had preceded her coming, whose decision it had been, Hester did not know. Her mother's one reply to a direct question had been a shrugging 'There was nothing for me there.'

Hester had a vivid picture of her mother's arrival and first years in New York, although this was drawn from only two clues. Her great-aunt, remarking once on Hester's looks in the dispassionate way of near relations, had nodded over

Hester's head to her mother. 'She is dark, like the father, no? Not like you were.' And Hester, with a naïve glance of surprise at her mother's sedate pompadour, had eagerly interposed, 'What was she like, Tante?'

'*Ach*, when she came off the boat, *war sie hübsch!*' Tante had said, lapsing into German with unusual warmth. 'Such a color! Pink and cream!'

'Yes, a real Bavarian *Mädchen*,' said her mother with a trace of contempt. 'Too pink for the fashion here. I guess they thought it wasn't real.'

Another time, her mother had said, in one of her rare bursts of anecdote, 'When I came, I brought enough linen and underclothing to supply two brides. At the convent school where I was sent, the nuns didn't teach you much besides embroidery, so I had plenty to bring, plenty. They were nice, though. Good, simple women. Kind. I remember I brought four dozen handkerchiefs, beautiful heavy linen that you don't get in America. But they were large, bigger than the size of a man's handkerchief over here, and the first time I unfolded one, everybody laughed, so I threw them away.' She had sighed, perhaps for the linen. 'And underdrawers! Long red flannel, and I had spent months embroidering them with yards of white eyelet work on the ruffles. I remember Tante's maid came in from the back yard quite angry and refused to hang them on the line any more. She said the other maids, from the houses around, teased her for belonging to a family who would wear things like that.'

Until Hester was in her teens, her mother had always employed young German or Czech girls fresh from 'the other side' – Teenies and Josies of long braided hair, broad cotton ankles and queer, blunt shoes, who had clacked deferentially to her mother in German and had gone off to marry their waiter's and baker's apprentices at just about the time they learned to wear silk stockings and 'just as soon as you've taught them how to serve a dinner,' returning regularly to show off their square, acrid babies. 'Greenhorns!' her mother had always called them, a veil of something indefinable about her lips. But in the middle drawer there was a long rope of blond hair, sacrificed, like the handkerchiefs, but not wholly discarded.

There was no passport in the drawer. Perhaps it had been destroyed during the years of the first World War, when her mother, long since a citizen by virtue of her marriage, had felt the contemporary pressure to excise everything Teutonic. 'If that nosy Mrs Cahn asks you when I came over, just say I came over as a child,' she had said to Hester. And how easy it had been to nettle her by pretending that one could discern a trace of accent in her speech! Once, when the family had teased her by affecting to hear an echo of 'public' in her pronunciation of 'public,' Hester had come upon her, hours after, standing before a mirror, color and nose high, watching herself say, over and over again, 'Public! Public!'

Was it this, thought Hester, her straining toward perfection, that made her so intolerant of me, almost as if she were castigating in her child the imperfections that were her own? 'Big feet, big hands, like mine,' her mother had grumbled. 'Why? Why? When every woman in your father's family wears size one! But their nice, large ears – you must have *those*!' And dressing Hester for Sunday school she would withdraw a few feet to look at the finished product, saying slowly, with dreamy cruelty, 'I don't know why I let you wear those white gloves. They make your hands look clumsy, just like a policeman's.'

It was over books that the rift between Hester and her mother had become complete. To her mother, marrying into a family whose bookish traditions she had never ceased trying to undermine with the sneer of the practical, it was as if the stigmata of that tradition, appearing upon the girl, had forever made them alien to one another.

'Your eyes don't look like a girl's, they look like an old woman's! Reading! Forever reading!' she had stormed, chasing Hester from room to room, flushing her out of doors, and on one remote, terrible afternoon, whipping the book out of Hester's hand, she had leaned over her, glaring, and had torn the book in two.

Hester shivered now, remembering the cold sense of triumph that had welled up in her as she had faced her mother, rejoicing in the enormity of what her mother had done.

Her mother had faltered before her. 'Do you want to be a dreamer all your life?' she had muttered.

Hester had been unable to think of anything to say for a moment. Then she had stuttered, 'All you think of in life is money!', and had made her grand exit. But huddling miserably in her room afterward she had known even then that it was not as simple as that, that her mother, too, was whipped and driven by some ungovernable dream she could not express, which had left her, like the book, torn in two.

Was it this, perhaps, that had sent her across an ocean, that had impelled her to perfect her dress and manner, and to reject the humdrum suitors of her aunt's circle for a Virginia bachelor twenty-two years older than herself? Had she, perhaps, married him not only for his money and his seasoned male charm but also for his standards and traditions, against which her railings had been a confession of envy and defeat?

So Hester and her mother had continued to pit their implacable difference against each other in a struggle that was complicated out of all reason by their undeniable likeness – each pursuing in her own orbit the warmth that had been denied. Gauche and surly as Hester was in her mother's presence, away from it she had striven successfully for the very falsities of standard that she despised in her mother, and it was her misery that she was forever impelled to earn her mother's approval at the expense of her own. Always, she knew now, there had been the lurking, buried wish that someday she would find the final barb, the homing shaft, that would maim her mother once and for all, as she felt herself to have been maimed.

A few months before, the barb had been placed in her hand. In answer to the telephone call, she had come to visit the family a short time after her mother's sudden operation for cancer of the breast. She had found her father and brother in an anguish of helplessness, fear, and male distaste at the thought of the illness, and her mother a prima donna of fortitude, moving unbowed toward the unspoken idea of her death but with the signs on her face of a pitiful tension that went beyond the disease. She had taken to using separate utensils and to sleeping alone, although the medical opinion that cancer was not transferable by contact was well known to her. It was clear that she was suffering from a horror of what had been done to her and from a fear of the revulsion of others. It was clear to Hester, also, that her father and brother had such a revulsion and had not been wholly successful in concealing it.

One night she and her mother had been together in her mother's bedroom. Hester, in a shabby housegown, stretched out on the bed luxuriously, thinking of how there was always a certain equivocal ease, a letting down of pretense, an illusory return to the irresponsibility of childhood, in the house of one's birth. Her mother, back turned, had been standing unnecessarily long at the bureau, fumbling with the articles upon it. She turned slowly.

'They've been giving me X-ray twice a week,' she said, not looking at Hester, 'to stop any involvement of the glands.'

'Oh,' said Hester, carefully smoothing down a wrinkle on the bedspread. 'It's very wise to have that done.'

Suddenly, her mother had put out her hand in a gesture almost of appeal. Half in a whisper, she asked, 'Would you like to see it? No one has seen it since I left the hospital.'

'Yes,' Hester said, keeping her tone cool, even, full only of polite interest. 'I'd like very much to see it.' Frozen there on the bed, she had reverted to childhood in reality, remembering, as if they had all been crammed into one slot in time, the thousands of incidents when she had been the one to stand before her mother, vulnerable and bare, helplessly awaiting the cruel exactitude of her displeasure. 'I know how she feels as if I were standing there myself,' thought Hester. 'How well she taught me to know!'

Slowly her mother undid her housegown and bared her breast. She stood there for a long moment, on her face the looming, pleading look of twenty years before, the look it had once shown under the theatre marquee.

Hester half rose from the bed. There was a hurt in her own breast that she did not recognize. She spoke with difficulty.

'Why . . . it's a beautiful job, Mother,' she said, distilling the carefully natural tone of her voice. 'Neat as can be. I had no idea . . . I thought it would be ugly.' With a step toward her mother, she looked, as if casually, at the dreadful neatness of the cicatrix, at the twisted, foreshortened tendon of the upper arm.

'I can't raise my arm yet,' whispered her mother. 'They had to cut deep. . . . Your father won't look at it.'

In an eternity of slowness, Hester stretched out her hand. Trembling, she touched a tentative finger to her mother's chest, where the breast had been. Then, with rising sureness, with infinite delicacy, she drew her fingertips along the length of the scar in a light, affirmative caress, and they stood eye to eye for an immeasurable second, on equal ground at last.

In the cold, darkening room, Hester unclenched herself from remembrance. She was always vulnerable, Hester thought. As we all are. What she bequeathed me unwittingly, ironically, was fortitude – the fortitude of those who have had to live under the blow. But pity – that I found for myself.

She knew now that the tangents of her mother and herself would never have fully met, even if her mother had lived. Holding her mother's hand through the long night as she retreated over the border line of narcosis and coma into death, she had felt the giddy sense of conquering, the heady euphoria of being still alive, which comes to the watcher in the night. Nevertheless, she had known with sureness, even then, that she would go on all her life trying to 'show' her mother, in an unsatisfied effort to earn her approval – and unconditional love.

As a child, she had slapped at her mother once in a frenzy of rebellion, and her mother, in reproof, had told her the tale of the peasant girl who had struck her mother and had later fallen ill and died and been buried in the village cemetery. When the mourners came to tend the mound, they found that the corpse's offending hand had grown out of the grave. They cut it off and reburied it, but when they came again in the morning, the hand had grown again. So, too, thought Hester, even though I might learn – have learned in some ways – to escape my mother's hand, all my life I will have to push it down; all my life my mother's hand will grow again out of the unquiet grave of the past.

It was her own life that was in the middle drawer. She was the person she was not only because of her mother but because, fifty-eight years before, in the little town of

Oberelsbach, another woman, whose qualities she would never know, had died too soon. Death, she thought, absolves equally the bungler, the evildoer, the unloving, and the unloved – but never the living. In the end, the cicatrix that she had, in the smallest of ways, helped her mother to bear had eaten its way in and killed. The living carry, she thought, perhaps not one tangible wound but the burden of the innumerable small cicatrices imposed on us by our beginnings; we carry them with us always, and from these, from this agony, we are not absolved.

She turned the key and opened the drawer.

COLM TÓIBÍN

ONE MINUS ONE

THE MOON HANGS low over Texas. The moon is my mother. She is full tonight, and brighter than the brightest neon; there are folds of red in her vast amber. Maybe she is a harvest moon, a Comanche moon, I do not know. I have never seen a moon so low and so full of her own deep brightness. My mother is six years dead tonight, and Ireland is six hours away and you are asleep.

I am walking. No one else is walking. It is hard to cross Guadalupe; the cars come fast. In the Community Whole Food Store, where all are welcome, the girl at the checkout asks me if I would like to join the store's club. If I pay seventy dollars, my membership, she says, will never expire, and I will get a seven percent discount on all purchases.

Six years. Six hours. Seventy dollars. Seven percent. I tell her I am here for a few months only, and she smiles and says that I am welcome. I smile back. I can still smile. If I called you now, it would be half two in the morning; you could easily be awake.

If I called, I could go over everything that happened six years ago. Because that is what is on my mind tonight, as though no time had elapsed, as though the strength of the moonlight had by some fierce magic chosen tonight to carry me back to the last real thing that happened to me. On the phone to you across the Atlantic, I could go over the days surrounding my mother's funeral. I could go over all the details as though I were in danger of forgetting them. I could

295

remind you, for example, that you wore a white shirt at the funeral. It must have been warm enough not to wear a jacket. I remember that I could see you when I spoke about her from the altar, that you were over in the side aisle, on the left. I remember that you, or someone, said that you had parked your car almost in front of the cathedral because you had come late from Dublin and could not find parking anywhere else. I know that you moved your car before the hearse came after Mass to take my mother's coffin to the graveyard, with all of us walking behind. You came to the hotel once she was in the ground, and you stayed for a meal with me and Suzie, my sister. Jim, her husband, must have been near, and Cathal, my brother, but I don't remember what they did when the meal was over and the crowd had dispersed. I know that as the meal came to an end a friend of my mother's, who noticed everything, came over and looked at you and whispered to me that it was nice that my friend had come. She used the word 'friend' with a sweet, insinuating emphasis. I did not tell her that what she had noticed was no longer there, was part of the past. I simply said, yes, it was nice that you had come.

You know that you are the only person who shakes his head in exasperation when I insist on making jokes and small talk, when I refuse to be direct. No one else has ever minded this as you do. You are alone in wanting me always to say something that is true. I know now, as I walk toward the house I have rented here, that if I called and told you that the bitter past has come back to me tonight in these alien streets with a force that feels like violence, you would say that you are not surprised. You would wonder only why it has taken six years.

I was living in New York then, the city about to enter its last year of innocence. I had a new apartment there, just as

I had a new apartment everywhere I went. It was on Nine-tieth and Columbus. You never saw it. It was a mistake. I think it was a mistake. I didn't stay there long – six or seven months – but it was the longest I stayed anywhere in those years or the years that followed. The apartment needed to be furnished, and I spent two or three days taking pleasure in the sharp bite of buying things: two easy chairs that I later sent back to Ireland; a leather sofa from Bloomingdale's, which I eventually gave to one of my students; a big bed from 1-800-Mattress; a table and some chairs from a place down-town; a cheap desk from the thrift shop.

And all those days – a Friday, a Saturday, and a Sunday, at the beginning of September – as I was busy with delivery times, credit cards, and the whiz of taxis from store to store, my mother was dying and no one could find me. I had no cell phone, and the phone line in the apartment had not been connected. I used the pay phone on the corner if I needed to make calls. I gave the delivery companies a friend's phone number, in case they had to let me know when they would come with my furniture. I phoned my friend a few times a day, and she came shopping with me sometimes and she was fun and I enjoyed those days. The days when no one in Ireland could find me to tell me that my mother was dying.

Eventually, late on the Sunday night, I slipped into a Kinko's and went online and found that Suzie had left me message after message, starting three days before, marked 'Urgent' or 'Are you there' or 'Please reply' or 'Please acknow-ledge receipt' and then just 'Please!!!' I read one of them, and I replied to say that I would call as soon as I could find a phone, and then I read the rest of them one by one. My mother was in the hospital. She might have to have an opera-tion. Suzie wanted to talk to me. She was staying at my mother's house. There was nothing more in any of them, the urgency being not so much in their tone as in their frequency and the different titles she gave to each e-mail that she sent.

I woke her in the night in Ireland. I imagined her standing in the hall at the bottom of the stairs. I would love to say that Suzie told me my mother was asking for me, but she said nothing like that. She spoke instead about the medical details and how she herself had been told the news that our mother was in the hospital and how she had despaired of ever finding me. I told her that I would call again in the morning, and she said that she would know more then. My mother was not in pain now, she said, although she had been. I did not tell her that my classes would begin in three days, because I did not need to. That night, it sounded as though she wanted just to talk to me, to tell me. Nothing more.

But in the morning when I called I realized that she had put quick thought into it as soon as she heard my voice on the phone, that she had known I could not make arrangements to leave for Dublin late on a Sunday night, that there would be no flights until the next evening; she had decided to say nothing until the morning. She had wanted me to have an easy night's sleep. And I did, and in the morning when I phoned she said simply that there would come a moment very soon when the family would have to decide. She spoke about *the family* as though it were as distant as the urban district council or the government or the United Nations, but she knew and I knew that there were just the three of us. We were the family, and there is only one thing that a family is ever asked to decide in a hospital. I told her that I would come home; I would get the next flight. I would not be in my new apartment for some of the furniture deliverers, and I would not be at the university for my first classes. Instead, I would find a flight to Dublin, and I would see her as soon as I could. My friend phoned Aer Lingus and discovered that a few seats were kept free for eventualities like this. I could fly out that evening.

You know that I do not believe in God. I do not care much about the mysteries of the universe, unless they come to me in words, or in music maybe, or in a set of colors, and then I entertain them merely for their beauty and only briefly. I do not even believe in Ireland. But you know, too, that in these years of being away there are times when Ireland comes to me in a sudden guise, when I see a hint of something familiar that I want and need. I see someone coming toward me, with a soft way of smiling, or a stubborn uneasy face, or a way of moving warily through a public place, or a raw, almost resentful stare into the middle distance. In any case, I went to JFK that evening, and I saw them as soon as I got out of the taxi: a middle-aged couple pushing a trolley that had too much luggage on it, the man looking fearful and mild, as though he might be questioned by someone at any moment and not know how to defend himself, and the woman harassed and weary, her clothes too colorful, her heels too high, her mouth set in pure, blind determination, but her eyes humbly watchful, undefiant.

I could easily have spoken to them and told them why I was going home and they both would have stopped and asked me where I was from, and they would have nodded with understanding when I spoke. Even the young men in the queue to check in, going home for a quick respite – just looking at their tentative stance and standing in their company saying nothing, that brought ease with it. I could breathe for a while without worry, without having to think. I, too, could look like them, as though I owned nothing, or nothing much, and were ready to smile softly or keep my distance without any arrogance if someone said, 'Excuse me,' or if an official approached.

When I picked up my ticket and went to the check-in desk, I was told to go to the other desk, which looked after business class. It occurred to me, as I took my bag over, that it might be airline policy to comfort those who were going home for reasons such as mine with an upgrade, to cosset them through the night with quiet sympathy and an extra blanket or something. But when I got to the desk I knew why I had been sent there, and I wondered about God and Ireland, because the woman at the desk had seen my name being added to the list and had told the others that she knew me and would like to help me now that I needed help.

Her name was Frances Carey, and she had lived next door to my aunt's house, where we – myself and Cathal – were left when my father got sick. I was eight years old then. Frances must have been ten years older, but I remember her well, as I do her sister and her two brothers, one of whom was close to me in age. Their family owned the house that my aunt lived in, the aunt who took us in. They were grander than she was and much richer, but she had become friendly with them, and there was, since the houses shared a large back garden and some outhouses, a lot of traffic between the two establishments.

Cathal was four then, but in his mind he was older. He was learning to read already, he was clever and had a prodigious memory, and was treated as a young boy in our house rather than as a baby; he could decide which clothes to wear each day and what television he wanted to watch and which room he would sit in and what food he would eat. When his friends called at the house, he could freely ask them in, or go out with them. When relatives or friends of my parents called, they asked for him, too, and spoke to him and listened avidly to what he had to say.

In all the years that followed, Cathal and I never once

spoke about our time in this new house with this new family. And my memory, usually so good, is not always clear. I cannot remember, for example, how we got to the house, who drove us there, or what this person said. I know that I was eight years old only because I remember what class I was in at school when I left and who the teacher was. It is possible that this period lasted just two or three months. Maybe it was more. It was not summer, I am sure of that, because Suzie, who remained unscathed by all of this (or so she said, when once, years ago, I asked her if she remembered it), was back at boarding school. I have no memory of cold weather in that house in which we were deposited, although I do think that the evenings were dark early. Maybe it was from September to December. Or the first months after Christmas. I am not sure.

What I remember clearly are the rooms themselves, the parlor and dining-room almost never used and the kitchen, larger than ours at home, and the smell and taste of fried bread. I hated the hot thick slices, fresh from the pan, soaked in lard or dripping. I remember that our cousins were younger than we were and had to sleep during the day, or at least one of them did, and we had to be quiet for hours on end, even though we had nothing to do; we had none of our toys or books. I remember that nobody liked us, either of us, not even Cathal, who, before and after this event, was greatly loved by people who came across him.

We slept in my aunt's house and ate her food as best we could, and we must have played or done something, although we never went to school. Nobody did us any harm in that house; nobody came near us in the night, or hit either of us, or threatened us, or made us afraid. The time we were left by our mother in our aunt's house has no drama attached to it. It was all grayness, strangeness. Our aunt dealt with us in her own distracted way. Her husband was mild, distant, almost good-humored.

And all I know is that our mother did not get in touch with us once, not once, during this time. There was no letter or phone call or visit. Our father was in the hospital. We did not know how long we were going to be left there. In the years that followed, our mother never explained her absence, and we never asked her if she had ever wondered how we were, or how we felt, during those months.

This should be nothing, because it resembled nothing, just as one minus one resembles zero. It should be barely worth recounting to you as I walk the empty streets of this city in the desert so far away from where I belong. It feels as though Cathal and I had spent that time in the shadow world, as though we had been quietly lowered into the dark, everything familiar missing, and nothing we did or said could change this. Because no one gave any sign of hating us, it did not strike us that we were in a world where no one loved us, or that such a thing might matter. We did not complain. We were emptied of everything, and in the vacuum came something like silence – almost no sound at all, just some sad echoes and dim feelings.

I promise you that I will not call. I have called you enough, and woken you enough times, in the years when we were together and in the years since then. But there are nights now in this strange, flat, and forsaken place when those sad echoes and dim feelings come to me slightly louder than before. They are like whispers, or trapped whimpering sounds. And I wish that I had you here, and I wish that I had not called you all those other times when I did not need to as much as I do now.

My brother and I learned not to trust anyone. We learned then not to talk about things that mattered to us, and we stuck to this, as much as we could, with a sort of grim stubborn pride, all our lives, as though it were a skill. But you know that, don't you? I do not need to call you to tell you that.

At JFK that night, Frances Carey smiled warmly and asked me how bad things were. When I told her that my mother was dying, she said that she was shocked. She remembered my mother so well, she said. She said she was sorry. She explained that I could use the first-class lounge, making it clear, however, in the most pleasant way, that I would be crossing the Atlantic in coach, which was what I had paid for. If I needed her, she said, she could come up in a while and talk, but she had told the people in the lounge and on the plane that she knew me, and they would look after me.

As we spoke and she tagged my luggage and gave me my boarding pass, I guessed that I had not laid eyes on her for more than thirty years. But in her face I could see the person I had known, as well as traces of her mother and one of her brothers. In her presence – the reminder she offered of that house where Cathal and I had been left all those years ago – I could feel that this going home to my mother's bedside would not be simple, that some of our loves and attachments are elemental and beyond our choosing, and for that very reason they come spiced with pain and regret and need and hollowness and a feeling as close to anger as I will ever be able to manage.

Sometime during the night in that plane, as we crossed part of the Western Hemisphere, quietly and, I hope, unnoticed, I began to cry. I was back then in the simple world before I had seen Frances Carey, a world in which someone whose heartbeat had once been mine, and whose blood became my blood, and inside whose body I once lay curled, herself lay stricken in a hospital bed. The fear of losing her made me desperately sad. And then I tried to sleep. I pushed back my seat as the night wore on and kept my eyes averted from the movie being shown, whatever it was, and let the terrible business of what I was flying toward hit me.

I hired a car at the airport, and I drove across Dublin in the washed light of that early September morning. I drove through Drumcondra, Dorset Street, Mountjoy Square, Gardiner Street, and the streets across the river that led south, as though they were a skin that I had shed. I did not stop for two hours or more, until I reached the house, fearing that if I pulled up somewhere to have breakfast the numbness that the driving with no sleep had brought might lift.

Suzie was just out of bed when I arrived, and Jim was still asleep. Cathal had gone back to Dublin the night before, she said, but would be down later. She sighed and looked at me. The hospital had phoned, she went on, and things were worse. Your mother, she said, had a stroke during the night, on top of everything else. It was an old joke between us: never 'our mother' or 'my mother' or 'Mammy' or 'Mummy,' but 'your mother.'

The doctors did not know how bad the stroke had been, she said, and they were still ready to operate if they thought they could. But they needed to talk to us. It was a pity, she added, that our mother's specialist, the man who looked after her heart, and whom she saw regularly and liked, was away. I realized then why Cathal had gone back to Dublin – he did not want to be a part of the conversation that we would have with the doctors. Two of us would be enough. He had told Suzie to tell me that whatever we decided would be fine with him.

Neither of us blamed him. He was the one who had become close to her. He was the one she loved most. Or maybe he was the only one she loved. In those years, anyway.

Or maybe that is unfair. Maybe she loved us all, just as we loved her as she lay dying.

And I moved, in those days – that Tuesday morning to the Friday night when she died – from feeling at times a great remoteness from her to wanting fiercely, almost in the same moment, my mother back where she had always been, in witty command of her world, full of odd dreams and perspectives, difficult, ready for life. She loved, as I did, books and music and hot weather. As she grew older she had managed, with her friends and with us, a pure charm, a lightness of tone and touch. But I knew not to trust it, not to come close, and I never did. I managed, in turn, to exude my own lightness and charm, but you know that, too. You don't need me to tell you that, either, do you?

I regretted nonetheless, as I sat by her bed or left so that others might see her – I regretted how far I had moved away from her, and how far away I had stayed. I regretted how much I had let those months apart from her in the limbo of my aunt's house, and the years afterward, as my father slowly died, eat away at my soul. I regretted how little she knew about me, as she, too, must have regretted that, although she never complained or mentioned it, except perhaps to Cathal, and he told no one anything. Maybe she regretted nothing. But nights are long in winter, when darkness comes down at four o'clock and people have time to think of everything.

Maybe that is why I am here now, away from Irish darkness, away from the long, deep winter that settles so menacingly on the place where I was born. I am away from the east wind. I am in a place where so much is empty because it was never full, where things are forgotten and swept away, if there ever were things. I am in a place where there is nothing. Flatness, a blue sky, a soft, unhaunted night. A place where no one walks. Maybe I am happier here than I would be anywhere else, and it is only the poisonous innocence of the moon tonight that has made me want to dial your number and see if you are awake.

As we drove to see my mother that morning, I could not ask Suzie a question that was on my mind. My mother had been sick for four days now and was lying there maybe frightened, and I wondered if she had reached out her hand to Cathal and if they had held hands in the hospital, if they had actually grown close enough for that. Or if she had made some gesture to Suzie. And if she might do the same to me. It was a stupid, selfish thing I wondered about, and, like everything else that came into my mind in those days, it allowed me to avoid the fact that there would be no time anymore for anything to be explained or said. We had used up all our time. And I wondered if that made any difference to my mother then, as she lay awake in the hospital those last few nights of her life: we had used up all our time.

She was in intensive care. We had to ring the bell and wait to be admitted. There was a hush over the place. We had discussed what I would say to her so as not to alarm her, how I would explain why I had come back. I told Suzie that I would simply say that I'd heard she was in the hospital and I'd had a few days free before classes began and had decided to come back to make sure that she was okay.

'Are you feeling better?' I asked her.

She could not speak. Slowly and laboriously, she let us know that she was thirsty and they would not allow her to drink anything. She had a drip in her arm. We told the nurses that her mouth was dry, and they said that there was nothing much we could do, except perhaps take tiny drops of cold water and put them on her lips using those special little sticks with cotton-wool tips that women use to put on eye makeup.

I sat by her bed and spent a while wetting her lips. I was

at home with her now. I knew how much she hated physical discomfort; her appetite for this water was so overwhelming and so desperate that nothing else mattered.

And then word came that the doctors would see us. When we stood up and told her that we would be back, she hardly responded. We were ushered by a nurse with an English accent down some corridors to a room. There were two doctors there; the nurse stayed in the room. The doctor who seemed to be in charge, who said that he would have been the one to perform the operation, told us that he had just spoken to the anesthetist, who had insisted that my mother's heart would not survive an operation. The stroke did not really matter, he said, although it did not help.

'I could have a go,' he said, and then immediately apologized for speaking like that. He corrected himself: 'I could operate, but she would die on the operating table.'

There was a blockage somewhere, he said. There was no blood getting to her kidneys and maybe elsewhere as well – the operation would tell us for certain, but it would probably do nothing to solve the problem. It was her circulation, he said. The heart was simply not beating strongly enough to send blood into every part of her body.

He knew to leave silence then, and the other doctor did, too. The nurse looked at the floor.

'There's nothing you can do then, is there?' I said.

'We can make her comfortable,' he replied.

'How long can she survive like this?' I asked.

'Not long,' he said.

'I mean, hours or days?'

'Days. Some days.'

'We can make her very comfortable,' the nurse said.

There was nothing more to say. Afterward, I wondered if we should have spoken to the anesthetist personally, or tried to contact our mother's consultant, or asked that she be moved to a bigger hospital for another opinion. But I don't think any of this would have made a difference. For years, we had been given warnings that this moment would come, as she fainted in public places and lost her balance and declined. It had been clear that her heart was giving out, but not clear enough for me to have come to see her more than once or twice in the summer – and then when I did come I was protected from what might have been said, or not said, by the presence of Suzie and Jim and Cathal. Maybe I should have phoned a few times a week, or written her letters like a good son. But despite all the warning signals, or perhaps even because of them, I had kept my distance. And as soon as I entertained this thought, with all the regret that it carried, I imagined how coldly or nonchalantly a decision to spend the summer close by, seeing her often, might have been greeted by her, and how difficult and enervating for her, as much as for me, some of those visits or phone calls might have been. And how curtly efficient and brief her letters in reply to mine would have seemed.

And, as we walked back down to see her, the nurse coming with us, there was this double regret – the simple one that I had kept away, and the other one, much harder to fathom, that I had been given no choice, that she had never wanted me very much, and that she was not going to be able to rectify that in the few days that she had left in the world. She would be distracted by her own pain and discomfort, and by the great effort she was making to be dignified and calm. She was wonderful, as she always had been. I touched her hand a few times in case she might open it and seek my hand, but she never did this. She did not respond to being touched.

Some of her friends came. Cathal came and stayed with

her. Suzie and I remained close by. On Friday morning, when the nurse asked me if I thought she was in distress, I said that I did. I knew that, if I insisted now, I could get her morphine and a private room. I did not consult the others; I knew that they would agree. I did not mention morphine to the nurse, but I knew that she was wise, and I saw by the way she looked at me as I spoke that she knew that I knew what morphine would do. It would ease my mother into sleep and ease her out of the world. Her breathing would come and go, shallow and deep, her pulse would become faint, her breathing would stop, and then come and go again.

It would come and go until, in that private room late in the evening, it seemed to stop altogether, as, horrified and helpless, we sat and watched her, then sat up straight as the breathing started again, but not for long. Not for long at all. It stopped one last time, and it stayed stopped. It did not start again.

She was gone. She lay still. We sat with her until a nurse came in and quietly checked her pulse and shook her head sadly and left the room.

We stayed with her for a while; then, when they asked us to leave, we touched her on the forehead one by one, and we left the room, closing the door. We walked down the corridor as though for the rest of our lives our own breathing would bear traces of the end of hers, of her final struggle, as though our own way of being in the world had just been halved or quartered by what we had seen.

We buried her beside my father, who had been in the grave waiting for her for thirty-three years. And the next morning I flew back to New York, to my half-furnished apartment on Ninetieth and Columbus, and began my teaching a day later. I understood, just as you might tell me now – if you picked up the phone and found me on the other end of the line, silent at first and then saying that I needed to talk to you – you might tell me that I had over all the years postponed too much. As I settled down to sleep in that new bed in the dark city, I saw that it was too late now, too late for everything. I would not be given a second chance. In the hours when I woke, I have to tell you that this struck me almost with relief.

AIMEE BENDER

MARZIPAN

ONE WEEK AFTER his father died, my father woke up with a hole in his stomach. It wasn't a small hole, some kind of mild break in the skin, it was a hole the size of a soccer ball and it went all the way through. You could now see behind him like he was an enlarged peephole.

Sharon! is what I remember first. He called for my mother, sharp, he called her into the bedroom and my sister Hannah and I stood outside, worried. Was it divorce? We twisted nervously and I had one awful inner jump of glee because there was something about divorce that seemed a tiny bit exciting.

My mother came out, her face distant.

Go to school, she said.

What is it? I said. Hannah tried to peek through. What's wrong? she asked.

They told us at dinner and promised a demonstration after dessert. When all the plates were cleared away, my father raised his thin white undershirt and beneath it, where other people have a stomach, was a round hole. The skin had curved and healed around the circumference.

What's that? I asked.

He shook his head. I don't know, and he looked scared then.

Where is your stomach now? I asked.

He coughed a little.

Did you eat? Hannah said. We saw you eat.

His face paled.

Where did it go? I asked and there we were, his two daughters, me ten, she thirteen.

You have no more belly button, I said. You're all belly button, I said.

My mother stopped clearing the dishes and put her hand on her neck, cupping her jaw. Girls, she said, quiet down.

You could now thread my father on a bracelet. The giantess' charm bracelet with a new mini wiggling man, something to show the other giantesses at the giantess party. (My, my! they declare. He's so active!)

My parents went to the doctor the next day. The internist took an X ray and proclaimed my father's inner organs intact. They went to the gastroenterologist. He said my father was digesting food in an arc, it was looping down the sides, sliding around the hole, and all his intestines were, although further crunched, still there and still functioning.

They pronounced him in great health.

My parents walked down into the cool underground parking lot and packed into the car to go home.

Halfway there, ambling through a green light, my mother told my father to pull over which he did and she shoved open the passenger side door and threw up all over the curb.

They made a U-turn and drove back to the doctor's.

The internist took some blood, left, returned and winked.

Looks like you're pregnant, he said.

My mother, forty-three, put a hand on her stomach and stared.

My father, forty-six, put a hand on his stomach and it went straight through to his back.

*   *   *

314

They arrived home at six-fifteen that night; Hannah and I had been concerned – six o'clock marked the start of Worry Time. They announced the double news right away: Daddy's fine. Mommy's pregnant.

Are you going to have it? I asked. I like being the youngest, I said. I don't want another kid.

My mother rubbed the back of her neck. Sure, I'll have it, she said. It's a special opportunity and I love babies.

My father, on the couch, one hand curled up and resting inside his stomach like a birdhead, was in good spirits. We'll name it after my dad, he said.

If it's a girl? I asked.

Edwina, he said.

Hannah and I made gagging sounds and he sent us to our room for disrespecting Grandpa.

In nine months, my father's hole was exactly the same size and my mother sported the biggest belly around for miles. Even the doctor was impressed. Hugest I've ever seen, he told her.

My mother was mad. Makes me feel like shit, she said that night at dinner. She glared at my father. I mean, really. You're not even that tall.

My father growled. He was feeling very proud. Biggest belly ever. That was some good sperm.

We all went to the hospital on delivery day. Hannah wandered the hallway, chatting with the interns; I stood at my mother's shoulder, nervous. I thought about the fact that if my father lay, face down, on top of my mother, her belly would poke out his back. She could wear him like a huge fleshy toilet seat cover. He could spin on her stomach, a beige propeller.

She pushed and grimaced and pushed and grimaced. The

doctor stood at her knees and his voice peaked with encouragement: Almost There, Atta Girl, Here We Go – And!

But the baby did not come out as planned.

When, finally, the head poked out between her legs, the doctor's face widened with shock. He stared. He stopped yelling Push, Push and his voice dried up. I went over to his side, to see what was going on. And what I saw was that the head appearing between my mother's thighs was not the head of a baby but rather that of an old woman.

My goodness, the doctor said.

My mother sat up.

I blinked.

What's wrong? said my father.

Hannah walked in. Did I miss anything? she asked.

The old woman kicked herself out the rest of the way, wiped a string of gook off her arm, and grabbing the doctor's surgical scissors, clipped the umbilical cord herself. She didn't cry. She said, clearly: Thank Heaven. It was so warm in there near the end, I thought I might faint.

Oh my God, said Hannah.

My mother stared at the familiar wrinkled face in front of her. Mother? she said in a tiny voice.

The woman turned at the sound. Sweetheart, she said, you did an excellent job.

Mother? My mother put a hand over her ear. What are you doing here? Mommy?

I kept blinking. The doctor was mute.

My mother turned to my father. Wait, she said. Wait. In Florida. Funeral. Wait. Didn't that happen?

The old woman didn't answer, but brushed a glob of blood off her wrist and shook it down to the floor.

My father found his voice. It's my fault, he said softly, and, hanging his head, he lifted his shirt. The doctor stared. My mother reached over and yanked it down.

It is not, she said. Pay attention to *me*.

Hannah strode forward, nudged the gaping doctor aside and tried to look up inside.

Where's the baby? she asked.

My mother put her arms around herself. I don't know, she said.

It's me, said my mother's mother.

Hi Grandma, I said.

Hannah started laughing.

The doctor cleared his throat. People, he said, this here is your baby.

My grandmother stretched out her wrinkled legs to the floor, and walked, tiny body old and sagging, over to the bathroom. She selected a white crepe hospital dress from the stack by the door. It stuck to her slippery hip. Shut your eyes, children, she said over her shoulder, you don't want to see an old lady naked.

The doctor exited, mumbling busy busy busy.

My mother looked at the floor.

I'm sorry, she said. Her eyes filled.

My father put his palm on her cheek. I grabbed Hannah and dragged her to the door.

We'll be outside, I said.

We heard her voice hardening as we exited. Nine months! she was saying. If I'd known it was going to be my *mother*, I would've at least smoked a couple of cigarettes.

In the hallway I stared at Hannah and she stared back at me. Edwina? I said and we both doubled over, cracking up so hard I had to run to the bathroom before I wet my pants.

* * *

We all drove home together that afternoon. Grandma in the backseat between me and Hannah wrapped up in the baby blanket she had knitted herself, years before.

I remember this one, she remarked, fingering its soft pink weave. I did a nice job.

My father, driving, poked his hole.

I thought it might be a baby without a stomach, he said to my mother in the front seat. I never thought this.

He put an arm on her shoulder.

I love your mother, he said, stroking her arm.

My mother stiffened. I do too, she said. So?

I hadn't gone to my father's father's funeral. It had been in Texas and I'd just finished with strep throat and everyone decided Hannah and I would be better off with the neighbors for the weekend. Think of us Sunday, my mother had said. I'd worn black overalls on Sunday, Hannah had rebelled and worn purple, and together we buried strands of our hair beneath the spindly roots of our neighbor's potted plants.

When they returned, I asked my father how it was. He looked away. Sad, he said, fast, scratching his neck.

Did you cry? I asked.

I cried, he said. I cry.

I nodded. I saw you cry once, I assured him. I remember, it was the national anthem.

He patted my arm. It was very sad, he said, loudly.

I'm right here, I told him, you don't have to yell it.

He went over to the wall and plucked off the black-and-white framed photograph of young Grandpa Edwin.

He sure was handsome, I said, and my father rested his hand on top of my head – the heaviest, best hat.

* * *

318

After we arrived home from the hospital, Hannah and I settled Grandma in the guest bedroom and our parents collapsed in the den: our father, bewildered, on the couch, our mother flat-backed on the floor, beginning a round of sit-ups.

Fuck if my mother is going to ruin my body, she muttered. Fuck that shit.

I brought a book on sand crabs into the living-room and pretended to read on the couch. Hannah promptly got on the phone. No really! I heard her saying. I swear!

My father watched my mother: head, knees. Up, down.

At least you can *do* sit-ups, he said.

She sat-up, grit her teeth, and sat-down. Some good sperm, she said, nearly spitting.

It's miracle sperm, my father said.

Excuse me, I said, I'm in the room.

Miracle? my mother said. Make it your dad then. Tell your fucking chromosomes to re-create *him*.

Her breasts leaked, useless, onto her T-shirts – cloudy milk-stain eyes staring blind up at the ceiling. She did a set of a hundred and then lay flat.

Mommy, I said, are you okay?

I could hear Hannah in the other room: She died in October, she was saying. Yeah, I totally saw.

My mother turned her head to look at me. Come here, she said.

I put down my book, went over to her and knelt down.

She put a hand on my cheek. Honey, she said, when I die?

My eyes started to fill up, that fast.

Don't die, I said.

I'm not, she said, I'm very healthy. Not for a while. But when I do, she said, I want you to let me go.

* * *

I was able to attend my mother's mother's funeral. I kept close to Hannah for most of it, but when the majority of relatives had trickled out, I found my mother huddled into a corner of the white couch – her head back, face drawn.

I sat next to her, crawled under her arm and said, Mama, you are so sad.

She didn't move her head, just petted my hair with her hand and said: True, but honey, I am sad plus.

Plus what I never asked. It made me not hungry, the way she said it.

She stopped her sit-ups at ten-thirty that night. It was past my bedtime and I was all tucked in, lights out. Before she'd fallen asleep, Hannah and I had been giggling.

Maybe I'll have you, I said, stroking my stomach.

She'd sighed. Maybe I'll have myself, she'd whispered.

That concept had never even crossed my mind. Oldest, I hissed back.

After a while, she'd stopped answering my questions. I prodded my stomach, making sure it was still there and still its usual size. It growled back.

I heard my mother let out a huge exhale in the den and the steady count: three hundred and five, three hundred and six, stopped.

Stepping quietly out of bed, I tiptoed into the hallway; my father was asleep on the couch, and my mother was neatening up the bookshelves, sticking the horizontal books into vertical slats.

Mommy, I called.

She didn't turn around, just held out her arm and I went right to it.

My baby, she said, and I felt myself blooming.

We sat down on the couch, curled together, my knees in

320

a V on her thigh. Her side was warmer than usual from the sit-ups, even a little bit damp. She leaned her head against mine and we both stared ahead, at the closed drapes that were ivory, specked with brown.

I'm hungry, I said.

Me too.

We stood and went to the refrigerator. I found some left-over spaghetti. My mother opened the freezer doors, rummaged around and brought out half a cake.

I never knew there was cake in there, I mumbled, stuffing a forkful of noodles into my mouth.

It was chocolate on the outside and sealed carefully in plastic.

This was from Grandma's funeral, she told me.

I blinked. No way, I said. The marzipan one? I *loved* that cake.

You tried it? My mother unwrapped it.

I ate at least three pieces, I said. It was the best food at the wake by far.

She cut me a thin slice and put it on my place mat.

Most ten-year-olds don't like marzipan, she told me. It's Grandma's favorite, marzipan is, she said. You must've gotten the taste from her.

I nibbled at its edge. It was cold and grainy from the freezer.

Delicious, I said, savoring the almond paste as it spread out in my mouth.

My mother cut herself a piece, grabbed a fork from the drying rack and sat down across from me.

Why do we have it? I asked.

She shrugged. You know some people keep pieces of wedding cake, she said, taking a bite.

* * *

In the morning, my father was holding the photograph of his father in his lap.

Edwin, I said. Handsome Grandpa Edwin.

He pulled me close to him. Grandpa Edwin had thick brown curls.

He really was an asshole, my father said.

I started laughing: loud, full laughter.

He put a hand over my mouth and I laughed into his palm.

Sssh, Lisa, he said. Don't laugh about it.

It's funny, I mumbled.

Don't laugh at a dead man, he said.

I had a few left in me and I let them out, but they were half their big belly laugh size by then.

How's the hole? I asked, when I was done. Does it hurt?

Nah, he said. It's no big deal.

Can I see?

He raised his thin undershirt.

Can I touch? I asked. He nodded. I gingerly put my fingertips on the inner circle; his skin felt like skin.

So where do you think it went? I asked.

What, he said, the skin?

Everything, I said: the skin, the ribs that were in the way, the stomach acid, all of it.

I guess it's all still in there, he said. I guess it's just pushed to the side.

I think it's cool, I said, imagining a new sports game kind of like basketball that revolved around my father.

He put his shirt back down, a curtain falling. I don't, he said. But it didn't kill me, he said, and I'm grateful for that.

At dinner my grandmother cooked her famous soup with tiny hot dogs floating in a thick bean broth.

I missed this soup, I said, I never thought I'd eat this soup again. This is my favorite soup in the whole world.

Hannah promptly lost a piece of bread inside and poked around the bowl with her fork.

Let's hold hands, said my mother, before we start.

I swallowed the spoonful in my mouth.

I grabbed Hannah's hand and my grandmother's hand. One was soft and mushy and the other one was soft and mushy, but different kinds of soft and different kinds of mushy.

My mother closed her eyes.

We never say prayers, I interrupted.

We are today, said my mother.

I bowed my head.

So what do we say? I asked, looking down into my soup which was bobbing along. Something about bread?

Sshh, said my father. It's a silent prayer.

No, it's not that, said my mother, I'm still thinking.

Ow, Hannah told my father, you're squeezing too hard.

I think we're supposed to be thankful, I hinted.

Hannah turned and glared at me. Shut up, she said. Give her a second.

My grandmother was quiet, smelling her soup.

Needs salt, she whispered.

My mother looked up.

I'm not sure what to say, she said. Her eyebrows furrowed, uncertain.

Let's make it up, I said. I squeezed Hannah's hand and my grandma's hand, and at the same time, they squeezed back.

I'll start it, I said, and we'll go around the circle.

My mother looked relieved. Good, she said, that sounds good.

I would like to say thanks, I began, for my parents and my

sister and for the special appearance of Grandma . . . I turned to Hannah.

. . . And for Grandma's soup which is the best soup and is way better than that fish thing we were going to eat. She faced my father.

He cleared his throat. There's usually something about survival in good prayers, he said. Thanks for that.

My mother gave him a look. That's so impersonal, she said.

He shrugged. I'm on the spot, he said. Survival is important to me.

My mother looked us all over and I could see the candle flame flickering near her eye. Her gaze held on her mother.

We all waited.

It's your turn, I said, in case she'd forgotten.

She didn't look at me. She stood up, breaking the hand-links she had made, and sat close to her mother.

My father began eating his soup.

I have a cake from your funeral, she said.

I felt myself lift inside. I squeezed down on Hannah's hand. She said Ouch.

Cake? my grandmother said. What kind of cake?

Marzipan cake, my mother said.

My grandmother smiled. Marzipan? she said. That's my favorite.

I stood up; I wanted to be the one; I went to the freezer, opened it, dug around and found the cake wedged beneath the third ice tray like a small football.

Here, I said. Here it is.

My mother grabbed it out of my hands.

Just a taste, she said.

Let's all have some! I said. We can all eat funeral cake!

Just a little, my mother said.

Oh come on! I said. Let's make it into five pieces.

My mother looked at me.

Okay, she said. Five pieces. Her face looked lined and tired as she cut up the cake. I passed a piece to each of us. My grandmother bit into hers right away.

Mmm, she said. That is good, now that is *good*.

My mother did not eat hers. She wrapped it back in the plastic.

My grandmother kept eating and oohing. I bit into mine. Hannah gave me hers; she hates marzipan. I nearly hugged her. My father ate his quickly, like an appetizer.

I remember, said my mother, we all thought you would've liked it. We said you would've loved it.

My grandmother licked her lips. I do love it, she said. She pointed. Are you going to eat your piece?

No, said my mother.

Can I have it? she asked. I haven't had such good marzipan in I don't know how long.

No, my mother said, closing her fingers over her piece. I want to keep mine, she said.

Oh come on, said my father, let the lady have her cake. It was her funeral cake for God's sake.

I finished my slice. I still had Hannah's.

Here, Grandma, I said, Hannah didn't want hers. I slid the whitish slab onto her plate.

Thank you dear, my grandmother said.

I want to keep mine, my mother repeated.

Hannah began on her soup. Her spoon made dull clinking sounds on the bowl.

The soup is good, Grandma, she said.

Mmm-hmm, said my father.

My mother sat still at her place. The plastic-wrapped cake sat next to her spoon. She didn't touch her soup. The hot dogs stopped floating and were still.

I'll eat yours if you don't want it, I said to my mother.

She pushed over her bowl. I pretended I was her while I ate it. I imagined I was doing the eating but she was getting nourished.

When I was done, I asked: May I be excused?

No one answered, so I stayed.

LORRIE MOORE

HOW TO TALK TO YOUR MOTHER (NOTES)

1982. Without her, for years now, murmur at the defrosting refrigerator, 'What?' 'Huh?' 'Shush now,' as it creaks, aches, groans, until the final ice block drops from the ceiling of the freezer like something vanquished.

Dream, and in your dreams babies with the personalities of dachshunds, fat as Macy balloons, float by the treetops.

The first permanent polyurethane heart is surgically implanted.

Someone upstairs is playing 'You'll Never Walk Alone' on the recorder. Now it's 'Oklahoma!' They must have a Rodgers and Hammerstein book.

1981. On public transportation, mothers with soft, soapy, corduroyed seraphs glance at you, their faces dominoes of compassion. Their seraphs are small and quiet or else restlessly counting bus-seat colors: 'Blue-blue-blue, red-red-red, lullow-lullow-lullow.' The mothers see you eyeing their children. They smile sympathetically. They believe you envy them. They believe you are childless. They believe they know why. Look quickly away, out the smudge of the window.

1980. The hum, rush, clack of things in the kitchen. These are some of the sounds that organize your life. The clink of the silverware inside the drawer, piled like bones in a mass grave. Your similes grow grim, grow tired.

Reagan is elected President, though you distributed donuts and brochures for Carter.

Date an Italian. He rubs your stomach and says, 'These are marks of stretch, no? Marks of stretch?' and in your dizzy mind you think: Marks of Harpo, Ideas of Marx, Ides of March, Beware. He plants kisses on the sloping ramp of your neck, and you fall asleep against him, your underpants peeled and rolled around one thigh like a bride's garter.

1979. Once in a while take evening trips past the old unsold house you grew up in, that haunted rural crossroads two hours from where you now live. It is like Halloween: the raked, moonlit lawn, the mammoth, tumid trees, arms and fingers raised into the starless wipe of sky like burns, cracks, map rivers. Their black shadows rock against the side of the east porch. There are dream shadows, other lives here. Turn the corner slowly but continue to stare from the car window. This house is embedded in you deep, something still here you know, you think you know, a voice at the top of those stairs, perhaps, a figure on the porch, an odd apron caught high in the twigs, in the too-warm-for-a-fall-night breeze, something not right, that turret window you can still see from here, from outside, but which can't be reached from within. (The ghostly brag of your childhood: 'We have a mystery room. The window shows from the front, but you can't go in, there's no door. A doctor lived there years ago and gave secret operations, and now it's blocked off.') The window sits like a dead eye in the turret.

You see a ghost, something like a spinning statue by a shrub.

1978. Bury her in the cold south sideyard of that Halloween-ish house. Your brother and his kids are there. Hug. The minister in a tweed sportscoat, the neighborless fields, the crossroads, are all like some stark Kansas. There is praying, then someone shoveling. People walk toward the cars and hug again. Get inside your car with your niece. Wait. Look up through the windshield. In the November sky a wedge of wrens moves south, the lines of their formation, the very sides and vertices mysteriously choreographed, shifting, flowing, crossing like a skater's legs. 'They'll descend instinctively upon a tree somewhere,' you say, 'but not for miles yet.' You marvel, watch, until, amoeba-slow, they are dark, faraway stitches in the horizon. You do not start the car. The quiet niece next to you finally speaks: 'Aunt Ginnie, are we going to the restaurant with the others?' Look at her. Recognize her: nine in a pile parka. Smile and start the car.

1977. She ages, rocks in your rocker, noiseless as wind. The front strands of her white hair dangle yellow at her eyes from too many cigarettes. She smokes even now, her voice husky with phlegm. Sometimes at dinner in your tiny kitchen she will simply stare, rheumy-eyed, at you, then burst into a fit of coughing that racks her small old man's body like a storm.

Stop eating your baked potato. Ask if she is all right.

She will croak: 'Do you remember, Ginnie, your father used to say that one day, with these cigarettes, I was going to have to "face the mucus"?' At this she chuckles, chokes, gasps again.

Make her stand up.

Lean her against you.

Slap her lightly on the curved mound of her back.

Ask her for chrissakes to stop smoking.

She will smile and say: 'For chrissakes? Is that any way to talk to your mother?'

At night go in and check on her. She lies there awake, her

lips apart, open and drying. Bring her some juice. She murmurs, 'Thank you, honey.' Her mouth smells, swells like a grave.

1976. The Bicentennial. In the laundromat, you wait for the time on your coins to run out. Through the porthole of the dryer, you watch your bedeviled towels and sheets leap and fall. The radio station piped in from the ceiling plays slow, sad Motown; it encircles you with the desperate hopefulness of a boy at a dance, and it makes you cry. When you get back to your apartment, dump everything on your bed. Your mother is knitting crookedly: red, white, and blue. Kiss her hello. Say: 'Sure was warm in that place.' She will seem not to hear you.

1975. Attend poetry readings alone at the local library. Find you don't really listen well. Stare at your crossed thighs. Think about your mother. Sometimes you confuse her with the first man you ever loved, who ever loved you, who buried his head in the pills of your sweater and said magnificent things like 'Oh god, oh god,' who loved you unconditionally, terrifically, like a mother.

The poet loses his nerve for a second, a red flush through his neck and ears, but he regains his composure. When he is finished, people clap. There is wine and cheese.

Leave alone, walk home alone. The downtown streets are corridors of light holding you, holding you, past the church, past the community center. March, like Stella Dallas, spine straight, through the melodrama of street lamps, phone posts, toward the green house past Borealis Avenue, toward the rear apartment with the tilt and the squash on the stove.

Your horoscope says: Be kind, be brief.

You are pregnant again. Decide what you must do.

1974. She will have bouts with a mad sort of senility. She calls you at work. 'There's no food here! Help me! I'm starving!' although you just bought forty dollars' worth of groceries yesterday. 'Mom, there is too food there!'

When you get home the refrigerator is mostly empty. 'Mom, where did you put all the milk and cheese and stuff?' Your mother stares at you from where she is sitting in front of the TV set. She has tears leaking out of her eyes. 'There's no food here, Ginnie.'

There is a rustling, scratching noise in the dishwasher. You open it up, and the eyes of a small rodent glint back at you. It scrambles out, off to the baseboards behind the refrigerator. Your mother, apparently, has put all the groceries inside the dishwasher. The milk is spilled, a white pool against blue, and things like cheese and bologna and apples have been nibbled at.

1973. At a party when a woman tells you where she bought some wonderful pair of shoes, say that you believe shopping for clothes is like masturbation – everyone does it, but it isn't very interesting and therefore should be done alone, in an embarrassed fashion, and never be the topic of party conversation. The woman will tighten her lips and eyebrows and say, 'Oh, I suppose you have something more fascinating to talk about.' Grow clumsy and uneasy. Say, 'No,' and head for the ginger ale. Tell the person next to you that your insides feel sort of sinking and vinyl like a Claes Oldenburg toilet. They will say, 'Oh?' and point out that the print on your dress is one of paisleys impregnating paisleys. Pour yourself more ginger ale.

1972. Nixon wins by a landslide.

Sometimes your mother calls you by her sister's name.

Say, 'No, Mom, it's me. Virginia.' Learn to repeat things. Learn that you have a way of knowing each other which somehow slips out and beyond the ways you have of not knowing each other at all.

Make apple crisp for the first time.

1971. Go for long walks to get away from her. Walk through wooded areas; there is a life there you have forgotten. The smells and sounds seem sudden, unchanged, exact, the papery crunch of the leaves, the mouldering sachet of the mud. The trees are crooked as backs, the fence posts splintered, trusting and precarious in their solid grasp of arms, the asters spindly, dry, white, havishammed (Havishammed!) by frost. Find a beautiful reddish stone and bring it home for your mother. Kiss her. Say: 'This is for you.' She grasps it and smiles. 'You were always such a sensitive child,' she says.

Say: 'Yeah, I know.'

1970. You are pregnant again. Try to decide what you should do.

Get your hair chopped, short as a boy's.

1969. Mankind leaps upon the moon.

Disposable diapers are first sold in supermarkets.

Have occasional affairs with absurd, silly men who tell you to grow your hair to your waist and who, when you are sad, tickle your ribs to cheer you up. Moonlight through the blinds stripes you like zebras. You laugh. You never marry.

1968. Do not resent her. Think about the situation, for instance, when you take the last trash bag from its box: you must throw out the box by putting it in that very trash bag. What was once contained, now must contain. The container,

334

then, becomes the contained, the enveloped, the held. Find more and more that you like to muse over things like this.

1967. Your mother is sick and comes to live with you. There is no place else for her to go. You feel many different emptinesses.

The first successful heart transplant is performed in South Africa.

1966. You confuse lovers, mix up who had what scar, what car, what mother.

1965. Smoke marijuana. Try to figure out what has made your life go wrong. It is like trying to figure out what is stinking up the refrigerator. It could be anything. The lid off the mayonnaise, Uncle Ron's honey wine four years in the left corner. Broccoli yellowing, flowering fast. They are all metaphors. They are all problems. Your horoscope says: Speak gently to a loved one.

1964. Your mother calls long distance and asks whether you are coming home for Thanksgiving, your brother and the baby will be there. Make excuses.

'As a mother gets older,' your mother says, 'these sorts of holidays become increasingly important.'

Say: 'I'm sorry, Mom.'

1963. Wake up one morning with a man you had thought you'd spend your life with, and realize, a rock in your gut, that you don't even like him. Spend a weepy afternoon in his bathroom, not coming out when he knocks. You can no longer trust your affections. People and places you think you love may be people and places you hate.

Kennedy is shot.

Someone invents a temporary artificial heart, for use during operations.

1962. Eat Chinese food for the first time, with a lawyer from California. He will show you how to hold the chopsticks. He will pat your leg. Attack his profession. Ask him whether he feels the law makes large spokes out of the short stakes of men.

1961. Grandma Moses dies.

You are a zoo of insecurities. You take to putting brandy in your morning coffee and to falling in love too easily. You have an abortion.

1960. There is money from your father's will and his life insurance. You buy a car and a green velvet dress you don't need. You drive two hours to meet your mother for lunch on Saturdays. She suggests things for you to write about, things she's heard on the radio: a woman with telepathic twins, a woman with no feet.

1959. At the funeral she says: 'He had his problems, but he was a generous man,' though you know he was tight as a scout knot, couldn't listen to anyone, the only time you remember loving him being that once when he got the punchline of one of your jokes before your mom did and looked up from his science journal and guffawed loud as a giant, the two of you, for one split moment, communing like angels in the middle of that room, in that warm, shared light of mind.

Say: 'He was okay.'

'You shouldn't be bitter,' your mother snaps. 'He financed you and your brother's college educations.' She buttons her coat. 'He was also the first man to isolate a particular isotope of helium, I forget the name, but he should have won the Nobel Prize.' She dabs at her nose.

Say: 'Yeah, Mom.'

1958. At your brother's wedding, your father is taken away in an ambulance. A tiny cousin whispers loudly to her mother, 'Did Uncle Will have a hard attack?' For seven straight days say things to your mother like: 'I'm sure it'll be okay,' and 'I'll stay here, why don't you go home and get some sleep.'

1957. Dance the calypso with boys from a different college. Get looped on New York State burgundy, lose your virginity, and buy one of the first portable electric typewriters.

1956. Tell your mother about all the books you are reading at college. This will please her.

1955. Do a paint-by-numbers of Elvis Presley. Tell your mother you are in love with him. She will shake her head.

1954. Shoplift a cashmere sweater.

1953. Smoke a cigarette with Hillary Swedelson. Tell each other your crushes. Become blood sisters.

1952. When your mother asks you if there are any nice boys in junior high, ask her how on earth would you ever know, having to come in at nine! every night. Her eyebrows will lift like theater curtains. 'You poor, abused thing,' she will say.

Say, 'Don't I know it,' and slam the door.

1951. Your mother tells you about menstruation. The following day you promptly menstruate, your body only waiting for permission, for a signal. You wake up in the morning and feel embarrassed.

1949. You learn how to blow gum bubbles and to add negative numbers.

1947. The Dead Sea Scrolls are discovered.

You have seen too many Hollywood musicals. You have seen too many people singing in public places and you assume you can do it, too. Practice. Your teacher asks you a question. You warble back: 'The answer to number two is twelve.' Most of the class laughs at you, though some stare, eyes jewel-still, fascinated. At home your mother asks you to dust your dresser. Work up a vibrato you could drive a truck through. Sing: 'Why do I have to do it now?' and tap your way through the dining-room. Your mother requests that you calm down and go take a nap. Shout: 'You don't care about me! You don't care about me at all!'

1946. Your brother plays 'Shoofly Pie' all day long on the Victrola.

Ask your mother if you can go to Ellen's for supper. She will say, 'Go ask your father,' and you, pulling at your fingers, walk out to the living-room and whimper by his chair. He is reading. Tap his arm. 'Dad? Daddy? Dad?' He continues reading his science journal. Pull harder on your fingers and run back to the kitchen to tell your mother, who storms into the living-room, saying, 'Why don't you ever listen to your children when they try to talk to you?' You hear them arguing. Press your face into a kitchen towel, ashamed, the hum of the refrigerator motor, the drip in the sink scaring you.

338

1945. Your father comes home from his war work. He gives you a piggyback ride around the broad yellow thatch of your yard, the dead window in the turret, dark as a wound, watching you. He gives you wordless pushes on the swing.

Your brother has new friends, acts older and distant, even while you wait for the school bus together.

You spend too much time alone. You tell your mother that when you grow up you will bring your babies to Australia to see the kangaroos.

Forty thousand people are killed in Nagasaki.

1944. Dress and cuddle a tiny babydoll you have named 'the Sue.' Bring her everywhere. Get lost in the Wilson Creek fruit market, and call softly, 'Mom, where are you?' Watch other children picking grapes, but never dare yourself. Your eyes are small, dark throats, your hand clutches the Sue.

1943. Ask your mother about babies. Have her read to you only the stories about babies. Ask her if she is going to have a baby. Ask her about the baby that died. Cry into her arm.

1940. Clutch her hair in your fist. Rub it against your cheek.

1939. As through a helix, as through an ear, it is here you are nearer the dream flashes, the other lives.

There is a tent of legs, a sundering of selves, as you both gasp blindly for breath. Across the bright and cold, she knows it when you try to talk to her, though this is something you never really manage to understand.

Germany invades Poland.

The year's big song is 'Three Little Fishies' and someone, somewhere, is playing it.

ACKNOWLEDGMENTS

AIMEE BENDER: "Marzipan" copyright © 1998 by Aimee Bender, from *The Girl in the Flammable Skirt* by Aimee Bender. Used by permission of Doubleday, a division of Random House, Inc. "Marzipan" from *The Girl in the Flammable Skirt* by Aimee Bender. Published by Random House. Used by permission of David Higham Associates.

ELIZABETH BOWEN: "Coming Home" from *The Collected Stories of Elizabeth Bowen* by Elizabeth Bowen, copyright © 1981 by Curtis Brown Limited, Literary Executors of the Estate of Elizabeth Bowen. Used by permission of Alfred A. Knopf, a division of Random House, Inc.

HAROLD BRODKEY: "Laura" from *First Love and Other Sorrows*. Reprinted by permission of International Creative Management, Inc. Copyright © 1958 by Harold Brodkey.

HORTENSE CALISHER: "The Middle Drawer". Reprinted by permission of Donadio & Olson, Inc. Copyright © 1948 by Hortense Calisher.

RON CARLSON: "Blood and Its Relationship to Water" from *A Kind of Flying: Selected Stories* by Ron Carlson. Copyright © 2003, 1997, 1992, 1987 by Ron Carlson. Used by permission of W. W. Norton & Company, Inc. "Blood and Its Relationship to Water" from *A Kind of Flying* by Ron Carlson. Copyright © 1987 by Ron Carlson. Used by permission of Brandt & Hochman Literary Agents, Inc. All rights reserved.